LIGHTNING RODS

First published in 2011 by New Directions, New York

First published in the UK by
And Other Stories
91 Tadros Court, High Wycombe, Bucks, HP13 7GF

www.andotherstories.org

ISBN 978-1-908276-11-7
eBook ISBN 978-1-908276-15-5

A catalogue record for this book is available from the British Library.

This book is a work of fiction. Names, characters, businesses,
organisations, places and events are either the product of the
author's imagination or are used fictitiously. Any resemblance
to actual persons, living or dead, events or locales is entirely
coincidental.

An excerpt from *Lightning Rods* was originally published in *n+1*.

Supported by the National Lottery through Arts Council England.

LOTTERY FUNDED

LIGHTNING RODS

Helen DeWitt

Introduced by David Flusfeder

CONTENTS

INTRODUCTION

Many readers will be familiar with Helen DeWitt's writing from her debut novel, *The Last Samurai*. A marvellous tale of a boy looking for a father, it was published in 2000, translated into about twenty languages, and was a bestseller in most of them. It's a big book, in the best sense, emotional and expansive, moving across geography and languages; and it is the sort of novel that readers fall in love with, accepting or rejecting possible new intimates by investigating how much they love it too.

Nothing about *The Last Samurai*, except the pleasures and quality of its prose, can prepare its readers for her second novel.

The protagonist of *Lightning Rods*, Joe, is a salesman down on his luck. Neither selling encyclopaedias in Eureka, Missouri, nor selling vacuum cleaners in Eureka, Florida, has brought him any money or success, and he spends most of his time in his trailer occupied in variations on a very precise masturbatory fantasy. Exciting and somehow consoling him is the image of a woman whose lower body is hidden behind a wall. Above the wall, she is immaculately dressed, seemingly unconcerned (she might be talking to a neighbour or quietly varnishing her fingernails); but hidden below is her unclothed lower half, which is being penetrated by an unseen buttock-clenched stud.

Joe's move towards success is to adapt this fantasy into a product for the corporate workspace: what he's selling is an anonymous sexual service, which, in the blithe logic of *Lightning Rods*, is a remedy for, among other ills, sexual harassment, absenteeism and low morale.

This novel is a delight. It has been hailed by American critics as a satire; and it can be seen as being one – a satire of, I suppose, American commodity capitalism – the way any fetish or obsession (or artist) can be turned into product. But that doesn't account for how good *Lightning Rods* actually is. And satire, anyway, is an angry, conservative form: a calling to account of institutions and people who have fallen away from an ideal standard of behaviour and morality established in a romantically remembered, or invented, better time (see for example the work of Jonathan Swift or the magazine *Private Eye*). Satire is the rage-fuelled comedy directed against politicians who spout on about ethics while corruptly lining their pockets; the humour lies in the disparity between things-as-they-are and things-as-they-ought-to-be.

Lightning Rods is smarter and tenderer than that. There have been satires of American mercantalism before, and satires of American sexual mores; but I don't remember such a successful comedy of middle America's imagined picture of itself, where people are always courteous, where mediocrity finds its appeasing accommodations and compensations, and where failure is only the presager to a vast world-bending success. DeWitt has been compared to, among others, George Orwell, Henry Miller and Aesop, as well as Swift. Nathanael West comes to my mind, for DeWitt's comedy can sometimes read like an upside-down version of West's, with his heartache and cataclysms transmuted into a slightly mad congeniality; but the only reason we're looking to make these comparisons, and become dissatisfied with them, is that DeWitt is doing something original here.

This is a comedy of procedure (or, as DeWitt might write, *procedure*), of how goods and people are engineered into becoming parts of a functioning world, and the result is much funnier than any gloss or introduction can possibly do justice to. It's a very American comedy, finding a sort of wonder in the way that American can-do Protestantism manages to overcome any shame or inhibition to produce and market a commodity, just so long as the thing is understood to be honestly produced with an urgency that is matched by the buyer's desire to consume it.

DeWitt's finest success, though, is not in her subject matter but in her *voice*. There's a delight in language and a constant humour in the way that she writes her outlandish, utterly believable fable of obsession rewarded. Maybe it's partly because she's a woman that she evades all the pitfalls one might expect from the subject matter – prurience, pornography, tedium are far away from anything in this book.

We never tire of Joe's company, and we adore his best employee, the ferociously efficient Lucille, who is absolutely firm in her ambitions (money, Harvard Law School) and impeccable in appearance and behaviour – and we should remember here the original meaning of the word 'impeccable', which is 'without sin'. This is a book of great delicacy and charm, and laugh-out-loud wit, written so deftly that the reader may find him- or herself not even noticing the precision and balance of the prose; yet, despite its ostensible subject matter, it is set in a world utterly without sin. Everything originates from Joe's world view, with its vocabulary and metaphors derived from self-help manuals and management guidebooks, its salesman tone of convivial yearning, where people are always on first name terms, even when they're talking to themselves:

> Humans are animals, he thought. All these instincts, these incredibly powerful instincts, are just thwarted by all these taboos. If you can break through some of those taboos *for* people, there's got to be money in it. A *lot* of money. But the money is big because those taboos are so strong. Do you have what it takes to break through that, Joe? Do you have what it takes to look someone in the eye when they're thinking it's disgusting? Because the thing is, Joe, a big idea is ahead of its time. That's *why* there's money in it. It's going to be a long, long time before people catch up with you. If they ever do. You've got to know you're right, because they sure as hell won't.

This is a world where a good deal is the ultimate good, in which the salesman makes a profit and the customer is satisfied, but, like DeWitt's grateful readers, will keep coming back for more.

David Flusfeder
London, April 2012

LIGHTNING RODS

1

FAILURE IS ALWAYS THE BEST WAY TO LEARN

HURRICANE EDNA

One way of looking at it is that it was just an unfortunate by-product of Hurricane Edna.

If you're in sales you know that life has its ups and its downs. He was living in Eureka, Mo., a district he'd been given only because nobody else wanted it, and with reason. He was supposed to be selling the *Encyclopaedia Britannica* to people who simply couldn't see how their lives would be transformed by instant access to the *Micropaedia* and the *Macropaedia*. He had been there six months and hadn't made a single sale.

One day it occurred to him that the problem was he was selling something people could do without. How much better to sell something people knew they needed anyway! Something that didn't make people give you weird looks! Something like vacuum cleaners. Because he just knew the problem wasn't with him. The problem wasn't even with the product. The problem was with the people.

He wasn't the kind to let grass grow under his feet, so he walked straight into the nearest Electrolux office.

Geographically speaking, it might not have been an office most people would have identified as even in the vicinity. Asked to name a state that's close to Missouri, very few people come up with Florida; those few tend to change their minds when they look at a map. Which just goes to show how easy it is to be misled by our assumptions, overlook the obvious, and jump to conclusions.

What most people assume is that you can answer a question like that just by *looking* at a map. And what they overlook is the fact that when you start a new job it's important to give it everything you've got.

It's important to give that new job 101%, 25 hours a day, 366 days a year. You simply can't afford to have any distractions. If the reason you gave up your old job was that it was not sufficiently remunerative to enable you to meet your commitments, you may well find yourself with some debts which it would be distracting to deal with at this time. It's absolutely vital to start the new job in an area where any difficulties you may have experienced in the past are unlikely to lead to unwelcome distractions. He needed to be based in a locality presenting no foreseeable distractions, and he selected the nearest Electrolux office which would enable him to meet that need, and he walked straight in.

When you're in sales you've always got one thing to sell, and that's yourself. He walked in and started talking about what he could do for Electrolux sales and they said You're that good. All I ask is the chance to show what I can do, he said, and they said All right, hot shot, let's see what you can do, and they gave him a district.

He familiarized himself with the product and moved to Eureka, Fla., and rented a trailer. The next day he got cracking.

By the end of the week he realized this was not going to be as easy as it looked. Because every single house he went to had the same story to tell. They already *had* an Electrolux, they'd bought it just after Hurricane Edna, and it was one of the best things they'd ever done. The customer would then insist on dragging out the faithful Electrolux and singing its praises. Yessir, the customer would say, reckon I'll break down before this thing does.

In fact, the place was every salesman's nightmare: a festering swamp of market saturation. A rep had come through and cleaned up in the wake of Hurricane Edna and every single item he had sold was still there in good working order.

He tried, obviously, to point out that time doesn't stand still, enhancements had been introduced, but once again Hurricane Edna blew him out of the water. The customer would explain loyally that she wouldn't dream of replacing her old model, you should have *seen* what we had to deal with, she would explain, the Electrolux had handled things you wouldn't normally ask of a vacuum cleaner.

He managed to make one sale to someone who had just moved into the area.

The result was that he spent a lot of time in the trailer trying to get up the energy to go out. He would lie in bed with a magazine, or sometimes he would watch a video, or sometimes he used fantasies of his own.

His first fantasy was about walls. The woman would have the upper part of her body on one side of the wall. The lower part of her body would be on the other side of the wall.

Sometimes, in fact most of the time, the upper part of the body would be fully clothed. There would be nothing to show what was going on on the other side of the wall.

Sometimes the woman would be naked from the waist down. Most of the time she would be wearing a short tight skirt that could be pushed up and underpants that could be pulled down. Sometimes he would have trouble deciding whether it was better with or without the pants. The high point was pushing the skirt slowly up to reveal a firm, tight, unsuspecting ass. Later a cock would go in and the vantage point of the fantasy would shift to the other side of the wall, where you would not know from the fully clothed upper body of the woman that a cock was hard at work on the other side of the wall. For some reason or other she would need to pretend that nothing was happening.

The problem with the fantasy was that it was hard to get the wall right. Could she be leaning across the counter of a kitchen that opened into the dining room? But then you would see what was behind her. Could there be a roll-down blind? But why would it be rolled down? And anyway you would still be able to see. Could she be leaning out an upstairs window? A partially opened window with the blind down. She stuck her head out, say, to talk to a neighbor. The window was too stiff to open any higher. Meanwhile her lodger, say, comes up behind her, slides his hands up her thighs, slides up the tight skirt, gives her an unexpected bonus on top of the rent. From the vantage point of outside the window you would see her talking brightly to a neighbor – brightly but with a strained expression.

This was a solution that seemed to work at the time, and yet later he would feel dissatisfied, as if some essential ingredient of the fantasy had dropped out. Was the problem with the neighbor? Would it help if it was her boss? An important client? Or was the problem on the other side of the wall?

He would get up and go out and tackle another street. To be fair, he never once had anyone who didn't look pleased to see him. He would go up to a door and ring the bell. Someone would come to the door, and there would be the usual initial hostility when they saw it was a salesman. One mention of the word Electrolux and it was a different story.

"Electrolux!" the target would exclaim. "Why didn't you *say*? You just come right in. Now what can I get you? Coffee? Tea? A soda? Now can I interest you in something to eat? What would you say to a piece of pumpkin pie with ice cream? Or I've got a chocolate cake. Or how *about* some chocolate chip cookies?"

Half an hour later he would escape clutching as likely as not a little Ziploc bag of chocolate chip cookies in a sweating hand.

When he was a boy he used to wish every day was Halloween. There is an old Chinese saying: May your enemy's wishes come true.

He would force himself to visit every single house on the street. Hours later, awash with coffee, stuffed with pumpkin, apple, cherry, pecan, chocolate meringue, lemon meringue, banoffee and blueberry pie, ears ringing with the praises of the Electrolux and stirring stories of its battles after Hurricane Edna, he would make his way back to the trailer, stopping only to pick up a magazine or two.

Back on the bed he would leaf rapidly through the magazines.

The problem was that the magazines never really had what he was looking for. Once in a while a magazine might show the naked bottom half of a woman cut off by a window. The problem was that the magazines never showed pictures of the clothed top half of a woman cut off by a window.

This was an area where you might expect videos to provide a better product, but in fact the videos also tended not to include the scenes where you saw the clothed half of the woman, or if they did the woman overacted so much it spoiled it.

He would lie on his side, hand jiggling quietly, trying to envisage the window, the skirt, the ass, the fully clothed upper body of a woman with a strained expression.

The funny thing about it was that at the time he felt really guilty about it. He kept thinking he should get up and go out and sell vacuum cleaners. He should get up and go out and make something of his life. It felt like he was just lying there wasting time. He kept doing it but he didn't feel good about it. He was thirty-three years old and he had zip to show for it. And here he was lying in bed in the middle of the day not even masturbating effectively but just twiddling until he got the fantasy set up to his satisfaction. He didn't feel good about it at all.

His feeling at the time was that the guy who had cleaned up after Hurricane Edna had probably been a completely different kind of guy. The kind of guy who goes out, buys a magazine, takes the magazine home, opens the magazine, looks at the tits of the month, jerks off, closes the magazine, and goes out and sells vacuum cleaners.

Sometimes he would lie there for fifteen minutes worrying about the roll-down blind and twiddling and he would think of the guy and he would think *This* has *got* to *stop*, I'm going to turn over a new leaf. How could he lie there for *fifteen minutes* worrying about the Goddamn roll-down fucking blind? It was disgusting. So he'd get out the magazine and turn to a pair of tits backed by Miss April and get on with the show. And go out and try to move some product.

Which just goes to show how blinkered we can be by our preconceptions. Because little though he knew it, it was the hours he spent trying to sell vacuum cleaners that were the waste of time, something he would remember with shame and self-loathing for the rest of his life. His well-meant efforts to develop an efficient masturbatory program, likewise, were completely misconceived.

What he didn't realize is that a genius is different from other people. A genius doesn't waste time like other people. Even when he looks like he is wasting time he may in fact be making the most productive possible use of the time. In fact the only time a genius wastes time is when he tries to follow the rules and act like ordinary people.

What he didn't realize was that all that time he spent twiddling and worrying about the roll-down blind would one day lead directly to a multi-million dollar industry that would improve the lives of millions of Americans.

Another fantasy was about a game show with three contestants with their upper bodies sticking through a hole in a wall. In the first part of the game, one contestant was penally challenged from behind. Panelists had to guess which. The contestants got points if the panelists guessed wrong. An inset in the screen showed the thrusting buttocks of a man giving the contestant the old Atchison Topeka. In the second stage of the game, any number could be involved, from zero (though this had never happened in the whole time he'd been watching the show), right on up to a full house (this was actually surprisingly common). The panelists had to guess how many, and which ones.

Each panelist got to ask questions, or set tests. The panelist then made a decision on the basis of the behavior of the contestants during the questions, and made his or her guess.

After a while one of the contestants started to get a personality. She was a consecutive winner for twenty shows. She wore a pink jacket and immaculate pink lipstick and make-up, and she had dark hair in a hairsprayed permanent. People looked at the heaving buttocks in the inset and they couldn't *believe* that someone that cool could possibly be getting the full-service 24-hour Revco from the rear. Then after she won the round the MC would say Let's just see that amazing performance again.

In her final play-off one of the panelists, a real bitch, said she'd like to see her put on nail polish. She took a bottle of pink nail polish and started on her nails, and everybody watched, and her nails were absolutely perfect. It turned out later that this was one of the times when all three contestants were getting the old Triple Jeopardy. One kept smearing her nail polish, and one dropped the bottle, but Suzie just kept quietly finishing her nails.

Afterwards the MC said: I've never seen anything like it. I take my hat off to you. Let's just see that again.

The screen divided in half, on one half the heaving buttocks on the other Suzie quietly painting her nails.

MC: Well, I see it and I still don't believe it. What's your secret?

Suzie: That's my secret.

He really liked her. And he always played fair. It was all right to replay highlights of her game career. But she'd won her million fair and square; she didn't have to play the game again, and he never brought her into any new episodes. Sometimes he'd think of her, out in the world, in her pink suit, with a million to blow. She did what she had to do, and then she did what she wanted to do.

He often wondered whether other men did this. Did they have participants that developed personalities? Did they have a sense of humor? Was there a story that developed over several episodes?

And being a salesman he could not stop analyzing in a really micro obsessive nitty-gritty way what got him off. It's not what you see it's what you know. Because it wasn't the bare buttocks or the thrusting cock into a tight wet cunt but Suzie in her pink jacket painting her nails that sent Old Faithful skyward every time.

For a while, anyway, he went on rerunning favorite episodes in Suzie's brilliant career, looking in once in a while on current episodes just to see how things were going and then going out from time to time when he felt like a piece of homemade pumpkin pie with ice cream.

Then one day he noticed that the game was rigged.

For some reason he hadn't noticed it before, but once you knew what to look for you couldn't miss it. The contestants varied, but there was always one with platinum blonde hair and pink lipstick and big tits in a tight top who had no self-control whatsoever. The thing was a joke. The MC would start the game and suddenly the girl's eyes would widen and her pink mouth would open with this ostentatious *Oh my God, there's a cock up my twat* kind of expression.

Is anything the matter? the MC would say in a syrupy voice and the girl would say No and then suddenly catch her breath or bite her lip or widen her eyes just to make sure everyone knew what was going on. How obvious can you get?

And the MC would say OK, we'll get on with the show then. Panelists, our stud for this session was Mr. Body for Arkansas four years running. As I speak Clint is giving one of the girls the kind of workout only a serious bodybuilder can provide. Let's have a quick look at the service offered by Clint, and there would be an inset of the thrusting buttocks.

Well, that's one bodybuilder who thinks there are no holds barred, he'd say, and the studio audience would laugh.

Ladies and gentlemen, your job is to decide which of our lovely ladies is enjoying this magnificent stallion of a man. Heloise, it's your turn to ask the first question.

And the blonde girl would whimper or shout Oh my God and the panel would laugh. Sometimes the panel wouldn't take it seriously. It would be absolutely obvious what the answer was but they'd laugh and guess wrong on purpose.

Sometimes he could enjoy it anyway and sometimes it was just irritating. They were only doing their job but sometimes it irritated him anyway, and he missed the days before he realized the whole thing was a set-up.

One day he lay on his side on the bed and they had yet another of these blondes on the show. He lay there wondering where they got them all. The studs today were three guys who were putting themselves through college. They had called the studio's 800 number in the aftermath of a frat party and left their names and when they got the follow-up call they all thought *Shit*. But in the end they agreed to go on the show because it was something different and because people only saw you from behind and because it was something to say you'd done, and because of the money. Would they do it again?

Jeff: No way. Don't get me wrong, I really enjoyed myself today, it's been a really unique experience and it certainly will be something to look back on, I'll say that, but I don't think I'd want to make a regular thing of it.

Shane (laughing): Is that an offer?

MC (laughing): No.

Duane: Well, the way I see it, Mike, there's a whole lot more goes into this than meets the eye.

MC (laughing): You can say that again! (studio audience laughs)

Duane: No, but seriously. On the one hand, you're there to do a job. It's up to you to take a professional approach. But on the other hand, it's important to have a good time. So would I do it again? Sure I would. Because there's no way you can bring everything to the game that it's possible *to* bring, on your first time on the show. And the other thing I'd like to say is, I'd just like to say thank you to all the girls, it was a pleasure to work with them and they definitely made it a day to remember.

Joe lay with his head on his arm. His hand, he realized, was holding a limp, wilted dick. *Jesus*, he thought. *Jesus*. This was *exactly* the *problem*. What *was* it with him? He was the type of guy to go out and try to sell vacuum cleaners and end up eating twenty fucking pieces of pumpkin fucking pie. *Jesus*.

He pulled a magazine out from under the bed, opened it to the central spread, stared narrow-eyed at the girl's tits and jerked off. *Jesus*.

He got up off the bed, zipped up his pants, and went outside to sit on the steps.

"Look, Joe," he said. "Things can't go on like this. Do you hear what I'm saying? This can't go on."

He sighed. The sun was setting behind the pines. Another day comes and goes.

"Look," he said. "The game is not rigged, OK? The only reason it's rigged, if it *is* rigged, is because you made it up that way. Nobody did anything behind your back. You decided, for reasons best known to yourself, to move in the direction of a rigged game, so you got a rigged game. You didn't *find* anything *out*. There was nothing *to* find out. You made the whole thing up in your head. And now you're talking to yourself. This has *got* to *stop*."

The sky was a dark clear blue, all except for the narrow band of blazing orange behind the black pines.

He said, "All I want is to be a success. That's all I ask."

The sky slowly blackened and the stars came out, and still he sat on the steps.

He had hit rock bottom. Because let's face it, the kind of guy who gets ahead in the world, the kind of guy who makes a mark, the kind of guy who makes a difference, is the kind of guy who deals with his sexual urges and gets on with the job. He is not the kind of guy who lies around obsessing about whether some completely imaginary game show is rigged. He is not the kind of guy who gets side-tracked out of his masturbatory fantasy into a non-masturbatory fantasy about three guys from college called Jeff, Shane, and Duane. *Duane.* Where the fuck did that *come* from? *Jesus.*

What he realized later was that this was exactly the mistake he had made all his life, assuming that if he was different in some way that was automatically worse. Assuming he'd be all right if he was just like everybody else. Assuming the thing he needed to work on was getting rid of all the things that stood out. Because after all the basic raw material of his fantasies was probably not all that different from a lot of guys, look at it this way you could find similar types of scenario with some of the elements in magazines and videos which had to mean they thought it would appeal to a lot of guys. The thing was just that most guys would not replay favorite episodes from the days when Suzie was on the show, and wonder what she was doing with herself now that she had a million bucks to play around with; most guys would not get involved in the personalities, they would not get pissed off because the MC was an asshole and start wondering how to get him off the show, they would not wonder why it had to be rigged, and they would not decide that the thrusting buttocks behind the screen belonged to three college guys named Jeff, Shane, and Duane.

What he should have realized is that if there is something that makes you different from everybody else it may be that that very thing is your unique selling point.

Because as it turned out, it was his tendency to gradually start seeing the personalities, to start bringing in all kinds of irrelevant stories to the point where people would have names, that turned out to be his hidden strength. Gradually the people would turn out to be ordinary people just like you and me, only involved in a situation most ordinary people would not put themselves into. And instead of getting obsessed with the sex, the way most guys would, he just happened to have this tendency to start seeing the whole picture with the sex as part of the picture. He happened to have this ability to imagine what it would be that would get ordinary people involved in something like that.

The sky was a velvety black. The stars were out and the moon had risen.

He said, "Come on, Joe. You can do better than this."

He started wondering what it was about sex. Because if you think about it the pornography industry is a multi-billion dollar industry. Some people use it as an adjunct to a fulfilling sexual relationship, sure, but what about the rest? If you could figure out a way to deliver the real thing you'd really be onto something. A way to deliver the real thing where people did not have to worry about running into the criminal element, or getting arrested, or just getting recognized.

He started looking at it another way. The way he looked at it was, why is this not a problem for homosexuals? A couple of guys could be just working together in an office and they can meet in the john and get back to work. A lot of guys would not have a problem with doing this kind of thing with a female partner, part of the problem obviously was segregated toilets and part of the problem was that a lot of women would have a problem with it.

Any salesman knows that you have to deal with people the way they are. Not how you'd like them to be.

The crickets were chirping in the long grass.

Joe sat on the steps, jingling the change in his pocket.

"Come on, Joe," he said. "There's got to be something you can do."

His thoughts turned again to the guy who had cleaned up after Hurricane Edna. Basically the guy had identified a disaster that had struck everyone and he had identified a problem that faced everyone who had been struck by the disaster. Then he had gone in with a solution to the problem.

Somewhere around midnight the idea came to him.

"Joe," he said, "you're in big trouble."

SPECIAL K

In the morning the sun was shining, birds were singing, and there was dew on the grass. The crazy thoughts of the night before did not look so bad. They looked crazy, but they did not look like crazy things he would seriously think about trying out. Everyone gets crazy thoughts from time to time, it's what you do about them that counts.

It was time to turn over a new leaf. Eat right. Get some exercise. For instance, instead of taking the car, why not *walk* to the store?

He walked over to the 7- Eleven and bought a box of Special K and a carton of skim milk.

On his way back to the trailer park he saw a heron fly over the lake and vanish in the reeds. "Now if you'd taken the car you wouldn't have seen that," he said. "It's a beautiful world. You have a right to be here. Now let's get back to the trailer, have us some breakfast, and get out there and sell some vacuum cleaners."

After breakfast he washed the bowl and left it to drain. He did not wash the rest of the week's dishes because it's important to be able to prioritize. He shaved and dressed and put the Electrolux in the car.

"Skooby dooby doo, exchanging glances, skooby dooby dooby dooby dooby," he sang, shifting to Drive. He pulled out of the trailer park and headed down the highway for the next neighborhood on his list.

The highway went along the beach. This was a part of the beach that never saw much action at the best of times, and at this time of day it was pretty much deserted. The tide was out. The sand just above the water gleamed white in the bright morning sun, and tiny sandpipers darted up and down. Out to sea a line of pelicans flew low over the waves.

"It's a beautiful world," said Joe again. "You have a right to be here."

He started singing the song "Everything is beautiful in its own way," which he had never expected to want to sing voluntarily and so had never learned past the first line. "Everything is beautiful in its own way," sang Joe. "Skooby dooby doo, dooby doo, dooby doo, dooby dooby by doo . . . " Maybe it had something to do with starting the day with Special K.

He kept driving along, one hand on the wheel, singing the first line of "Everything is beautiful in its own way" and grinning and looking out to sea. The pelicans were just tiny specks in the distance, but the sandpipers were still running up and down.

Years later he could always get a laugh out of an audience telling the story. Because the thing of it is, this is a thing that crosses generations. You take a bunch of guys and maybe for some of them The Man was Elvis, and for some of them it was Jimi Hendrix, and for some of them it was Kurt Cobain, but the thing they all have in common is that they would never sing "Everything is beautiful in its own way" unless someone held a gun to their head (and maybe not even then). Except that every one of those guys will have had the experience of being up at sunrise and going out and being alone in the world and wanting to sing something. He could get a laugh because he only knew the first line of "Everything is beautiful in its own way," and the other way he could get a laugh was by explaining that he went on to sing "Oh what a beautiful morning," and he actually knew all the words because his mother drove him crazy playing the record when he was a kid, but he couldn't quote them in his autobiography because he would have had to have paid a lot of money.

Well, he finished singing "Oh what a beautiful morning" and he found that he had taken his foot off the accelerator. The car was slowing down and he found that he was putting his foot on the brake and turning off the road. He stopped the car on the sandy shoulder and parked it and turned off the engine. He could hear the soft whisper of the waves and the piping of the sandpipers.

There are things that you spell out in words for an audience that you don't think in words at the time. In his mind he was just seeing the heron with its long sharp beak and spindly legs. He was seeing the sandpipers running up and down the wet sand. He saw the pelicans with their big beaks that could hold a whole fish. They were flying low over the waves because they knew where to find the kind of fish they could put in their beaks.

He opened the door and got out of the car. The Electrolux, with its accessories, sat in the back seat.

He closed the car door and folded his arms on top of the car, looking out to sea. "I don't have what it takes," he said. He had never said it before because saying it would be like admitting he couldn't make the grade. But now he said it and he wasn't blaming himself. Does a heron go around complaining because it doesn't have the kind of beak you can stick a whole fish in? Does it say "Where there's a will there's a way" and go flying low over the waves, beak or no beak? Like hell it does.

There are guys who can persuade someone they want a new vacuum cleaner even if they have only just bought one. There are guys who can persuade someone they want a new vacuum cleaner even if the vacuum cleaner they have now is more a member of the family than an appliance. In all probability half the people who bought an Electrolux after Hurricane Edna had a perfectly good vacuum cleaner that had come through the hurricane miraculously unscathed. The reason they had bought a new vacuum cleaner was that they had come up against a guy who was born to sell vacuum cleaners. The reason they did not want to buy another vacuum cleaner now was that they were dealing with a guy who did not have what it takes to sell vacuum cleaners.

Well, if you don't have what it takes you can go on trying to sell vacuum cleaners till the cows come home. When you look back over your life, what you're going to see is that you ate a lot of pumpkin pie.

If you're a salesman, you have to deal with yourself the way you are. Not how you'd like to be.

If you don't have what it takes, you can waste a lot of time asking yourself "How can I *get* what it takes?" The question you should be asking yourself is, "Is there something else that takes what I have to offer?" Because if there's something you can succeed at, just the way you are, you won't have to waste a lot of time trying to change yourself. Which you're never going to be able to do, anyway.

If you ask most people what's the hardest thing about being a salesman, they will usually say the rejection. "People always trying to get rid of you," they say, "that's what I'd hate."

Or sometimes they say it's the travel that would really get to them, all those hotel and motel rooms blurring into each other, it must get really lonely. Or sometimes they think it would bother them to be selling things to people that they didn't really need, pressurizing people into buying things they were not really able to afford.

Well, at one time or another every salesman has probably felt all of those things. But the thing that's hardest about the job is something you can't leave behind you by getting another job. A salesman has to see people as they are.

Most people spend their lives trying to *avoid* doing that very thing. Most people see what they want to see. But a salesman can't afford to see people the way *he* might like them to be. He has to see them the way they actually are. And he also has to see them the way they'd like to be. Because no matter how badly people want something, if they don't want to be the kind of people who want that kind of thing you're going to have an uphill battle persuading them to buy it. He has to see what it is they don't like about the way they are and convince them that the way they are is OK. Or he has to see what it is they don't like and persuade them that he has just the product to fix it. That's the hardest thing about the job.

Now if you're selling encyclopedias it's obvious you're selling people the idea that they can be what they want to be. But even if you're selling vacuum cleaners you're selling people the way they could be – they could be people who will clean their stairs and the furniture and curtains using appropriate attachments, instead of people who could save themselves a couple of hundred bucks by just borrowing a vacuum cleaner for Thanksgiving and Christmas from their next-door neighbors. You're selling the chance to fix something that's wrong. What you're selling, basically, is the idea that there's nothing wrong with the *customer*; maybe they don't know as much as they should, or maybe they happen to live in a dirty house, but that's just because they don't have the one thing lacking to put it right.

What you're selling, obviously, is the idea that if they don't buy that one thing there *is* something wrong with them. They could put something right that needs fixing and they chose not to.

The reason it takes a salesman to do this is that left to their own devices most people will just drift along thinking I really should do something about that one of these days. That's the way people are, and it takes a salesman to get them out of the rut and take some action to actually achieve their goals. It takes a salesman to show them that something they hadn't thought of as a goal, such as reading the *Encyclopaedia Britannica* on a regular basis, could *be* a goal. An achievable goal. The longest journey starts with a single step. In this case, the step of buying the *Encyclopaedia Britannica*.

What this means is that a salesman is constantly confronted with the human capacity for self-deception. He has to recognize that most people will do just about anything rather than face up to the truth about themselves. That's the hardest thing about the job.

He looked out to sea over the roof of the car. The waves threw down their veils of foam and drew them back, and the sandpipers ran piping over the glistening sand.

He thought: An animal has no shame.

It hunts what it eats and it eats it.

It shits when it needs to. It pees when it needs to. That's why a parked car gets covered in bird shit. The bird doesn't wait to find a bathroom. It doesn't understand the concept of bathroom. It just goes when it needs to.

Then he started to think: But wait a minute, if you see a dog or a cat trying to shit while someone's watching they look kind of embarrassed. And afterwards a cat will scrape dirt over it. Is that just because it's left over from the days when the animal would be vulnerable to a predator, or a predator could track it, or something?

And the really interesting thing was that instead of getting side-tracked the way he usually did he just thought: Screw that.

In other words, when something was genuinely important he didn't get side-tracked. There was something inside him that was able to tell when something was genuinely important.

The thing that was important was that animals have the instinct to mate and they do it without shame.

He thought: Humans do nothing without shame.

Even eating is shameful because it makes you fat. And some things are so shameful you can't even use a word for them without swearing. You say "go to the bathroom" and "sleep with" because the actual words would be bad language.

What he was thinking, as he watched the sea and the birds, was Look how strong the impulse is! Because you can sell people just about anything if you can convince them it will give them a better chance to get sex. You can sell people just about anything if you can convince them it's a *substitute* for sex. The only thing you can't sell is the actual thing itself. That is, obviously people sell it, but you can't sell it without shame.

Well, just look at how much time people waste because they *can't* get it without shame! Look how much time people waste in conversations, asking people about their interests. Look how much time people waste fantasizing. And just look at the risks people take! Because he had read about a case where a man had harassed a woman by dropping M&M's in the pocket of her blouse and getting them out, and his firm had to pay her a million dollars. Or it might have been more.

Well, if people are willing to take those kinds of risks you *know* there's got to be money in it. And if people are going to do things that put their *company* at that kind of risk there's got to be money in it. Plus, if you could give people a way to get it out of their system they would be a whole lot more productive. They'd be happier about themselves. Because there had to be a lot of guys like himself, guys who didn't want to be spending the amount of time they were spending thinking about sex, guys who given the chance would rather get it out of their system and concentrate their energies on achieving their goals.

Now the way he saw it was, gay men seemed to be able to get it out of their system without too much trouble. *Their* only problem was there were not that many of them around. But normal men could be in an office full of women without finding an outlet. You have to deal with people the way they are, not the way you'd like them to be, and unfortunately most women did not seem to have the same urges. Or if they did, they wouldn't admit it. They probably didn't, anyway. But if they did they wouldn't admit it.

Because you have to deal with people the way they are, not the way you'd like them to be, and unfortunately most men tend not to respect women who have the same urges they have. Or even if a woman doesn't have the same urges, but just provides an outlet, men tend not to respect her. Because if you take people the way they are, most men tend to see sticking their dick into someone as a form of domination. To be honest, if you take people the way they are, that's what they like about it. It's not just the physical sensation. That's exactly why masturbation is so unsatisfactory. The physical sensation is pretty much the same. But the domination is all in your head.

So even if a woman wanted the physical sensation just as an outlet she would probably not admit it because of all the aggro.

But the thing to remember was that some women were prepared to provide an outlet, in *spite* of all the aggro, if the money was right. And lots of guys were prepared to pay, in spite of the aggro. And what the aggro boiled down to, if you thought about it, was the shame of being known to be the person who had been involved. That was why prostitution was so degrading. A prostitute knew that somebody knew she was a prostitute. So whatever else she did with her life, there was always the chance that it would come back to haunt her. And likewise, even if nobody else knew, a man knew that a prostitute knew that he had been to a prostitute.

If you could work out a way to offer anonymity you would have a solution to a disaster that made Hurricane Edna look like a variable breeze.

Now the night before, sitting on the steps, he had thought of a way to offer anonymity and he had decided he was crazy.

What he thought now was: An animal knows no shame.

In other words, the reason he had decided he was crazy was just because he was human. A salesman knows you have to deal with yourself as you are, and that includes a tendency to be ashamed to sell things that society has decided are shameful.

Well, the question to ask yourself is, are they right? And in this case the answer had to be no. A physical urge is a physical urge. What's shameful is to look the other way and let the devil take the hindmost, instead of dealing with it responsibly. Because the fact was, these unsatisfied urges were causing an incredible amount of wastefulness and suffering. Women were being molested in the workplace solely because their colleagues did not have a legitimate outlet for urges they could not control. Men who had worked hard and who had a valuable contribution to make were being put at risk, through no fault of their own. And it was shame, false shame, that had kept people from dealing effectively with the situation.

Humans are animals, he thought. All these instincts, these incredibly powerful instincts, are just thwarted by all these taboos. If you can break through some of those taboos *for* people, there's got to be money in it. A *lot* of money. But the money is big because those taboos are so strong. Do you have what it takes to break through that, Joe? Do you have what it takes to look someone in the eye when they're thinking it's disgusting? Because the thing is, Joe, a big idea is ahead of its time. That's *why* there's money in it. It's going to be a long, long time before people catch up with you. If they ever do. You've got to know you're right, because they sure as hell won't. People are going to give you a lot of grief. A *lot* of grief. So if you can't take it, Joe, let's call it quits right here and now.

What he thought was: I don't know if I have what it takes or not. I've never really been tested. I've never had the chance to find out what I'm capable of. But I know one thing. It's one thing to try, and do your best, and fail. All you can ever do is give something your best shot, and sometimes that's just not enough. But it's another thing to not even try. This is the first time I've had a chance at something really big. If I just walk away from it, what does that make me?

"Look, Joe," he said. "Let's not get too serious here. I'm not saying it won't be a lot of work. But it should be a lot of fun, too. Are you having such a good time selling vacuum cleaners? And OK, you may get some funny looks. But just try to see the humor in it. Besides, at the end of the day, you're doing everybody a favor. That's something to feel good about. So just do the best you can, and remember, if it all goes horribly wrong, you can always shoot yourself."

He was grinning. He slipped off his shoes and socks and rolled up his pants, and he walked up the cool soft sand of the low bank beside the road, and then down onto the beach. The sand near the road was choppy, warm where the sun hit it, cool where the hollows were in shade. Then the sand was firm and ribbed, and then it was flat and wet.

The line of pelicans was coming back along the waves. He watched them, shading his eyes.

"Look at those beautiful birds," he said. "Is there one single thing wrong with them, Joe? Does a pelican have one single thing to be ashamed of?"

He was walking along in the shallow water. He turned to face the sea and put his hands around his mouth.

"MY NAME IS JOOOOOOOOE!" he shouted. "Yabba dabba DOOOOOOOOOOOO!"

SO LONG ELECTROLUX

The first thing he did was he returned the Electrolux and its accessories.

"Well if it isn't the hot shot!" The head of the sales reps was in a meeting. His secretary had been interrupted in the middle of a book by Danielle Steel and was none too pleased at having to break off and check the vacuum cleaner back in.

"Not such a hot shot after all, I guess," he said.

The girl was looking at him mockingly.

"I guess I just don't have what it takes."

He said this with a quiet conviction that is rare in salesmen.

"Don't be so hard on yourself," the girl said. She was still looking at him mockingly, but there was a kind of undercurrent of sympathy.

"Now the guy who was there before me was a real operator," said Joe.

"Believe me, I know," said the girl.

"If you ever want some testimonials for the product, you should talk to some of the people there. They've all got these stories about how it saved their life after Hurricane Edna."

"Yeah, we keep getting letters from them. That's why I'm saying, don't be too hard on yourself. Billy Graham couldn't have sold a vacuum cleaner in Eureka. Billy Graham could have gone door to door telling people he had vacuum cleaners that were personally endorsed by Jesus K. Christ, and he would not have sold one single one. Ed has a kind of mischievious sense of humor is all. If he'd have given you the chance to show what you could do in some other district it might have been a different story."

"Well, it may turn out to be a blessing in disguise," said Joe. He was looking at the girl. His eyes kept being drawn to her breasts and then he would smoothly keep moving his gaze on as if it had just happened to travel past her breasts en route to checking out the pencil sharpener. He'd spent a lot of time on his own, after all. This kind of thing must happen all the time when the sales reps came in after a long time on the road. "Do you have much trouble with sexual harassment in your job?" he asked.

"What?" said the girl.

"With the sales reps, maybe? They spend all that time on the road and I just wondered if you ever had any problems."

"Well, it's not a job for shrinking violets if *that's* what you mean," said the girl. "But the way I see it is, and this is no disrespect to you, it takes a certain type of personality to succeed in sales. And it takes a certain type of personality to be able to deal with that type of personality. If you look at the skills, there's a lot of people could do my job. But what it really boils down to is being able to deal with people. You have to be able to give as good as you get. There's things about the job that would bother a lot of people. But that's taken account of in the package they offer. The way I see it is, I'm quite a strong person. If I can get a salary that takes that into account, why would I want to settle for a job that doesn't need those strengths?"

One of the things that's perennially fascinating about the world is the way people sell things to themselves. If people feel the need to sell something to themselves, that tells its own tale.

"That's very interesting," said Joe. "But doesn't it ever get to you? What I mean is, just suppose for the sake of argument that a guy like me, a guy you *know* is never going to make it to the top, comes up to you at the Xerox machine and does something inappropriate. Drops some M&M's in the pocket of your blouse and tries to get them out. What would your reaction be?"

"Well, if you've ever had a secret ambition to sing with the sopranos I suggest you try it and see."

"But say a top sales rep, say *the* top sales rep did something like that. You might have feelings about it that you would not feel free to express in the way you would to a guy who was not in that kind of position."

"I see what you're saying," she said. "But the way I look at it is, every job has its drawbacks. You can make yourself miserable dwelling on them and thinking if you go elsewhere you're going to find the perfect job. The fact is there *is* no perfect job. *The* perfect job does not exist. People are people. Any job you go to, you're always going to find people. And the way I look at it is, let's say somebody steps out of line. You've got to keep a sense of proportion about these things. I don't care *what* he's making, I don't care *how* many Goddamn vacuum cleaners he shifts, he can't *force* me to do anything I don't want to. As long as we're here during office hours I don't have to do anything not specifically covered by my job description. And as soon as I leave the building my time is my own."

"Well, there's a lot in what you say," said Joe.

But what he was thinking was this. A guy could be the top earner in a company and have a house and a car to reflect that, but when it came to something our instincts have programmed us to want more than almost anything else you can name he was basically no better off than Joe Schmoe.

If he wanted an outlet for his sexual urges he would have to invest the time talking to someone about her interests, with no guarantee that anything would come of it, or he would have to go home and jerk off to a magazine or video, or he would have to pay someone, with all the risks that entailed. But how much time does the top earner in a company realistically have to talk to someone about her interests? If he hires someone, on the other hand, a guy in that kind of position has a lot to lose. He has a reputation that can be damaged. What real choices does he have? If he's at the office he can't even put M&M's down somebody's blouse. Let alone get any kind of real sexual satisfaction. And a guy like that is going to be spending a lot of time on the job. He works his butt off and at the end of the day he can go home to a magazine. Just like Joe Schmoe sitting on his butt all day in a trailer.

If you're Joe Schmoe in the trailer you tend to think if you got off your butt and got your act together you could have real girls just like the ones in the magazines. You wouldn't have to do anything. They'd be yours for the asking. Well if it was actually *like* that you wouldn't get guys trying to get off on behaving suggestively in the office.

Well, if you have a situation where the top earner in a company *still* can't get what he wants, and where he can jeopardize his career trying to *get* what he wants, jeopardizing the profits of the *company* in the *process*, you *know* there's got to be money in it.

"Well, I've enjoyed talking to you," said Joe.

"What are your plans?" said the girl.

Joe was standing in front of her desk. Behind her desk the wall was a floor-to-ceiling mirror, with potted rubber plants along the base. In the mirror, between the rubber plants, he could see a guy wearing a tired brown polyester suit. It wasn't rumpled or wrinkled because that's the whole point of polyester. But it wasn't crisp, either, because polyester does not have it in it to be crisp. The guy was standing there among the plants with this suit wilting on his shoulders. If a guy like that came up to you and tried to sell a vacuum cleaner you might feel sorry for him and offer him a piece of pumpkin pie, but you would not buy a vacuum cleaner. If a guy like that came up to you and made an innovative suggestion for rewarding the top earners in your company you would reject it out of hand. He was just the kind of guy you'd *expect* to come up with the kind of dirty idea that was totally inappropriate to your company.

"I'm going to buy a new suit."

2

THE NUMBERS GAME

FIRST IMPRESSIONS

Joe was the first to admit that he made a lot of mistakes when he started out. He worried about all the wrong things. The way he looked at it at first was, take it slow, build up gradually. So the first thing he decided to try, if you can believe it, was a kind of office-orientated version of Spin the Bottle.

But one thing he got right was that it was important to look good. In the trailer he had only seen himself in the bathroom mirror that he used to shave in. Seeing himself in the office mirror had come as a shock. In fact it had made him wonder whether he had actually been sane when he bought that suit in the first place. Why would *anybody* buy a shit-colored suit? Why would that have seemed even *momentarily* a good idea? All right, it was on sale at the time. Originally a $99.99 suit, it had been reduced to $49.99 with choice of tie. But wouldn't you think you would at least *wonder* why they hadn't been able to sell it at $99.99? Wouldn't you think you would look at it and think Oh, I'll bet the reason they couldn't sell it at $99.99 was that nobody wanted to buy a suit that went with their turds. But no, he'd just gone in and said, "Hey! $49.99! And it fits! And it's 100% polyester so it won't get wrinkled!" *Jesus*.

Anyway, now that he had come to his senses he realized

that for what he was trying to achieve it was impossible to look too good.

He bought a thousand-dollar suit on the installment plan. It was a dark, silky charcoal, so dark it was almost black in certain lights. He bought a deep red silk tie. He bought ten white shirts and a pair of heavy silver cufflinks. He bought ten pairs of black silk socks. He bought a pair of three-hundred-dollar English shoes. He bought ten pairs of Jockey underpants and ten Jockey T-shirts because it's important to be clean. He bought a box of crisp white handkerchiefs. It's important not just to look like a rich man, but to feel the way a rich man feels in his clothes.

Then he had some stationery printed up. He wrote to a lot of businesses in the area explaining that he was doing research in personal interaction in occupational psychology, and asking whether members of staff would be prepared to participate in a simple study.

Seventy-five companies didn't bother to reply. Fifteen wrote to say they weren't interested. Ten said they would need to know more about it. He went in to Number 91 and he explained:

"As you know personal inter- and intra-gender interaction is a minefield in the modern office. Studies in Germany have shown that the tensions generated by an environment where the sexual is taboo have been eased by what I call a lightning rod."

"A what?" said the personnel officer.

"An arbitrary device permitting yet limiting interpersonal interactions. A common example is the mistletoe. Persons walking beneath it may be kissed. Persons who avoid it are exempt. Studies in Germany have shown that a similar device, installed in the office environment, removed much of the ill feeling which had previously been generated by, on the one hand, unwelcome advances and, on the other hand, unanticipated rejection."

He explained that the study would examine the effects of such a device in an American business environment.

Nine out of ten were not interested. One agreed to the study.

Now the way he had set it up – and this was a *long* way from the hole in the wall – was this. Participants would be placed in a computer-generated random-selection procedure. In phase one, the selection would take place once a day at 5. In phase two, there would also be a lunchtime selection. In phase three, there would be hourly selection. Two names would be chosen, one male and one female. These two persons would then be required to kiss in full view of the office, say under the main clock. In other words, Spin the Bottle.

Everyone in the office agreed to play.

Interesting.

SPIN THE BOTTLE

Right," said Joe. "This is D-Day. I'm going to go activate the program and generate our first draw and then we'll see who's the lucky couple."

He was standing under the clock of an open-plan office. Some of the employees were watching him; some weren't. There was a little laughter; not enough. He was wearing his thousand-dollar suit, but it didn't seem to make much difference.

He turned to the computer which had been put at his disposal, and clicked the icon of the program he had written. This was the tricky part. Joe would have been the first to admit that he knew nothing about writing software, but where there's a will there's a way. Anyway he sure as hell couldn't afford to have someone else write it. So he had bought a book called *Beginning Programming for Dummies*, and he had worked his way through it.

It was a real departure from the ordinary call of duty, because normally a salesman doesn't have to come up with the product. Somebody else has the job of making the product the best possible product for the money. It's the salesman's job to persuade people that they succeeded. It helps, obviously, if they at least got halfway there. But even if they didn't, that's not the *salesman's* fault.

There's a lot to be said for that feeling of limited responsibility. On the other hand, if you have actually produced the product yourself, you can't help but know it inside out. Besides which, one of the frustrating things about *being* a salesman is the fact that if there *is* something wrong with the product, there's not a damn thing you can do about it. Whereas if you made it yourself you can always go back to the drawing board if need be.

On the other hand again, a salesman tends not to turn on a vacuum cleaner thinking: It's in the lap of the gods.

On the *other* hand again, at least one good thing had come out of it, because if it all came to nothing at least he'd learned a new skill.

The little hourglass on the screen turned over and over and over, and a little message box appeared. It said: The persons selected in today's draw are Sharon Blake and Jeff Smith.

Joe tried to look as if he had known all along it would work. He looked out of the corner of his eye at the screen on the nearest occupied desk, and that too said "The persons selected in today's draw are Sharon Blake and Jeff Smith."

Now that he was pretty confident he knew the answer he was able to move around the office asking, "Right, now did everyone get the results of the draw on their screen? Great. We're in business."

"So are we supposed to do it right now?" A girl with shoulder-length brown hair and brown eyes was looking up at him. A mug on her desk said SHARON.

"That's right," said Joe. "As soon as the draw comes through the two selected persons are supposed to make their way to the clock."

"Well, here goes nothing," said the girl. She got up and walked to the clock. A tall, gangling guy with a big Adam's apple and an acne problem walked up to the clock and pecked her on the mouth. There was scattered applause and laughter in the office. And they walked back to their desks.

Am I just wasting my time here? thought Joe. Something told him he was barking up the wrong tree.

But he said, "Thank you. See you tomorrow, same time, same place."

"Look, Joe," he told himself that night. "Will you stop being so negative about everything? Just look at what you've achieved. For starters, you wrote a program that worked! Plus, you got people to do something they wouldn't necessarily have thought of themselves that was a little embarrassing. Not one single person asked to see your credentials. Nobody even *questioned* your right to make that kind of suggestion. And this is just Day One."

"I know," he said. "I know I'm off to a good start. It's just that I can't see there ever being much money in it if this is all there's ever going to be *to* it. But if there's ever going to be more to it there's one hell of a long way to go."

"Well, that's true in *one* sense," he said. "But in another sense this might actually be the harder of the two to swing. Because with *this* kind of set-up people can see what they get. They go in it with their eyes open. The gals know there's a guy in the office with a face like Mount Vesuvius, you gotta get them to agree to a potential involvement, even if a pretty *superficial* involvement, with someone who looks like that. Whereas in the longer term you're talking about an arrangement where nobody has to see anything unpleasant. The only thing you've got to overcome is the initial prejudice against engaging in intercourse in an unfamiliar set-up."

He sighed. "Say what you will," he said. "This was a real anti-climax."

So he spent a lot of time getting arbitrarily selected individuals to kiss each other. The longer it went on, the more he felt like he was on the wrong track. He thought he could probably add a random selection for tongue in mouth but he couldn't see how to get from there to the hole in the wall. Or maybe you could get to the hole in the wall but it would take a long time.

Still, he kept notes on the experiment and it was not without interest. There were three attractive women in an office of ten; there was one good-looking guy, two passable again out of ten. The unattractive you could say had an obvious interest in taking part. But even the attractive were prepared to play as long as they had a one in three chance of someone attractive. For this they were willing to run a two in three chance of someone unattractive. At the end of the three weeks they all said they'd enjoyed it but once an hour was too disruptive.

He thought: Wait just a second.

What if it worked like this?

You randomly select two members of staff who may kiss at their own discretion. By the end of the day! As soon as they have kissed they set off the selection device. But again, the persons selected may respond in their own time! Within a 24-hour period!

So he held a meeting with the staff putting forward the suggestion and it was received with enthusiasm. It meant another head-to-head with *Beginning Programming for Dummies*, but the thing that separates the sheep from the goats is the willingness to go that extra mile. They tried it for a week and they really liked it. They felt that management had responded to their concerns. After all, they all said, anyone who didn't want to could drop out. They all agreed that it was a lot of fun.

The head of the company said he would like to keep the random selection device, since it seemed to be having a good effect on staff morale.

Joe said: "I'm sure you'll appreciate that a lot of work has gone into this. Also, this is just a prototype and I'm concerned about releasing it too soon. But I appreciate your letting me work with your staff. They have been a lot of fun to work with. They've been a big help. I can let you have it for $1,000."

The guy bought it.

Interesting.

LOOKING FOR HIGHLY
QUALIFIED PROFESSIONALS

So far Joe hadn't done much more than extend the spirit of the Christmas party throughout the year. He hadn't broken any taboos, or at least not in a major way. But his confidence was up. Just succeeding in making a sale, and a sale, at that, of a product that wasn't self-explanatory, like a vacuum cleaner, had boosted his confidence to the point where he felt able to tackle something more demanding.

So he went out on a limb.

He took an office in an expensive building for just one month.

He advertised some positions for which women might be expected to apply. They called for good qualifications and offered good salaries. Basically he had just plagiarized from ads by legitimate businesses.

A woman answered the ad and he gave her an appointment. She was not ballooning but it would not be the end of the world if she walked out. Good practice material.

He said: "I'm afraid the position you are applying for has been filled. I do have another one which calls for someone with your qualifications. The pay is good, we are offering $60,000 a year, but I have to say I'm very doubtful about mentioning it to you."

The woman said: "Please go on."

He said: "It involves an unusual range of responsibilities."

She said: "Please go on."

He said: "I'm sure you are aware of the dilemma the issue of sexual harassment poses for many employers. It is a source of very serious concern, and rightly so. A woman has the right to go into her place of work without being subjected to unwelcome attention of a sexual nature. A woman has the right to be assessed purely on the qualifications which are relevant to the job, and not on her sexual availability, for example."

She said: "Do you mean, is it some sort of position as sexual harassment officer?"

He said: "Not exactly."

He said: "As you know, many offices have introduced codes of practice in an effort to eliminate behavior which might lead to litigation. This is of limited value. Breaches are not reported. The persons it is meant to protect are *not* protected. At the same time the atmosphere of the office is poisoned. A cloud of suspicion hangs over the most innocent encounters."

He added: "It is an unfortunate fact of life, also, that some of the worst offenders have been among the most successful in purely job-related terms. Employers are anxious not to lose the services of these valuable individuals."

She said: "I don't understand."

He said: "Many firms are now supplementing their sexual harassment policies with what we call lightning rods."

She said: "Lightning rods?"

He said: "Let me explain. Typically, a firm will have a range of openings for which women typically apply. They may choose to hire an individual for a limited range of tasks – word processing, xeroxing, and so on. But they may choose to pay an individual a very substantial premium – typically the amount of the original salary – to carry out these tasks and also act as a lightning rod. The individuals concerned would be randomly selected perhaps two or three times a week to provide contact of a sexual nature to selected members of the firm."

She said: "*What!*"

He said: "It's not for everybody. That's why I hesitated to mention it to you. I think everyone would agree that if you could get double the salary for holding somebody's hand a few times a week it would be a good deal. Perhaps one woman in a thousand would see this as no more than holding hands. We're looking for that one in a thousand. I need hardly say that the difficulty of finding such individuals is reflected in the pay."

She was staring at him and saying "I've never heard anything like it."

She said: "You mean it would be like the advertised job and you would also sleep with people?"

"No no no no no!"

Joe was horrified that she could even *think* such a thing.

He explained: "It is of the utmost importance to avoid anything approaching personal contact. Absolute confidentiality is essential. The man must never know which member of staff has been involved. The women must never know which man has been selected. Typically a cubicle is specially built leading off the men's and women's lavatories. The man is only ever in contact with the body below the waist."

The woman seemed unconvinced.

Joe elaborated: "I should add that this confidentiality extends to the highest levels. The appointment of lightning rods is not made by personnel; it never appears on a woman's file. They are administered by an exterior body. To all intents and purposes, as far as personnel is concerned, they are ordinary members of staff."

The woman said distastefully that it was too much like prostitution and she would not like to work in a place where something like that was going on.

He said: "We are not looking for prostitutes. We are looking for highly qualified professionals."

He said: "I have strong views on sexual harassment. A properly run organization protects its employees. You are better off working in an office with a system of lightning rods than in the type of environment which makes no realistic effort to manage the sexual impulses of its employees."

The woman said suddenly: "How could the job advertised have been filled? The ad was in the paper yesterday."

He said: "The fact is we are conducting a survey of attitudes."

He said: "Thank you very much for cooperating. Would you be willing to take a few moments to complete a questionnaire?"

The woman said angrily that he had wasted too much of her time already.

So it was quite helpful. He let a few days go by before making any more appointments, and then he was able to say they had found what they wanted on the first day.

The next candidate was younger and blonde. He seated her at the computer for a word processing test and from his desk watched the material of her skirt which pulled tight when she sat down.

She tested at 70 wpm.

Joe explained the dilemma facing many companies today.

He added persuasively: "It's not for me to tell people what their goals are."

He said: "I believe women identify their own objectives. Why, I could tell you stories – we had one woman, a very bright gal, had her heart set on law school. She was looking at five, six years of night school. When I outlined the package we were offering she said, 'That's me taken care of then. In two years I can earn enough to pay for a full-time program.' But it's not just for the career-minded. Many women today find themselves bringing up a family alone. A woman with a young family to support may find herself working several jobs, evenings, weekends. Through no fault of her own she is not there to give the moral guidance of a responsible adult. The children drift into drugs, crime. If I can give a woman the opportunity to make her own choices you can bet I'm going to do it."

She said: "I don't know."

He said: "It's not for everyone. We're looking for the kind of woman who is confident about herself. The kind of woman who has aims she wants to achieve. We're looking for someone with maturity. We're looking for someone who wants to make a real contribution to the company and expects to be compensated accordingly."

She said: "I just don't know what to say."

He said: "Are you in a relationship?"

She said: "Well, no."

You want to hear something scary?

You want to hear something really scary?

She bought it.

AN ATMOSPHERE OF
MUTUAL RESPECT

One of the mistakes that Joe made in the beginning was to assume that the biggest problem would be finding women who would be willing to do the job. The way he looked at it was that there were all *kinds* of reasons why anyone who had the skills to do straight office work would not want to branch out, no matter *how* big the pay-off. Whereas finding companies to install the facility would, he assumed, be relatively straightforward. Everybody *knew* sexual harassment was a major problem; everybody *knew* that issuing directives and guidelines that stayed, like as not, in the bottom of people's In tray was not the answer to that problem. *Especially* since the results-orientated type of guy who tended to transgress the boundaries was the *least* likely to waste time reading memos on sexual harassment. In fact, if somebody has time to spend reading that kind of garbage that's probably not an individual you want on your workforce in the first place. If cuts have to be made, that individual is going to be one of the first to go, thus further eroding the number of people in the workplace who have familiarized themselves with the sexual harassment policy.

The result was that Joe seriously underestimated the time he was going to need to get this baby off the ground.

When he had talked nineteen women into believing that they could be the woman in a thousand, all in just under two weeks, he began to feel he could do no wrong. All the self-doubts that had plagued him in the days of selling encyclopedias and vacuum cleaners just slipped away. If he could sell this he could do *anything*. Every salesman knows the feeling of incredulous euphoria that comes when you have miraculously managed to shift a product nobody in their right mind would buy. Every salesman knows the feeling of rapturous disbelief that comes when you've gone through the pitch you came up with for that unshiftable product and somebody actually *swallowed* it.

Multiply that feeling by nineteen and Joe's conviction that he could do no wrong will not seem so far-fetched. But as every salesman knows, that's a dangerous conviction to have. You're only as good as your last sale. What works in one context won't necessarily work in another. If you get to thinking you can sell things standing on your head with one arm tied behind your back, sooner or later a customer is going to start to wonder: Why would I want to buy something from some idiot standing on his head with one arm tied behind his back?

If someone had asked Joe, when he first rented the office, whether he genuinely believed this was something that could happen, Joe would probably have said, "I don't honestly know." But once he had nineteen ladies signed up, every one of whom had accepted every word he said as the Gospel truth, there seemed to be absolutely no reason why all should not come to pass exactly as he had described it. All he had to do was find some people prepared to hire those nineteen ladies, and it was a done deal.

It was time to approach the business community.

He made a point of going straight to the top. People who have worked in personnel for a number of years, he felt, tend to think in clichés and be resistant to new ideas.

He presented the product as a solution to the issue of sexual harassment. Without, obviously, going into a lot of unnecessary detail in his introductory letter.

He wrote to 1,000 companies. 800 didn't bother to reply.

A lot of people said they had everything under control.

Twenty agreed to see him.

The first time was the hardest. He had thought it over a million times, but he had never gone into someone's office where he had made an appointment and sat down and explained it out loud. He had deliberately gone straight to the top, which meant he was talking to a guy who had what it takes to succeed in a competitive industry and had made it to the top. The guy was wearing a suit as expensive as Joe's. He stood up and shook hands when Joe came in and then he invited Joe to tell him what it was about.

Joe covered the points he had to cover. The guy was in his early fifties. He listened without much expression, putting in a couple of questions. When he was sure he understood what was being suggested he said, "I'm afraid you've come to the wrong place. I won't take up any more of your time." And he buzzed through to his secretary and asked her to show the gentleman out.

That was the only appointment for the day. Joe went home and took off the thousand-dollar suit and hung it up. He took off the red silk tie and unbuttoned his collar.

He lay on the bed. This time he had a fantasy about a football team that had a hole in the wall of the locker room. The locker room was next to the changing room for the cheerleaders. One way of doing it would be for the cheerleaders to take it in rotation to provide an outlet for the players. Another way of doing it would be for each cheerleader to go once, and each player to go once. Another way would be to have an initiation for new cheerleaders, where a new cheerleader would be serviced by the whole team. They would have the try-outs for the cheerleaders, and the girls would work their butts off to make the cut, and then the head cheerleader, a real bitch, would have a new girl kneel on some kind of thing that rolled through the hole. The hole could be either right out in the open in the locker room where the players would line up to take their turns, or it could be in some kind of cubicle like a toilet stall.

Or you could have a row of holes in the wall, with all of the girls lined up, and the whole team could tackle them at the same time. You could have two installments. Offense and defense.

You could see them being rewarded in that way if they won. But what if they lost? What if there was a really major defeat?

The coach would probably be pretty pissed off.

Are you a bunch of asskickers or pussylickers? he'd shout, and when the cheerleaders were lined up he would order the team to go in with their tongues.

Aw but *Coach*

Move it! the coach would shout. Anyone who's not in there in the next five seconds is off the team, and that means you, Jerkovsky!

On the other side of the wall, an expression of incredulous bliss would gradually spread over the faces of the cheerleaders.

Or it might be that one guy screwed up royally. Dropped a pass. Missed a kick.

All right, the rest of you can go, the coach would say. Jackson, you're not leaving until each and every one of those girls has had ten minutes by the clock.

Aw but *Coach*

Get moving.

But what if one of them has her period?

Do it.

Jackson would get started and every time he came up for air the coach would ram his face back down. A good coach knows that sometimes you have to be cruel to be kind. Because at the very next game Jackson would be in a completely different league. He would be spotted by a talent scout, and in a few years he'd be playing at the Superbowl. And all because, throughout the game, the coach had the cheerleaders showing their pants in a routine that had more than its fair share of triple back flips. It was pretty good motivation for the rest of the team, too.

Joe lay on his side and he realized that he had gotten side-tracked yet again. Instead of beating up on himself, the way he usually would have, he just sent the victorious team back to the locker room for its reward.

Afterwards he sat up and put his feet on the floor. He thought suddenly Wait just a minute.

Something was bothering him.

It took him a while to put his finger on it. The thing that was bothering him was whether it could actually *happen* that way. Given the initial starting position of the cheerleaders. Because as he saw it those little short skirts definitely came ass backwards through the wall, allowing the team to go in for a quick forward pass. But it just didn't seem realistic to have oral sex applied from behind, was that even *possible*?

Sometimes the best thing you can do with a fantasy is just accept that some of the details may be a little unrealistic. In the old days, before he started getting his life together, he would have thrashed out the problem just in case he might want to utilize the fantasy on some future occasion. Already he had moved on from that. The main thing was that he had gotten whatever it was out of his system. The fantasy, with all its undoubted flaws, had enabled him to achieve that.

There was a lesson to be learned from this.

Because as a salesman the question you have to ask yourself, when you do anything, is, "Why did I do that?" If you can find out the answer, you'll understand just that much more about how other people tick, too.

He had thought he was prepared to face rejection, but the truth of the matter was it had been humiliating. The guy hadn't even said anything. He'd just made up his mind that somebody who could come up with this kind of idea was some kind of human cockroach. You don't waste time explaining to a cockroach that it's not welcome, you just want it gotten out of the way without making a mess on the kitchen floor.

Well, it's just a feature of the human psyche that when we undergo humiliation of some kind we tend to look for somebody else to humiliate, even if it's just in our imagination.

"Well, let me ask you this, Joe. Do you think for one second that other people in that organization don't face humiliation? Do you think people don't fail? Do you think people aren't made to feel inadequate? You *know* that's not so."

He looked at the thousand-dollar suit on its hanger.

"The only difference is, people in an organization tend to take *out* their humiliation on someone lower than themselves. One person is made to feel bad, and before you know it that feeling has been passed on, poisoning the atmosphere of the organization. Look at that study of baboons in captivity. The office is a *form* of captivity. The difference is, a baboon isn't trying to achieve anything. Whereas people in the business world have a job to do. But when people go around taking out their frustrations on their subordinates, it impacts negatively on the way they do their job. It undermines their self-esteem, for a start. Maybe it makes them defensive, unwilling to take risks. Or maybe it makes them reckless, taking *unnecessary* risks. Maybe somebody never accepts their suggestions, so they just decide to present them with a fait accompli. Whereas if people had a way of siphoning off all that hostility they could go back to the office and get on with the job. But that's exactly what a lightning rod offers the opportunity to do.

"So the lesson we can learn is, providing a safe outlet for sexual urges is just the tip of the iceberg. We're offering people the chance to *insulate* their negative emotions, instead of directing their aggression and hostility at their colleagues. That's a valuable service. Don't you ever forget that."

What he realized was that it was the fact that he was *able* to be humiliated that gave him such an insight into the reaction of the ordinary guy to a typical work environment. There are people who don't let things get to them – but those people are the exceptions. It's by understanding, and addressing, the problems of the average guy that you can make a real contribution to society.

The second place he went, the guy he talked to was wearing jeans and a sweater with holes in the elbows and no shoes.

Joe covered the points he had to cover and the guy started to laugh.

He said: "Well, I gotta hand it to you, that's a very original idea."

He started laughing again.

He said: "And the hell of it is, you could be on to something. I'd be interested to see how you do."

He went outside. It was a soft, bright day, and the wind was pulling leaves off the willows. A dog trotted by, lifted his leg, and trotted on.

There was a statue in the center of the square of General Lafayette. His green bronze three-cornered hat and the green bronze shoulders of his coat were white with pigeon shit.

On the sidewalk beside a fire hydrant were a couple of dried dog turds.

He thought: You know, if people went around doing that it would be really disgusting. If some guy just squatted down by the fire hydrant and left a couple of turds it would be really gross. And can you imagine what it would be like if everyone did that?

He walked down the steps to the sidewalk. The wind was ruffling the fine grass of the lawn like the fur of a glossy green animal.

He thought: Maybe this isn't such a good idea.

Now previously, in the days when he was selling, or trying to sell, vacuum cleaners, he would have thought this kind of self-doubt was a sign of weakness. He would have thought the problem with him was that he kept having doubts, and that the way to solve the problem was to just pretend they didn't exist and hope they would go away. He would have thought that he would have been a better salesman if he didn't have doubts. He would have thought being the type of guy to have doubts was exactly what made him relatively unsuccessful as a salesman.

The fact is, every great salesman has doubts. In fact, a great salesman has more doubts than anyone else. Because what those doubts are, is the questions *other* people are going to be asking *you*. A great salesman is able to anticipate a wider range of questions than other people. And instead of just hoping they'll go away, a great salesman *uses* those doubts as a chance to tackle those questions head on. Which is why a great salesman is never taken by surprise.

This time, anyway, instead of just ignoring his doubts, he asked himself: "OK, if it isn't a good idea, *why* isn't it a good idea?"

And by actually looking at the question he was able to come up with an answer.

Of *course* it would be disgusting if people went around depositing turds in the street. That's what we have toilets for. Nobody wants to look at something like that, so you put it out of sight so they don't have to.

But that was *exactly* what a lightning rod was supposed to do. Instead of a young girl jeopardizing herself by standing on the street in a dangerous neighborhood, putting herself at risk and in all likelihood being exploited by a pimp, you give her the opportunity to work in the safety of an office environment. Instead of acquiring a criminal record she is able to work at filing or some other clerical task and improve her skills. Her pay reflects the fact that she is providing an outlet for men who would otherwise be putting *themselves* at risk. But the whole thing is conducted in the privacy of a toilet cubicle. As far as her fellow workers are concerned, she is no different from anyone else. As far as *his* fellow workers are concerned, he is just going to the john. The whole *point* of the arrangement is to avoid giving anyone cause for offense.

●

So he went on to work his way through the other companies on his list.

Once he had a foot in the door he explained, "It's not for me to make moral judgments. I'm a businessman. I deal with people as they are, not as they ought to be."

"Speaking as a businessman," he went on, "I know that it is often the most valuable individuals in a company who present the greatest vulnerability to sexual harassment related issues. We know that a high level of testosterone is inseparable from the drive that produces results. Speaking of people as they are rather than as they should be I know that a high-testosterone-level individual has a high likelihood of being sexually aggressive; if the individual is working twenty-hour days as a driven results-orientated individual often does, that sexual aggression will find an outlet in the office."

"Well."

"You invest in training. A man is bringing in $100 million of business. You leave him open to the danger of momentarily forgetting himself with a little $25,000-a-year secretary?"

"Well ..."

"A properly run organization protects its employees."

"Sure, but ..."

"I have strong views on sexual harassment. I believe that those in a place of work who do not welcome sexual advances should not be subjected to them. I also believe that a man who is producing results in today's competitive market place has a right to be protected from potential undesirable side effects of the physical constitution which enables him to make a valued contribution to the company."

At this stage he might be asked, "Are you suggesting we hire prostitutes?!" Or "Surely you are not suggesting . . . !"

"Certainly not," he would protest, "prostitution is degrading to all concerned, an atmosphere of mutual respect is indispensable in the modern office."

"I don't understand," he would be told.

The concept was so revolutionary at the time that prostitution was the only thing people could think of. That was how original he was. He had to explain the whole thing from the word Go.

He would explain the concept of the lightning rod in the face of skepticism.

He would explain the importance of confidentiality.

He would say: "The last thing we want to do is ghettoize a certain class of women. What we are doing is introducing highly qualified professionals to the workplace. These are women who on their credentials could walk straight into an opening of a more conventional nature, women with goals to pursue who are willing to make a real contribution to the company."

He would say: "The average man things of sex every five seconds."

"The average employee," Joe would add, "spends two minutes in the course of a year reading the sexual harassment policy. If that. This is not, in my opinion, the level of protection which is appropriate to a high-testosterone performance-orientated individual."

He would sometimes add that access to the lightning rods could be restricted to high performers, acting as an incentive to less driven individuals.

He would sometimes cite, if the occasion seemed to warrant it, a study on the orangutang or the baboon. Primates in captivity, he would explain, form hierarchical societies in which place is established by humiliation and aggressive sexual behavior. Humans are primates. The office is a form of captivity. Every precaution must be taken to avoid stigmatizing persons providing this valuable service. Those using them must never see their faces. They must be indistinguishable from their colleagues.

He generally just made up whatever research he wanted on the baboon, since actual studies of the baboon might not support the point he wanted to make.

Similarly with statistics, a good salesman has a *feel* for the statistics that will carry weight in a particular context, and will tend to go with his feeling rather than with what scientists have come up with in some totally unrelated context.

One man said he was not exactly disputing the points made but he did not think he could reward his top earners with titless sex.

Another said: "What if the man wanted to be naked from the waist down and whipped?"

"Why would anyone want that?" asked Joe.

Thinking *What a weirdo.*

The guy said: "Well, some guys like that."

Joe thought: What if it turned out most high-performing individuals liked to be whipped on the bare butt? *That* would be something to see.

One guy said he would give it a try.

ANONYMITY GUARANTEED

Now it was Joe's belief that in the long run a company that wanted to include lightning rods in its team for the twenty-first century had only one option: to outsource *all* personnel recruitment. Otherwise how are you going to guarantee anonymity? If you just outsource the lightning rods *somebody* in the company is going to know which employees are handled by personnel and which are handled by an outside firm, and if that person happens to know why the outside firm was taken on that person is going to be able to identify the members of staff who are providing an extra service for the company.

The thing was, though, that there was no way in the world that he was going to persuade a company to hand over its entire personnel operations to an outsider. The actual service he was providing was radical enough without challenging received opinion on personnel.

The important thing is not necessarily to persuade someone straight off the bat to do something in some totally different way; the important thing is that you need to be aware of what your ultimate aim is.

What Joe did, anyway, was he left the whole question of personnel strictly out of bounds. He simply explained that, given the importance of anonymity, his company would have to handle all *temporary* personnel requirements. Some of the temps provided would be lightning rods; some would not. At the end of a six-month period they would review the success of the program.

The client obviously put up a fight. He said that this was a lot more far-reaching than he had originally anticipated.

Joe said, "Look, Steve. I'm not even going to try to persuade you. I'm just going to ask *you* to think about this for a minute. I've said it before, and I'll say it again. These women are not prostitutes. Now just think about what that means. These are qualified professionals who could walk into any job you care to name and get top dollar. I don't need to tell you that they're being asked to accept an *element* of risk. All they've got is my word for it that their anonymity will be respected; that the choice they've made goes no further than my office. I'm not about to do anything to jeopardize that for a short-term gain. I don't want it on my conscience if some gal who's made a big contribution to a company in good faith ends up being stigmatized because of short-sighted personnel arrangements. Nossir. It's of the utmost importance that any administrative arrangements made to process this personnel should appear to be no different from the arrangements made to process single-function members of staff."

"I see what you're saying," said Steve. "But as I'm sure you'll appreciate this is quite an upheaval for something that is just a trial flight."

"I certainly do appreciate that, Steve," said Joe. "But if you think about it, in the longer term this represents an opportunity for substantial savings. I don't need to tell *you* what it costs to hire as permanent staff someone who has initially worked for you as a temp. That's not the way I do business. If at the end of the six-month period you decide not to pursue the provision of lightning rods at that time, that's fine. If you decide to hire one or more of the ladies we've introduced to the organization, that's fine too. No strings. No introduction fee. The only thing you won't be getting is the lightning rod provision. All I ask is that as long as you *do* make use of the service, you pay a flat fee for a fixed number of lightning rods which is not associated with any one individual or individuals in any way. My agency will distribute remuneration in accordance with the services being provided; you don't need to know which particular individuals are providing them."

"Huh," said Steve.

"I think I need to think about it," said Steve, after a pause.

Any salesman knows that the *last* thing you want is for the target to think about it.

"Tell you what," said Joe. "Let's go and have a look at the disabled toilets."

They went down the hall to the Men's Room. There was a big cubicle at the end of the room for disabled users. The Ladies Room was next door. They didn't go into the Ladies Room but Steve explained that it too included a large cubicle for disabled users.

The Ladies Room was obviously not labeled "Ladies," but Steve, as head of the company, got irritated whenever he passed female toilets labeled "Women," so he had put his foot down. There was just a little icon on the door. Since the Ladies Room just had an icon on the door this meant the Men's Room had to have an icon on the door too, and then the disabled stall had an icon of a wheelchair.

Steve and Joe went into the cubicle to look around.

"You know," said Steve, "we provide better facilities for a type of employee who would be in a minority if we even happened to *have* one, which we don't, than for the hundreds of able-bodied employees we actually happen to have."

"Exactly," said Joe. "There's absolutely no reason why this space should not be put to use to promote the well-being of employees actually on the staff. Now speaking for myself I have every sympathy for individuals who have the misfortune to be crippled or malformed in some way which interferes with the normal function of going to the toilet, I think they have a tough row to hoe and I give them a lot of credit for that. A *lot* of credit. I mean, I personally wouldn't like to have to manoeuver myself out of a wheelchair every time I wanted to use the john, and I think it's up to those of us who are more fortunate not to put any unnecessary obstacles in their way. At the same time, when all's said and done, I think it's possible to go too far the other way."

"Next thing you know they'll be wanting me to put in a jacuzzi," said Steve. "It's not that I'm unsympathetic, but this kind of PC crap really gets my goat. Next thing you know they'll be taking me to court for not installing a sauna."

"You said it," said Joe. His eyes scanned the room. "Now the way I see it," he said, "is this could be modified to suit our purposes at a very reasonable cost. You said it backs onto the disabled cubicle in the Ladies; couldn't be better. We knock a hole in the wall connecting the two compartments, and install an inconspicuous transporter for the gal. We also install a simple dispenser for condoms and lubricant, disguised as a unit for dispensing extra toilet rolls, and a simple disposal unit."

"I think I need to think about it," said Steve.

"You bet," said Joe. He put his hands in his pockets. "You know, I really gotta hand it to you," he said, surveying the cubicle. "You really provide a first-class facility. You may not know this, but not all disabled toilets provide a sink at the right level."

"You don't say," said Steve.

"Of course, having a sink in the cubicle could be quite convenient from a hygienic point of view for individuals using the cubicle for purposes for which it was not originally designed," said Joe. "We would hope that individuals would take care to clean up after themselves so as not to inconvenience or offend legitimate disabled users of the toilet."

Steve laughed. "You son of a bitch," he said. "Hell, *I* don't know."

He opened the door of the cubicle to pace up and down along the urinals.

"You may have a point," he said. The fact that he had already agreed was neither here nor there, often it's only after agreeing to buy something that a customer begins to realize how much he would like not to buy it.

"You should see some of the hot shots we get these days," he said. "Straight out of college and they're on a hundred grand a year. In my day you didn't see that kind of money till you were thirty. In my day you thought you had something to prove. Well, you'd think the positive side of it would be you'd get staff who knew how to deal with liberated women. I know *I'm* too old to learn, but at that age they should have been growing up around women expecting to be treated as equals. Instead we get behavior that — well, all I can say is, we wouldn't have expected to get away with it *thirty* years ago, and that was before they started taking people to court for opening a door or some damn thing."

A good salesman knows when to let the customer do the talking. Joe waited sympathetically at the door to the disabled cubicle.

"I tell you frankly I've seen things that made my hair stand on end. The whole thing is a minefield. I've explained to a couple of the more egregious offenders that there are no certainties, the fact that a young woman is wearing high heels does not mean she can be guaranteed not to sue you. I don't mind telling you that some of these men are a lawsuit waiting to happen. This idea of yours may not be in the best of taste, but from where I'm standing it looks like more of a solution to a genuine problem of nightmare proportions than anything *else* I've seen. To be honest, it's something a man of my generation has trouble with, but the younger men are a different breed. We can't do business without them, or we'll lose our competitive edge; but I have to say I'm getting sick and tired of wondering when some girl is going to get awarded $1 million in damages because the firm didn't protect her from their shenanigans. How the hell am I or anyone else supposed to protect her, for the love of Mike? Well, if they want protection I'll give 'em protection. Send me a contract and we'll get the builders in."

3

TRIAL BALLOONS

MORE HIGHLY QUALIFIED
PROFESSIONALS

Joe had said he had well-qualified individuals who were ready
to walk through the door, which in retrospect had been over-
stating the case somewhat. It was one of those things a salesman just *has* to say. You get a sense for what someone wants
to hear, and sometimes there's something that you just *know*
is going to clinch the deal. You say what you have to say, and
then afterwards you clear it with head office. If you yourself
are head office it makes it easier in some ways, because you're
obviously not going to give yourself a lot of shit, but on the
other hand in some ways it gives you a whole new perspective
on what head office has to put up with. Because the buck stops
here. Whatever it was you said you could do, you personally
are going to have to do it.

Anyway he had to come up with staff fast.

While it was not strictly untrue that he had well-qualified
individuals who were ready to walk through the door, the
individuals who were ready to walk through the door had
answered ads for permanent jobs. Most were not prepared to
leave their present jobs for a six-month position with the possibility of renewal. Luckily one of the best qualified applicants,
a very bright gal, well turned out, good skills, unflappable,
hadn't turned a hair when he explained the nature of the job,

said she would be willing to take a six-month assignment on one condition.

"If at the end of the six months they decide not to go ahead with the program," said Lucille, "I want the option of staying on in the position for an additional six months at a salary 30% above the notional rate for the position, or, alternatively, a separation fee equivalent to 30% of the salary for six months *plus* one month's salary, to compensate for the inconvenience to me of having to look for another job for the second time in a year."

Joe had to hand it to her, she was one tough cookie. As long as none of the other gals got wise it was no skin off his nose.

"You got it," he said.

"I'd like that in writing, obviously," said Lucille.

"You got it," said Joe.

One thing that you soon learn in business is that you should learn from your mistakes and stop kicking yourself. Making mistakes is *how* we learn. If you're not making any mistakes, chances are you're not taking enough risks, and sometimes just not taking risks is the biggest mistake you *can* make.

That was what Joe told himself when he discovered that his hard work in recruiting eighteen other women who thought they could be the woman in a thousand had all been for nothing, because all eighteen had answered ads for permanent jobs. In retrospect, that had been a mistake. Granted. But there's no point kicking a dead horse.

So he picked himself up and started recruiting again, and within a week he had five gals prepared to try it out on a six-month contract, plus another five for camouflage. He wrote a new software program for the occasion. And he prepared himself for the last hurdle: a series of motivational talks with the individuals whom the package was designed to benefit.

Joe knew he would have to talk to the first beneficiaries of the program himself. He was going to have to talk to them one at a time, and he was going to have to choose his words carefully. One thing was for sure, if he explained it to a group it would never get off the ground. Everybody would be looking at everybody else to see how they were reacting, and it would be touch and go.

What he did was he arranged a day of brief appointments with the men in question. He explained about the dangers of inadvertently committing sexual harassment in the modern office. He explained that research had shown that the highest-performing individuals in a company were often the very ones who were put at risk. He commented that the thing about drive is you either have it or you don't, and if you have it you can't just turn it off at the flick of a switch. He explained that in view of these findings the company was placing a facility at the disposal of its highest-ranking performers, on an experimental basis.

Participants would be offered the opportunity anywhere from two to five times a week at randomly generated times of finding release for any pent-up physical needs. A notification would appear on a participant's computer screen. It would be entirely up to the participants whether they took action or not. Administrators of the program would have no information as to uptake on the part of individuals. Participation or non-participation would be entirely confidential.

As Joe spoke on, the client would, typically, not say anything at first in case it turned out to be a joke. So Joe would flesh out the rationale of the program with material on the baboon in captivity, amplifying if necessary with other findings in primatology. He would point out that the ventro-ventral, or so-called "missionary," position was virtually unheard of among other primates; that the ventro-dorsal position, or mounting from behind, was the preferred method of entry among virtually every primate known to man; and that we ignore nature at our peril.

While the client digested this unfamiliar material, Joe would continue to outline the logistics. A participant who had received notification, he explained, would be entitled to make use of the facility at his own convenience at any time before the end of the working day, at which time, unfortunately, the entitlement would no longer be valid. Should the participant choose to avail himself of the opportunity, he could either accept immediately or select the LATER option on the menu, in which case he would be allowed to either specify a later time, or simply wait until a convenient moment occurred and then click on the I'M READY NOW icon.

Any form of acceptance, Joe would explain, would activate a notification for a lightning rod; if the time was convenient she would report for duty, if it was inconvenient she would return the assignment to the pool for someone else to pick up. The identity of the lightning rods would remain confidential at all times.

Someone like Bill Gates could probably do this amount of programming standing on his head, but for Joe it represented a real challenge. He would have appreciated some sign that his clients were impressed by the sophistication of the product. For the most part, though, they seemed to focus on other things.

In fact he knew from the first moment he set eyes on them that the guys were a bunch of assholes. They all reacted in exactly the same stupid way.

"Let me get this straight," they would say. "The company is offering this as part of its sexual harassment policy? Hoo boy!"

He had to remind himself that these people were keeping him in business. It was the fact that they *were* assholes that had left the CEO of a competitive company at his wits' end how to deal with them. If they *hadn't* have been Grade A assholes the CEO would probably not have taken a giant step for mankind in being the first American executive to introduce lightning rods to the workplace.

Besides, the thing to remember was that it was probably not their fault that they were assholes. They were not to blame for their upbringing. All you had to do was talk to them to realize that these were people with no class. It wasn't their fault. They had just been brought up that way. The way to look at it was, if a guy, through no fault of his own, has not been brought up to treat women with respect, is it fair that his whole career should be put in jeopardy? Is it fair that on top of the disadvantage he has *anyway* in competing against guys who have been to Harvard and Yale, he should have the additional handicap of endangering his career every time he is in the vicinity of female personnel?

No. That *isn't* fair, and an egalitarian employer with a commitment to democracy will do everything in its power to remove the obstacles in the path of disadvantaged employees. Hell, they're legally *obligated* to provide a disabled toilet, well just because the law doesn't compel an employer to consider the needs of socially disadvantaged employees doesn't mean an enlightened employer can't be ahead of his time.

That was how Joe got himself through it as he talked to one prize asshole after another.

It was hard work, no two ways about it, but it was worth it.

Besides, it was nothing as compared to the almighty hassle of writing another software program.

SOMETHING WRONG

Joe had once failed to sell a single set of the *Encyclopaedia Britannica* in six months. He had once sold a single Electrolux and eaten 126 pieces of homemade pie in a time frame where most salesmen would hope to reverse the ratio of vacuum cleaners to pie. And now, after at first not succeeding, he had tried, tried, tried again and he had placed an innovative system of proactive sexual harassment management on a six-month trial basis.

It was all systems go. It was a product he believed in. His immediate money worries were over. He should have been having the time of his life. But something wasn't right. At some very basic level, something was wrong.

There's an old saying in show business: Never marry your mistress.

What the saying means is, if there's something you do for fun, don't turn it into something you have to do. If you turn it into a job that you get paid for, so that you have to do it whether you like it or not in order to get paid, chances are it will stop being fun.

This turns out to be true even of something like a sexual fantasy. If there's something that turns you on, it may not have the same effect if you have to do it even if you're not in the mood.

Joe had not been running the lightning rods for long before he discovered the truth of the old saying.

You might think that nothing could possibly beat acting out a fantasy that you have imagined hundreds of times in different guises. You might think that actually experiencing the situation you had fantasized about would be the ultimate erotic sensation.

Well, it ain't necessarily so.

If you think about it, maybe that's not so surprising. Why does coffee never taste as good as it smells? Why does bacon never taste the way it smells? Why does toast smell so good only to taste like dry toast? Why do frying onions always smell so good, when they're nothing to write home about when you actually put them in your mouth?

Nobody knows the answer, but these are universally recognized phenomena. So maybe it's *not* so surprising if other things don't live up to expectations.

After the facility had been installed Joe obviously had to make sure it functioned correctly. He had expected it to be a real turn-on to act out a fantasy with a real live flesh-and-blood girl at the other end, but to tell the truth it wasn't as good as his fantasies, because he was just stuck on one side, facing the wall in the disabled toilet, throughout.

Part of the problem was that the whole thing was so obviously prearranged. He'd never really stopped to think about it before, but one of the things that gave the fantasy a buzz was the element of the unexpected. It was the fact that the gal had her head out a window or whatever and wasn't expecting anything to happen. But the whole point of *having* a lightning rod was that this was a gal who'd signed on the dotted line, it was the fact that clients could find release with a gal who *was* expecting something to happen that freed them from the spectre of sexual harassment suits.

The other problem was that a key part of the fantasy was the look of sudden realization on the gal's face at the moment of impact, something that was, obviously, not accessible from behind. If he could have had access to the face on the other side of the wall it might have been a different story. But he couldn't have that because it would defeat the whole object of the exercise. He had randomized selection so even he would not know which member of the team he was test-driving – that was only fair. So while it was going on he kept feeling that the really interesting stuff was going on on the other side of the wall. Funny.

Anyway he simply reminded himself that he was not there to enjoy himself but to do a job. The only thing was, it was important that the facility should be something that people *would* be able to enjoy. Everything was in place, exactly according to specification, and that did give him a good feeling – he'd had to work hard to get things to this stage. But would the experience really do what it was meant to for the men who would be using it on a daily basis?

If you're in sales you know that confidence *creates* confidence. If you can convey to the customer that *you* consider yourself to have a first-class product, nine times out of ten the customer will see the product that way too.

"Besides, look at it this way," Joe reminded himself. "Right now they're getting exactly *nothing*. They're in no position to get critical."

He disposed of his condom in the receptacle provided, fighting off a feeling of let-down. Maybe it would have been better if the girl had been wearing clothes below the waist so he could have pushed her skirt up, he speculated. But any kind of clothes would have compromised the anonymity. That was probably why it had felt kind of clinical and impersonal.

We live in a flawed world. We can't always have everything the way we want it. It's important to be able to compromise.

And like they say in show business, never marry your mistress.

He tried, in other words, to deal with his sense of let-down by being philosophical about it, and by making jokes about it, which is what we all do when life doesn't live up to some picture we had in our minds.

The transporter went back through the hole, and the panel closed. Joe was alone in the disabled cubicle.

He thought: *No*. I'm *not* going to walk away from this. Something about this doesn't feel right. *Now's* the time to work out what it is. Before it's too late.

He paced up and down the cubicle. Something was wrong. *Something* was *wrong*.

As a salesman, he knew that if you go around with your head in the sand, sooner or later someone is going to give you a swift, hard kick in the butt. A good salesman knows you can't afford to look the other way. If there is something wrong with the product, you sure as hell better know about it.

Joe paced up and down. It's just not right, he thought. Something is just not right.

Suddenly it came to him.

That toilet has got to go.

Joe left the cubicle and paced gloomily up and down by the row of urinals. Had some momentary insanity taken hold of him when he came up with this? Because you'd think he would have noticed an obvious detail: In all the times he had been experimenting with the fantasy, not once had he set the scene in a lavatory. There was a reason for this. The reason is that even in a fantasy there is nothing even remotely erotic about a toilet bowl. In fact, considered as an accoutrement to a sexual encounter, a toilet bowl is a real cold shower.

The problem is that life is so different from fantasy. In a fantasy you can try out a toilet bowl as part of the picture, and if it doesn't work you can just relocate to the kitchen. In life, if you knock a hole in the wall of a disabled toilet, that hole will go right on being there until you brick it up again. If there's a toilet you don't care for, someone is going to have to physically disconnect and remove it to get it out of there.

"Look, Joe," he told himself. "Like it or not, the toilet has got to stay. They are legally obligated to provide that toilet for disabled persons in the building. If you take it out, you'll be breaking the law."

THE GUINEA PIGS

Meanwhile, out in the company, twenty results-orientated individuals were thinking I don't *believe* it.

And fifteen of them were thinking guiltily that they knew why the company had decided to do it.

Fourteen of them were suddenly thinking Nah. OK, I may have stepped over the line, but I'm *nothing* compared to Ed Wilson.

Five had a clear conscience. They just thought Ed Wilson. That's what it is, it's Ed Wilson.

And Ed Wilson thought, This is all because of me.

One thing about results-orientated individuals is that they are highly competitive, which means that they are always alert to the possibility that some other individual may be achieving better results than they are. The conclusion everyone drew was that Ed Wilson must be really out of sight. They knew he was good, but they didn't know he was *that* good. Otherwise no way would Steve Jackson have shelled out for something like this. If someone was egregious enough that something like this was necessitated, and he wasn't out the door ... hoo boy.

EARLY DAYS

In later years, when it got really big, one of the things people couldn't really get their heads around was how it got off the ground in the first place, given the nature of what Joe was actually providing in the early days. In the form it ultimately took, sure, whatever your personal views on the legitimacy of a service of this nature you could at least see what it was that might appeal to people. Let's say you could see what might appeal to people who were prepared to avail themselves of something like that. But people would try to set the scene, they'd try to imagine the set-up with the toilet just *there* because after all it was in a toilet cubicle, they'd try to imagine some guy coming in to try it out, and the mind just boggled. Even so, if the setting had been the *only* problem they could *kind* of see how you could get so you could just not notice it. But the thing people really had a hard time with was those first three weeks, before Joe cracked the packaging problem.

There was once a classic joke on the Bob Newhart Show in its heyday about a deodorant called Armpit, and something about the product as Joe initially introduced it to the world reminded people of Armpit. *How* could *anybody* go into a toilet stall and just wait for the naked half of a half-naked woman to come through a hole in the wall ass backwards? Nobody could see why something like that wouldn't kill the project stone dead. Apart from anything else, it was insulting to the people meant to be using it. The message something like that sent was "You're so desperate you'll take *anything*. And I mean *anything*. So screw you, Bozo."

The fact was that people were so used to all the features that everybody later came to take for granted that they couldn't really recapture the whole novelty of the situation. It was like trying to imagine what it was like in the days when flush toilets were aspirational.

Mike Newsome was one of the original guinea pigs, and as he said later he was initially skeptical. If you're in accounting, it's your job to be skeptical, and that's not something you can just turn off. The way Mike initially saw it was that it was some gimmick to deflect legitimate requests for pay increases. Or it was some cock-eyed motivational guru-type plan. Next thing you knew they would have them all out in the woods banging drums. Or somebody had decided they had to do something to appease the feminists, and this was what they had come up with.

Still, when the message came up on his screen the first time he went along to the disabled toilet, if only to satisfy his curiosity. Because frankly he couldn't believe they were serious. He had seen some pretty dumb things in his time, but this took the fruitcake.

Anyway, he had gone along to the disabled, and closed the door, and sure enough there was a dispenser beside the toilet paper containing a supply of condoms. Then a panel opened in the wall.

Well, it was for real, all right. And his reaction was exactly what people would have predicted who would also have predicted that the show would fold on day one. The total absence of packaging was a real turn-off. Mike had this impulse to pat the girl on the behind and tell her to go home, except there was no way to communicate with her. Where did they get them anyway? So he just stood there with his hands in his pockets. For some reason the fact that you were just looking at a wall, where ordinarily you would have seen someone's shoulders and head, made you aware that on the other side of the wall was someone's shoulder and head, the head of someone you had probably actually seen around the office. On the other side of the wall someone was just waiting for you to get on with it. For some reason, maybe it was something to do with the tiles and the stall and the bare functionality of the environment, something about it made him think of a concentration camp or something. It kind of gave him the creeps.

His other reaction was also exactly what people would have predicted, which was that this had to be aimed at people who were so desperate they'd screw anything that moved, and weren't too particular about the movement. In other words, Ed Wilson. It was something put together by someone with no class, for someone with no class. In other words, Ed Wilson. In fact, it wouldn't have surprised Mike to find that management had let nineteen other guys use the facility purely to camouflage an exercise in Ed Wilson containment.

Anyway he just stood there, realizing he was going to have to do something, and also that the one thing he couldn't do was go around to the Ladies to say case dismissed. From what he could see, this was absolutely typical of the half-assed way the thing had been set up. It didn't seem to have occurred to anybody that if for some reason things didn't go according to plan, there could be a need to get the message across. All they would have had to put in was a light switch with some prearranged signals, or a slot with some preprinted messages, but no, that was too easy. So that was part of it, just the sheer aggro of the fact that there was no other option available. And then, when he thought about why it was giving him the creeps he realized it was a knee-jerk reaction with no real justification in reality. It was a free country. Nobody was making anybody do anything they didn't want to; in fact the company was probably paying a lot of money to compensate them for their time. Besides. This was something experts had determined was helpful in increasing the productivity and job satisfaction of male employees. Wasn't there a chance that these guys were on to something?

Because let's face it, whatever else you might think of Joe, he'd really done his homework. The guy knew his stuff. All this research on baboons in captivity – you can't just shrug something like that off. And it suddenly occurred to Mike – of course, later he realized he was giving Joe too much credit, but this was what he thought at the time – that maybe it was clinical and unvarnished for a *reason*. Maybe it wasn't *meant* to be erotic. The point was not to plug into whatever mental trip someone might want to be on, the point was to provide a physical release for physical needs.

And then he thought Well, since it's *there*.

So he set aside his skepticism for the moment and availed himself of the facility. It was quite a strange experience in some ways. Still, it was enjoyable enough for what it was.

Anyway, almost straight away he noticed that he was experiencing an unusual sense of well-being. He hadn't been aware of his attention straying while he was trying to concentrate, whether to sex or to anything else, but for a significant period of time afterwards he felt more focused on the job in hand than he had for a long time.

Also, instead of hurrying away after work to go to the gym, he ended up staying an extra hour to finish off something that had been pending.

Obviously somebody knew exactly what they were doing. They had worked out that the human male animal needs a release. Even if he isn't actually aware of it, getting that release would improve his performance. You had to give them credit for going ahead with something a lot of people would consider unorthodox. They had probably come up against a lot of skepticism before people had had the chance to experience first hand just how helpful it could be.

It later turned out that seventeen out of the first twenty responded in exactly the same way.

They went in expecting something hot and found the reality fell a long way short of their expectations. But there was no way to tell the girl to go away. And while they were mulling that one over, and thinking it was so crude no one but Ed Wilson would see anything in it at all, they would suddenly remember all the information they'd been given on the baboon in captivity. They would realize that the clinical, unerotic environment was there for a reason. And they would remember that experts had determined that the male animal performs best if certain physical needs are given a release.

Being competitive, results-orientated individuals, they took a professional approach: If something will improve your performance, *go* for it.

What about the other three?

Well, two out of three wanted nothing to do with it.

The third was Ed Wilson.

TAKE OFF

Pete was one of the men who wanted nothing to do with it. There are all kinds of crazy people out there; who was there higher up in the organization who would be crazy enough to listen to them? And no matter *who* was that crazy, the obvious question you had to ask yourself was, is this something I want to be seen to be involved in? Is this something I even potentially want anyone to know I had anything to do with? Screwing someone from behind in the disabled john? To say this was a question you had to ask yourself implied that there was a possibility in a million years that you would be that dumb. But he had kept his counsel to himself, because this is the kind of thing where if anyone does it other people can't afford to be seen to disapprove.

What he actually said was that he was in a relationship. The fact was that even if it hadn't been a stupid idea for other reasons it would not be a good idea for anyone in a relationship. Not that he noticed that stopping some of the others. But if you're in a relationship it's important not to have anything you would rather the other person didn't know, because sooner or later they will sense that something is going on. Also, there are some things that there is no point expecting a woman to see in the light you might see it.

As far as he was concerned it was offered as a purely physical convenience, to be availed of in the spirit it was intended. Questions of fidelity would not really apply in that kind of situation. But if you were to try to explain that to someone you were serious about you would be wasting your time. Anything you might say to show why it *wasn't* infidelity would only make matters worse. You might think a woman would get upset if you fell in love with someone else, and that it would be completely obvious that screwing someone through a hole in the wall was not a meaningful activity in that context. Unfortunately it doesn't work that way. If you know what's good for you you'll leave well enough alone.

Besides, if you're actually in a relationship it's important to be able to satisfy the needs of the other person.

He wouldn't have minded trying it just once, to see what it was like, but safety first. You never know where there may be a concealed camera these days. You can't be too careful.

In his opinion this attitude was justified after just one week.

It was getting on for 11 o'clock in the morning, everything pretty much as normal, a day like any other day, when suddenly the fire alarm went off. It wasn't the time of day when they usually had drills, and at first everyone just assumed it was a mistake, but it kept going, and finally an announcement was made telling everyone to get out of the building. So they all cleared out of the building and stood around on the lawn, and after about fifteen minutes a car turned up, and the guy who had explained about the facility got out of the car and entered the building. He was gone about ten minutes, and then he came out and told everyone they could go back to work.

Later word started to get around. What had happened was that some asshole had tried to ski off-piste. Lose the condom. Or go anal or something. And the lightning rod had set off the alarm. Once that happened, apparently, the cubicle could only be opened from the outside. The anonymity of the offender was preserved by clearing the building of all other personnel, while a representative of lightning rods came to reprimand the individual and inform him of the suspension of privileges he had incurred.

At first everyone had just assumed it was Ed Wilson, but it turned out Ed Wilson was actually out of town, so nobody knew *who* the guy was. So you could say anonymity was protected. But as far as Pete was concerned, this was not a situation you even potentially wanted to be in. You could see where they would have to have something like this for the girls' protection, but the potential for having your cover blown was such that he personally wanted nothing to do with it.

Bill was initially suspicious. He had already experienced difficulty in concealing the fact that he was gay; he suspected that this was really a covert ploy to flush out gay members of staff, while ostensibly doing nothing more sinister than keeping Ed Wilson under control. Even though he was suspicious he couldn't help but be amused. The thing was so absolutely typical of the way straights would pick up on something introduced by the gay community and rob it of all the things that had made it worth doing in the first place. In fact what it just went to show was what pathetic sex lives straights had, they had to be really desperate. If it had come right down to it he might have been able to use the facility if he had had to, but he noticed one or two other guys said they were in relationships. So he just said he was in a relationship. He had a laugh about it with Luke afterwards.

Ed Wilson thought that people had overreacted to some incidents that had gotten blown way out of proportion. All he had done was make the mistake of thinking he was working with people with a sense of humor. But the way he looked at it was, if people were going to take it that way, why look a gift horse in the mouth?

EUREKA!

A couple of weeks went by. No one had complained about the toilet. No one had complained about the fact that there was no element of the unexpected. But it kept bothering Joe. He tried not to let it bother him. He went on selling the product with all the force and eloquence at his command, just as if he had unshakable confidence in a product that featured a disabled toilet standing by. But all the time it was there, at the back of his mind. Something wasn't right.

A good salesman pays attention to his instincts. Even if a product is selling, even if the customer appears satisfied, if you're dissatisfied with some feature of the product sooner or later the public is going to catch up with you. Or, to put it another way, a competitor is going to come along who has ironed out that particular wrinkle. If you can get to the wrinkle first, while building on the brand loyalty you have hopefully established, you're way ahead of the game.

An ordinary salesman, of course, can only voice his concern to head office in the hope that it gets passed on to product development. Joe being Head Office, Product Development, and Sales all in one, all he had to do was let his salesman's instincts carry out their war of attrition at a subconscious level. Finally it was just too much. Law or no law, something was going to have to be done.

For once, Joe made a point of not taking any paperwork home. He was going to take the evening off and just brainstorm for a while and see what came of it.

He decided to just take it one thing at a time. The first thing was all this nudity. For whatever reason, an already naked body is just not as big of a turn-on as one where there is some nudity yet to be achieved. The perennial appeal of the striptease relies on this very fact. Now, for purposes of anonymity it was obviously of the essence that female staff should not have any of their *own* clothes visible. Shortsightedly, he had been just assuming that meant they shouldn't have any clothes visible at all. Whereas there was absolutely *no* reason why they shouldn't be actually *wearing* a tight skirt such as he used in his fantasies – the type of skirt that wouldn't ordinarily be worn to an office anyway, so there wouldn't be a chance of unfortunate misunderstandings. He could just bulk buy a supply of short, tight skirts in manmade leopardskin, and they could be kept in some kind of storage container in the Ladies disabled, and the gals could slip into one before going on duty.

Once he'd cracked that one he wished he'd taken the time to confront the problem earlier. Because the toilet was another kettle of fish.

He kept thinking and thinking and thinking, but somehow the solution eluded him.

By this stage the rest of the guinea pigs had adjusted somehow, and the project had gotten through the initial rough patch. The way the guinea pigs saw it was, you don't expect Vitamin C to taste like an orange. You take it because it's good for you. And after they'd tried it a few times they didn't really notice most of the features that at first had seemed strange.

Then Joe introduced the short skirts and the high heels and the whole thing took off.

But one of the things that people commented on later was just how little had been done to prepare people psychologically for the kind of outspread a scheme like this might have. In the early stages virtually nothing was known about the effect of using lightning rods on individuals whom the facility was meant to protect. The least Joe could have done, people felt, was to monitor participants carefully for adverse collaterals. One of the many things people couldn't get their heads around was the fact that Joe had basically gone into business after a *single study* involving getting members of an office to play computerized Spin the Bottle. And frankly, to call it a study was stretching it. Basically all he'd been doing was seeing what he could get away with. Responsible employment psychology this was *not*.

It was hardly surprising, in the circumstances, that there were some painful surprises in store for some of Joe's guinea pigs. The only thing that was surprising was that anyone could have been surprised.

LET DOWN

Chris was one of the first to discover that the seemingly straightforward sexual harassment preventative could lead to unanticipated and tragic consequences.

The funny thing was that he just thought it was funny to begin with. He had no strong feelings about it one way or another. It could be that it would be helpful for guys who were not getting satisfaction elsewhere. This was not really a problem for him, and when he was at work he liked to think one hundred percent about work, so he did not really expect to make much use of the facility.

What he privately thought to himself was that it sounded like the kind of idea someone would come *up* with who was not getting satisfaction. But there's no point in needlessly alienating someone who has gotten the go-ahead from higher up, so when it was explained to him he just said Hoo boy and kept his thoughts to himself.

But a funny thing happened. He tried out the facility a couple of times just to see what it was like, and what he noticed suddenly was just how much the urge to get instant gratification had been dominating his relations with the opposite sex. For instance, he had tended to go to the kind of venue where you would expect to find women who were also interested in instant gratification. Most women operate on a different time scale from men, but not all, and he had tended to seek out the ones who would not take offense if you took things at your own speed.

What this meant was that he had actually been very limited in the kind of women he met. Marketing is not something that gives you a lot of time to stop and think, it's a fast-moving game, but every once in a while he would vaguely think that someday he was going to want to get to know some other kind of girl. Because obviously you don't want your kids when the time comes being brought up by the kind of girl who would go home with a complete stranger she just met in a bar. Then every once in a while his mother would arrange for him to meet some girl who looked exactly like a dachshund. Given the choice he had always felt he would rather not have children with genes that were fifty percent dachshund. So he had always known vaguely that one day he was going to have to do something himself, only the same drive that made him such a success in marketing kept pushing him into going after the kind of girl who responds instantly to a guy with drive.

Anyway after one of his trial sessions he went to a bar as per usual and he noticed a table of girls, only this time the one he noticed was the quiet one. He went over and struck up a conversation, and then a couple of the louder girls were asked to dance. So they went off and he suggested dancing to the quiet one and she said No, and then he said What about going out on the deck? They went out and found a table overlooking the lake. There was a full moon in the sky and ducks quacked softly in the reeds. It turned out that she was a librarian. The other girls at her table lived in the same apartment building and they had persuaded her to come out with them but it was not the kind of thing she usually did.

They talked for a while and they discovered that they shared an interest in Philip K. Dick. So they got into a long conversation and when they went back inside the other girls had gone, leaving her with no way to get home. He had offered her a ride, and he had driven her home, and he hadn't even tried to kiss her goodnight.

What he realized afterwards was that unlike the way he usually approached things he had not been mentally at some subliminal level calculating his chances and then managing events to move them in a certain direction and interpreting everything that went on in terms of how well he was doing in terms of getting things to turn out a certain way. This time he had been able to step aside from those preoccupations and realize that Louise was actually not seeing anything that went on in those terms. The reason he was able to do this was not just the fact that he had obtained satisfaction earlier in the day, but that he had the certainty that he could get it again the following day if he wanted it, without any of the undoubted hassle of persuading someone to go back with him, persuading someone that they were both adults, and then in the morning getting rid of her without a lot of hassle. The disability facility lacked a lot of the features you typically looked for in sex – tits, for example. The possibility of things developing in an oral direction. But it wasn't bad for what it was. And somehow it had enabled him to get to know Louise without coming across as obnoxious. If you're in marketing you tend to be pretty direct, and that can spill over to parts of life where it is not really adaptive. Somehow he had gotten around that pitfall for a change.

One thing you soon realize in marketing is that there's a lot goes on in people that they themselves don't necessarily understand. That applies to you just as much as anyone out there. Once he had recognized how much his drives were coloring his life he was able to see that he would have to do something about it if it was not to affect his developing relationship with Louise.

So he made a point of going to the disability after that, and he started going out with Louise — dinner, movies, concerts — and he was able to give her the space she needed without getting impatient the way he otherwise might have.

Now the thing was, Louise was not the kind to go home with someone from a bar, but she was no dachshund. She wasn't what you would call a babe, but that wasn't to say she wasn't attractive. The more Chris got to know her and the more she relaxed, the more attractive she became.

They discovered they had lots of other things in common, like sharing a liking for R.E.M. and spaghetti Westerns. The relationship gradually deepened. One day Chris picked Louise up at the library on a Saturday, and she was reading to the little kids in the children's section. It was obvious that this was somebody who would take a lot of trouble with her own kids. Chris had had to fight every step of the way to make himself what he was, with no help from his family, and he had always promised himself that if he ever had kids it would be different for them.

He decided that he was ready to settle down and he asked Louise to marry him and she said yes. So it's funny the way things work out, because none of that would have happened if he hadn't been able to let her take her time. Once they were engaged there was no longer any need to make use of the facility, it had served its purpose. It was just for those few crucial weeks that it had helped to keep drives he had not been fully aware of under control.

But one day they were talking about something and Louise said if there was one thing she hated it was being lied to. "I can stand anything but a lie," she said. "Don't ever let there be any secrets between us, Chris."

Afterwards he could never work out how it happened. Maybe he had had too much to drink, so that he had felt as though he could tell her anything and it wouldn't matter. Whatever it was, Louise had suddenly sensed that there was something he wasn't telling her and she had said the thing about a secret was that not telling it made it much worse than it actually was. So he had said it wasn't anything really, it was just a facility they had at work that he had made use of a couple of times, and Louise said you mean like corporate hospitality or something and he said kind of and he explained and Louise just totally freaked out.

It was at a time like this that the facility really came into its own. There are times when you just want something completely uncomplicated. There are times when you just don't feel like talking. There are times when all you want is something that will take your mind off things. If it hadn't been for the disability the whole Louise thing would probably have really gotten in the way of work. Instead he was able to just put it behind him and concentrate on achieving his goals.

Others, of course, had stories of their own. Something that had looked completely uncomplicated, a purely physical convenience, turned out to have far-reaching psycho-social repercussions.

Whether Joe could have circumvented these problems if he had done a follow-up study on the Spin the Bottle participants will never be known. Long after the lightning rods had become a standard fixture in a wide variety of corporate environments somebody got the idea of going back to talk to the people who had taken part in the Spin the Bottle trial; to his surprise he found that the Spin the Bottle installation was still in place ten years after Joe signed off on the project. A couple of members of staff who were more computer savvy than Joe had doctored the software to introduce a couple of new twists, but essentially the proto-lightning rod was still going strong, with no noticeable negatives that anyone could see. Nobody had to do it who didn't want to. Most people thought it was fun.

Nobody had made a connection between the application and the lightning rods they had heard or read about in the media. When the researcher pointed out that their device had been developed by the same guy, who had gone on to develop the more hard-core service immediately after, people were taken aback and disgusted; they all agreed that something like that would have poisoned the office atmosphere. What they *had* was just something for fun, something to lighten up the day. They certainly were *not* going to upgrade.

So even if Joe had taken a more responsible attitude toward checking for fallout, it's possible that the net result would have been just the same.

As for the lightning rods, relatively few aspects of their experience could in any case have been satisfactorily modeled through extrapolation from the earlier Spin the Bottle trial.

LET THE CHIPS FALL
WHERE THEY MAY

Lucille had always thought of herself as pretty unflappable. The way she saw it was, she was the kind of person who could take things in her stride. She didn't let things get to her. Whatever might be going on around her, she just got on with whatever it was she had to do. Also, she prided herself on her attention to detail. More specifically, she prided herself on paying attention to detail without getting obsessed about it. Basically she was the kind of person who could just get on with the job without making a fuss about it. Give her something to do and she would get the job done.

When she had started working she had taken all these things for granted. You're there to do a job. So see what needs to be done, and do it. Can't get much more obvious than that, right? Wrong.

What she had started realizing after a while was that most people just flew apart over things that she just took in her stride. The longer you work, the more you realize how many people can't deal with things. Even if they're *paid* to deal with them, they *still* can't deal with them. So that somebody who just does what they're paid to do really stands out.

Well, that's fine. And it wasn't that people had been unappreciative. People were always saying how much they appreciated working with someone they could trust to do the job right. They were always saying how great it was to work with someone who didn't lose her head in a crisis. She'd worked in quite a few places, and each time word would get around and she'd be asked to help out by people she didn't normally work for when something big came up, because if it was really big they wanted someone with an attention to detail who didn't lose her head in a crisis. *Fine.*

It wasn't exactly that the pay was bad, either. Her salary usually *did* reflect the value people put on her work. She would tend to be getting 20%, maybe 30% more than someone who was nominally in the same position – it wasn't exactly that people weren't prepared to put their money where their mouth was. And it wasn't that she had to gouge it out of them, either. By the time she'd worked for someone a couple of months he couldn't do enough for her; he'd be champing at the bit for the next chance to throw a bonus at her, or a raise. She'd never quit a job without being offered more money to stay.

The thing is, though, there's recognition and recognition. The way Lucille saw it was, to be perfectly honest, she wasn't 30% better than everybody else. What's 30%, after all? Three-tenths. About a third. A *third*? I.e. her work was a *third* better than average? In your dreams. The way she saw it, she was about *thirty* times as good as the average PA, and *ten* times as good as the average senior PA, and she sure as heck wasn't earning anything like *that* differential.

What actually tended to happen was she would end up picking up a lot of overtime.

In other words, the result of being head and shoulders above the rest was that she didn't have a life to call her own.

What the new position seemed to offer, anyway, was some kind of recognition of the ability to take things in your stride. It was a way to parlay that ability into a remuneration package that went some way toward acknowledging its scarcity. In the longer term, it offered the chance to move up into a different sphere where her qualities would get something like their market value. Something about the woman who wanted to go to law school had struck a real chord. "What's to stop *me* doing that?" Lucille had thought. "I could save up some money and go to Harvard Law School."

The first few times were actually rather unpleasant. She had insisted on Joe putting in various safeguards which apparently hadn't occurred to him, Joe not really being blessed with that kind of attention to detail. So she knew nothing could go seriously wrong. But there was something about taking off all your clothes below the waist and going backwards through a hole in the wall that felt quite uncomfortable. But the way she looked at it was, it was no different from what you put up with when you go to the gynaecologist. You just had to learn to take it in your stride. The way to look at it was, we all have to do things we don't like in life. The important thing is to do something that offers appropriate compensation that enables you to do something you *do* want to do.

Besides, the thing to remember is there are two ways of looking at things you don't like that life throws at you. One way is to emphasize the negative and just fall apart because every little thing isn't exactly the way you like it. The other way is to look at it as an opportunity to practice dealing with things you don't like. It's a chance to practice not letting things get to you. You start out on little annoyances like the bus being late or running out of coffee when you don't have time to go to the store, and you get to the point where you just don't notice. Then you work up to slightly bigger annoyances, like just missing a bus when there won't be another for an hour. You get to the point where you just take *that* in your stride. And each time something goes wrong you practice just dealing with the situation without getting worked up about it. If something comes along that you *really* don't like, this is a chance to see how strong you are. If you can get through something potentially unpleasant without letting it interfere with your peace of mind, that tells you something about yourself. No matter *what* happens, nothing is going to drag you down. That's an incredibly strong position to be in. You don't get to that position by shrinking from a little unpleasantness.

So Lucille got through the first few weeks without any serious difficulties, and then Joe introduced the skirts. For some reason just the fact of wearing the skirt felt more protected somehow. From her own point of view, it was definitely an improvement. But the fact that she'd gotten through those first weeks without it meant she knew she could do anything, and that's always a good thing to know.

The other early lightning rods found the practicalities of the job harder to adjust to. In later years, looking back on their experiences, a common theme was a feeling that they had been inadequately prepared. Basically Joe had just demonstrated how the message would appear on their screen and then taken them back to the disabled stall and demonstrated how the transporter worked, and that was *it*. Lucille by that stage had put it all behind her and was making a million a year as a litigation lawyer, but every once in a while she would pick up a paper and see a story about someone who hadn't been able to put it behind her. Someone who had spent an unpleasant three weeks back in 1999 and had never recovered from the shock. Well, just reading between the lines Lucille could tell that this was someone who should never have gone in for that kind of work in the first place. If anyone had asked her, which they hadn't, she'd have said it was a job where you definitely *needed* strength. To put people without that strength in the line of fire was just asking for trouble.

4

AS FUR AS YOU KIN GO

WORD OF MOUTH

What Joe would explain, when later confronted with this kind of criticism, was that at the outset the success of the facility was by no means the foregone conclusion it might with hindsight appear. In an ideal world he would obviously have wanted to spend more time making sure no one was doing anything she didn't feel comfortable with. Unfortunately our world is very far from ideal, sustainable client development was absolutely vital to the success of the business, and it was up to him to singlehandedly pursue that goal for *all* their sakes. Regrettably, he had had to make some difficult decisions. If the ship went down, they would all go down with it. So he had to make some tough choices.

So while the early lightning rods were going through a period of adjustment, Joe was back out there gunning for the product. He had sent out some more letters while the builders were working, and he had made some more pitches. Just the knowledge that he had actually made a sale and that installation was underway gave him an edge. You can fake confidence in the sense that you can put on a good show, but what you can't fake is the inner confidence that comes from success. Because no matter what you say to the customer, *you* always know the score. If the score is Sales: 0, let's face it: you're going to have to put on one hell of a good show.

One thing that really boosted his confidence, anyway, was that about a month after he introduced the short skirts he got a couple of calls from some guys who played golf with Steve. Joe had been absolutely right: Once Steve had committed to the project he had wanted to convince himself he had done the right thing.

In a lot of ways, obviously, he would have been better off just keeping it to himself, but that's not the way people work. It's lonely at the top; a guy who has made a big decision like this wants other people to make that decision too. So Steve had told a buddy of his, an older man who shared Steve's conservative instincts and was not really comfortable with the mores of the younger generation.

"We're businessmen, Al," Steve had said. "At the end of day, we've got to be realistic. We've got to deal with people the way they are, not the way we might like them to be. If we can't do that, hell, we might as well retire right here and now."

The way Joe knew Steve had said this was that Al passed it on to explain his own reason for calling. Al had gone on to explain that he wasn't ready to push up daisies yet, and that he appreciated an honest approach. It was like a breath of fresh air. "Let's call a spade a spade," said Al.

"I couldn't agree with you more," said Joe.

So Al had made an appointment for Joe to come and see him at a mutually convenient time.

Steve had also spread the good word to an up-and-coming younger businessman, who by the sound of it had said something that Steve had taken to imply that his management style was somewhat dated. Again, this is really not a good reason to go sharing information of a relatively delicate nature, but as it turned out no harm had been done. The kid called Joe and explained that he was opening a new office in Kansas City. Some of his key players from New York would be going over to get things started. The way he saw it was, their style might come as something of a shock to people from the Midwest; the last thing he wanted was for people to get their backs up just when they were supposed to be working together as a team. If he could get some lightning rods in place it might ease the tension, as well as making it easier on the out-of-towners.

"You bet," said Joe.

"The way I see it is, now's the time to get the installation in place, so it's there when the office opens."

"I couldn't agree with you more," said Joe.

"I think it plays better if we fly 'em in. It's all fairly new, and I can see some problems if we try to recruit out in Kansas. Ever been to Kansas?"

"I was saving it," said Joe.

"Great place. *Great* place. And some really great people. But they're not what you would call sophisticated, you know, they see stuff on TV that they wouldn't necessarily expect to come across in real life. You know? I mean, that's why I think these lightning rods would be such a great idea in the first place. No point offending local sensibilities. But if you start recruiting locally it kind of defeats the object. Any problem getting staff to relocate?"

"No problem at all," said Joe.

"Great. *Great.* So when can we get you out to the Big K? This weekend suit you?"

The Big *K*? thought Joe. *Give* me a *break.*

"Suits me just fine," he said.

•

That's sales for you. One minute you're killing yourself just trying to get your foot in the door. The next minute someone is chasing you down the street because their mother's uncle's cleaning lady told them something about the product that made them feel life without the product would not be worth living.

PASTURES NEW

Joe flew out to the Big K that weekend to look at the new office and make arrangements for installation of the transporters and what have you. He should have been walking on air. Another sale, further easing of cash flow situation, what more could you ask? But the fact is that the whole time he was flying out to Kansas City the issue of the disabled toilet kept getting at him. He'd tried to get it out of his mind, but it just kept coming right on back. It was like the old roll-down blind debate, only magnified by a factor of a thousand.

He got in late Friday night. All he had was his carry-on luggage, so he went straight to the shuttle service that connected up to the Hilton. At this stage in the game he certainly couldn't afford to stay at a Motel 6, with all that implied about cash flow being a cause for concern; no, the Hilton it had to be. At least his suit would look right at home.

Then a funny thing happened. He was standing in line for the shuttle, and the person ahead of him bent down to get something out of her suitcase, and he realized that the person standing in front of her was a dwarf. The guy couldn't have been more than four feet tall. If that. He wasn't really doing

much of anything, just standing there being short. Then the shuttle bus drew up beside them.

The thing was, never having actually come across a dwarf in real life before, and only having seen *Time Bandits* a long time ago, Joe had never realized just how short a dwarf's legs can be. The shuttle bus had a fairly low step, but it was *way* too high for that dwarf. Well, obviously the guy had had to deal with this type of situation before, he just took hold of the pole in the middle of the door and swung himself right on up, no problem. He had to hand the driver money to put in the fare dispenser, which was also *way* too high, and then he went back into the bus and he had to swing himself up *again* just to get onto one of the seats – what kind of a way is that to go through life?

Joe paid his fare and then he went back into the bus and sat down, a long way from the dwarf. One of the first lessons you learn in life is to avoid men of below-average height. There's something about being short that makes a man feel he has something to prove, say he stopped growing at 5'6", a couple of extra inches would have made all the difference, instead of going with the flow he tends to be aggressive if not downright mean. Take away another couple of inches, and you're into mean son of a bitch territory. Take it right on down to 3'11" and God only *knows* what you're up against. Best to keep a safe distance.

Anyway, the bus pulled out, and Joe's mind reverted to its bête noir: the disabled toilet. And the thing he suddenly realized was that the disabled toilet would be *way* too high for someone like this dwarf. No better than any of the other toilets, in fact, except that it had a rail he could use to climb up onto the seat. And if you stop and think about it for a minute, when was the last time you saw a toilet with a *dwarf* icon on the door? Well, what kind of world do we live in when we give people no option but to climb up onto the seat whenever they need to answer the call of nature?

Joe was still thinking this indignantly when one of the other passengers, a big fat guy with a paunch, decided to pick on the dwarf. The fat guy had also had to sit at the front of the bus, on one of the long seats that back onto the side rather than facing the front, because it was the only seating that would accommodate him comfortably. Not that the guy was so big he couldn't take the *width* of the other seats. He was big, but he wasn't *that* big. No, the problem was the distance between the seats was such that a guy with that size of paunch wouldn't have been able to squeeze it in between the seat he was sitting in and the back of the seat in front. So the guy was sitting up front, where he had a whole aisle to let the paunch breathe freely, and he was sitting facing the dwarf, who was reading a book.

Fat Guy: "Watcha reading, big guy?"

Joe was thinking I don't *believe* it. I *don't believe* it. *Big guy*? What kind of insensitive pig comes right out and says something like that to someone you *know* has got to be sensitive about his *height*? It wasn't even that the guy was out to torment, looking at him you could tell he thought he was just being friendly. *Jesus.*

Joe waited for the dwarf to pull a switchblade and sling it straight into the unsuspecting paunch. Or stamp his heels to reveal a line of razor blades in the soles of his shoes. Wanna try a little kick boxing, *big guy*? the dwarf would say, and before the guy knew what hit him the dwarf would be in the air, slashing out –

"*The John Foster Dulles Book of Humor*," said the dwarf.

"Huh," said the guy. "Any good?"

"I'm only up to page two."

"Well, to tell you the truth, John Foster Dulles is not someone I would have tended to associate with humor. Or anything else, come to think of it."

"That's a mistake a lot of people make. There's a lot more to JFD than meets the eye."

JFD? thought Joe. JFD?

"Is that a fact. The name's Paul, by the way."

"Ian."

"Pleased to meet you, Ian."

Joe was wondering why it was that Kansas had never acquired a reputation for being strange. If somebody can go around calling John Foster Dulles JFD and nobody bats an eyelash you have to ask yourself what are the *rest* of them like? And no sooner had he asked himself why word hadn't gotten out than the answer came to him, just like that. The reason nobody knew about it was that normal people never came to see what was going on. Not realizing what the state had to offer they went elsewhere for their kicks. People from out of state tended not only to *be* but to *stay* just that: out of state.

"People tend to not know a lot about him. The fact is that he was quite an interesting guy, it's just that Ike hogged the limelight."

"Ike?"

"Eisenhower?"

"Oh, right, right. Right." There was a short pause. "You know," said Paul, "history was never my strong point, but for some reason I always thought Eisenhower's first name was Dwight. Am I getting him mixed up with someone else?"

"Ike was a nickname," said Ian.

"*Oh. I see.*"

"As in 'I like Ike.' It was his slogan when he ran for president."

"You don't say. Now I never knew that."

"Where you from, anyway?" asked Ian, which was exactly what Joe had been wondering.

"Well, I've been all over the place, but I was born in Keene, New Hampshire."

Joe mulled this over. Maybe Kansas wasn't so strange after all. Maybe Keene, New Hampshire was the outpost of the Twilight Zone.

Ian closed his book and stuck it in the pocket of his carry-on bag. "I've never been that far east, myself," he said. "I hear the autumn leaves are quite a sight."

"They certainly are," said Paul. "They're a sight to behold."

"Well, it's been nice talking to you," said Ian. "This is where I get off." He pushed a button in the pole by the seat. The bus pulled to a stop. "Hope you enjoy your stay in Kansas City."

"Why, thank you," said Paul. "And the same to you."

Ian got off the bus. The bus moved on.

Joe thought suddenly: Instead of a *fixed* alternative toilet, what we need is something with an adjustable *height*, like a dentist's chair! Something you could pump up and down! Or maybe just raise electronically! But if you can raise it up and down, what's to stop you from taking it *right* down? So it's completely out of sight! Under a panel in the floor! Should the cubicle be required for some *other* purpose, such as answering a call of a *different* nature!

And he thought: Maybe the adjustable height toilet *already exists*!

The bus was moving swiftly down a broad, straight, empty street with no traffic to get in its way. Every second was bearing him further away from someone who would almost certainly have the answer to this crucial question.

Joe sprang into action. "*Driver!*" he shouted. "*Stop the bus! That was where I wanted to get off!*"

"I thought you said you wanted the Hilton," said the driver, with the helpfulness for which Jayhawkers are famous.

"I need the exercise!" said Joe desperately, while the bus bore him further and further along.

"I can let you off at the next stop," said the driver.

"I think I'm going to throw up!" said Joe, clapping a hand over his mouth.

The bus pulled silently to the curb.

Joe could tell the driver knew he was lying and was just too polite to say so. He hurtled out the door before the driver could change his mind.

He turned and ran back in the direction of the last stop, cursing his carry-on luggage.

One good thing was that Ian would not have covered a lot of ground in the interim.

Sure enough, five minutes of sprinting brought him gasping up behind an unmistakable figure.

"Wait!" gasped Joe. "Wait!"

And he stopped at last, panting, by his side.

"Can I help you?" asked Ian.

"I hope so," panted Joe. He stood panting. He really needed to be getting more exercise. Maybe he should lay in a supply of Special K. Walk to the store instead of taking the car. Or maybe more serious measures were called for. Join a gym. Work out for an hour every day ...

"Uh," said Joe. No way this was not going to be embarrassing. "Please don't take this the wrong way," he said. "I, uh, I'm helping a friend who's opening an office here. I, uh,

I thought as long as we're starting from scratch we should have a toilet with adjustable height in the alternative cubicle, and I, uh, I just wondered if you happened to know of such a thing."

"No," said Ian. "I don't think I've ever come across anything like that."

"Oh," said Joe. "Oh, well, I'm sorry to have troubled you."

"That's all right," said Ian. "Was there anything else?" He was obviously itching to go home and get back to *The John Foster Dulles Book of Humor.* Well, it takes all kinds to make a world.

"No," said Joe. "Thanks for your help. That is, do you happen to know how I would get to the Hilton from here?"

"The *Hilton*?" said Ian. "That's *way* across town. Were you planning to walk?"

"Unless you have a better idea," said Joe. Interestingly, now that he was actually talking to the guy he was beginning to see that underneath all the shortness was a real human being. A human being who called John Foster Dulles JFD, but a human being for all that.

"I think your best bet is to go right back the way you came," said Ian. "Fourth set of traffic lights, take a right, keep going, I think it's a couple of blocks, could be three, you come to a strip mall with a KFC. You should be able to get a taxi there. Otherwise there's the bus, but at this time of night they only come once an hour."

"OK," said Joe. "I think I got that. Fourth set of lights, right, two or three blocks. Thanks. You've been a big help."

He turned back the way he came. Fourth set of lights, right, two blocks. No problem.

His mind returned to its current preoccupation.

•

Walking back toward the Kansas City Kentucky Fried Chicken, carrying his carry-on luggage, Joe realized that he had had a very narrow escape.

For some reason, the whole time he'd been thinking about lightning rods he'd been thinking of people using the facility as people pretty much like himself. He hadn't anticipated users in wheelchairs. He hadn't anticipated users of significantly lower height. Well, in this day and age you can't afford not to anticipate that kind of eventuality. There is absolutely no reason why someone in one of those categories should not be the kind of high-performance results-orientated individual whose services a company would want to retain. Which means any facilities made available to other employees have to be potentially available to individuals in the relevant categories.

Besides, there was more to it than just some kind of abstract fairness. If you think about it, it stands to reason a disabled person is going to spend a lot of time being frustrated. A guy who spends his life climbing up onto bus seats is going to be frustrated a lot of the time. And it stands to reason that sexual frustration is going to be part of the package. Which means that these are individuals who could well benefit from access to lightning rods, if their employer has not been too blinkered by his preconceptions to provide it.

The other thing he realized was that this adjustable toilet idea had real potential, even apart from solving his own particular disabled toilet problem. Why *wasn't* something like that widely available? This could be his own small contribution to easing the lives of people whose needs were too readily overlooked. He could insist on an adjustable toilet being part of every lightning rod installation; sooner or later, you just *knew* something like that would catch on.

Think how much mothers with little kids would appreciate it. In fact, if the whole lightning rod thing didn't take off, he could just concentrate on developing and marketing his adjustable toilet.

And the third thing he realized was that he now knew why it was that he had never made a career out of sales. All right, he'd had his successes, but something just hadn't clicked, and now he knew why. Basically, he wasn't a salesman. He was an ideas man. And those are two very different animals. He just happened to have a talent for thinking up things no one had thought of before, and then persuading people that something they hadn't happened to have thought of was indispensable. Sales is obviously a *part* of that. A *big* part. But it's only part of a larger whole. And the thing that made that whole possible was that knack for coming up with ideas.

Having come up with the idea of the adjustable toilet, Joe was able to sell it to Jerry without too much trouble. Jerry said he thought Kansas City was just the place to introduce this novelty to the world. He started singing the Kansas City song from *Oklahoma!* and Joe joined right in, because you should never pass up an opportunity to bond with the client.

The fact that Jerry would sing the song about Kansas City, *Kansas* just showed how uneducated he was, because any idiot knows the Kansas City referred to in *Oklahoma!* is Kansas City, Missouri – the phrase "Kansas City, Mo." is actually *in* one of the other songs. While the two cities are admittedly contiguous, though on opposite sides of the river, this just makes it all the more annoying for residents of Kansas City, Ka. when people make this kind of mistake. But any salesman knows you can't afford to get pedantic with the client. The old saying, "The customer is always right," harks back to this common knowledge. If you're the kind of person who has to correct someone every time they make a factual mistake, you might just want to stop a moment and compare the average take-home pay of a teacher and that of a halfway competent salesman. Truth be told, you can make a hell of a lot more money by being wrong at the right time than by being right at the wrong time.

Most American kids know this instinctively, which is why they're so often caught off-base when asked without warning to name the capital of Peru. They know that if it comes to the crunch, and they actually need to know the name of the capital of Peru, they can quickly retrieve the information from the *Encyclopaedia Britannica*. But there are more important things in life than impromptu identification of obscure foreign capitals, and when it comes to those things Americans are second to none. When it comes to making somebody feel good who is going to give you hundreds of thousands of dollars worth of business, an American will be shaking hands on the deal while the smart-ass is still waiting for a round of applause because he knew whatever it was without having to look it up.

The main thing was that the adjustable toilet was a done deal. And for that, Joe would have sung just as wholeheartedly in Kansas City, Mars.

The result was the Joe was much busier than he had expected to be just getting Jerry's outfit up and running. He had to fly out to recruit unifunctional staff, and then he had to fly back to get the prototype toilet installed, and what with one thing and another he wasn't really able to keep his finger on the pulse at his first installation. He had other things on his mind.

Joe gradually got more and more involved in his adjustable toilet project over in the Big K, and by the time the whole installation was in place the cubicle also featured an adjustable sink, an adjustable hand dryer, and an adjustable towel rack, not to mention an adjustable condom and lubricant dispenser and adjustable transporter. The place was so designed that a person of sub-average height would be just as comfortable as anybody else. Joe kept wishing there was some way he could track down Ian and show him what he'd accomplished, since he was probably the only person Joe knew who was capable of appreciating it.

It wasn't that Joe was spending all his time in the Big K, obviously. He was back and forth. But that was where the focus of his attention was. For some reason, the more he worked on the project, the more aware he became of just how unique it was in terms of the world at large. Every company is required to have conveniences for disabled users, but if somebody happens to be an unusual size the message is "Why didn't you go before you left home?"

In some ways it was easier to get fired up about something like this than it was about the actual lightning rods. With the lightning rods, in a *sense* you were protecting people from something that was no fault of their own, i.e. a tendency to insult female staff through some kind of testosteronal imbalance. But that does seem to be something people could in *some* sense do something about. Whereas what kind of a world is it that acts like height was something you could change if you had the willpower? It wasn't even as if you were talking about a *minority*, or something you were expecting to go away, there were millions of kids in the world and the situation wasn't likely to change so *what* was the *problem*? In some ways Joe was tempted to just leave the whole lightning rods thing and go with the new idea, which obviously had huge potential since nothing like it had ever been tried before.

The problem was, there's a difference between selling a solution to a perceived problem and selling a solution to something that is not perceived as a problem. People perceive million-dollar sexual harassment suits as a problem. They do not perceive the struggles of persons of short height as a problem, or at least, if it *is* a problem, it's not *their* problem. So whereas Joe knew that as long as he stuck with the lightning rods cash flow would not be a problem, he also knew, unfortunately, that if he put all his eggs in the basket of the adjustable toilet he'd be back killing time in a trailer before you could say Jack Robinson – without even the chance of a free pumpkin pie.

Still, there's more than one way to skin a cat. Joe always made a point of having complete control over his lightning rod installations, and he had now made a vow to have height-friendly facilities in every single one. The way he saw it was, if the lightning rods took off the way it was starting to look like they were going to, the adjustable features would gradually become familiar to people, and sooner or later they would just be standard in all public conveniences.

And in the meantime, the disabled toilet was a real weight off his mind. With his new installations what happened was, the same mechanism that activated the transporter automatically took the toilet right down into the floor, where a sliding panel covered it for the duration. Since he was starting from scratch, he was also able to achieve an ambience that was a little less clinical than the one he had had to offer his original clients.

Unfortunately nobody has worked out a way to be two places at the same time. While Joe was otherwise occupied, the pot was starting to notice that no one was watching.

TROUBLE

If you're in personnel one of the things you learn is never to be surprised by anything people do. Because it doesn't matter *how* long you've been in the business, you think you've seen everything, and they can still surprise you.

This applies even more if you have been in personnel since the days when it was *called* personnel. If you have spent a lifetime dealing with people, at first in the context of a personnel department, and later, moving with the times, in a human resources task force, you get to the point where you think there's *nothing* new they can throw at you. You've seen the nicest people you could imagine engaging in systematic theft of supplies, you've seen the shameless use of the office phone to distant parts of the globe, and again it's often the nicest people who are the guilty parties. The fact is there is something about an office environment that tempts people to operate with a completely different moral code from the one they were brought up with. If they actually *were* brought up with a moral code, which to be honest sometimes you really have to wonder.

Roy had been dealing with people, one way and another, for over thirty years, so it did not surprise him to discover that something was going on. If you're used to dealing with people you know how important it is not to let abuses go unchecked. If something irregular gets established and taken for granted, to the point where everybody does it, you are only going to be able to stamp it out with a lot of bad feeling. An experienced human resources operator knows the cost of bad feeling. Sometimes it's the price you have to pay. But it does come with a price tag, make no mistake about that, so if you can stamp out whatever it is before people have started thinking of it as a God-given right, believe you me you had better hop to it.

Roy was not surprised to find that *something* was afoot. But in spite of all his years dealing with humans in all their manifold variety, what that something might be never crossed his mind in his wildest dreams.

What happened was that Roy, over the years, had taken to using the disabled cubicle in the Men's. Even as a boy Roy had been what the Sears Roebuck catalog called husky, and over the years he had gone on quietly expanding. Sears did not have a name for adult men with a six-foot waist, and eventually Roy had had to stop ordering his clothes from a catalog; for a while he had taken to buying his clothes at Walmart. Then he had come to his senses. As a personnel officer he knew none better that it's important to accept yourself the way you are. If you look at Minnesota Fats in the movie *The Hustler*, Minnesota Fats is actually better dressed than the Paul Newman character. Fats knew he was the best, and he dressed the part. So Roy had bought a five-hundred-dollar tailored suit at a time when five hundred dollars was a lot of money, and he always flew first class when he flew, and he always used the disabled cubicle in the Men's Room.

One day he was sitting on the toilet in the disabled cubicle, taking his time, when a couple of guys walked in and started taking a leak. One of them laughed to the other, "Jeez, it's fucking 9:15 and somebody's on a disability. Hoo boy."

That was all Roy heard. He got up with help from the bar, and thought no more of it. But the next day he was in the cubicle and a couple of guys came in and they were talking again.

One said he was going to take his disability and call it quits for the day.

The other guy said, "Hoo boy."

Now what Roy naturally thought was that this was some kind of variation on calling in sick for the day. The fact that this practice, whatever it might be, had developed its own slang, showed how far things had spread. Something was afoot that was going to have to be nipped in the bud.

The first thing Roy did was to go back to his office and check up on absenteeism patterns in the past month. Plenty of men his age swore *at* computers. Roy swore *by* them. You could get an overall picture of what was going on in a place of work in five minutes that you couldn't have gotten in a *year* fifteen years ago. The thing to remember is, a computer is a tool. It's there to help you do what *you* want to do. Used properly, a computer can be a valuable aid in determining what exactly it *is* that you want to do. But at the end of the day it's just something to take care of things that would bore a human because they would take too long. It's a machine, if you will. Neither more nor less.

Anyway, in five minutes Roy had gotten a picture of absenteeism in the past month that had him staring and scratching his head. "Holy son of a gun," said Roy, looking at the little chart the computer had produced on his screen. In thirty years he'd never seen anything like it.

Absenteeism in the firm had reached an all-time low. In a building that housed 500 employees, ten had had a sick day in the last month. The rate was the same for the previous month. Roy went back six months. Month after month it was the same story. Then six months ago the figures were back up to where he would have expected them to be.

Something had been going on for six months and it had taken him completely by surprise.

"Holy moly," said Roy. He took out one of the jumbo bags of peanut M&M's that he kept in his bottom drawer and tore a small hole in the corner.

He decided that today he would start with green.

He shook a few M&M's onto his pad, ate the green one, and put the rest in a bowl.

"Darned if I ever seen anything like it," he said, popping another green M&M and tossing a few more into the bowl.

One of the great things about a computer is it can tell you just about anything you might want to know without even getting up out of your chair. All you have to do is ask it the right question is all.

Roy decided that he would do a breakdown by number of days off work. He got through three or four M&M's setting up the search parameters, and then he ran the search.

"Jumping Jehoshophat!" exclaimed Roy.

Nobody had been off work for more than one day except a guy who had broken his leg.

He ran a search according to age without throwing up anything of interest. Then he ran a search by department and that didn't throw up anything either.

Roy ate five green peanut M&M's and swept a confused jumble of yellow, brown, red, and blue M&M's into the bowl.

Roy always saved the blue for last. When he was down to the blue he would put them in a separate bowl and put it out at Reception for visitors to help themselves to. No matter how many visitors they had the level in the bowl never went down that fast. It just went to show what a mistake Mars had made in departing from its tried-and-true formula. You couldn't blame them for trying, but Roy couldn't help wishing someone in that company would be man enough to admit he had made a mistake.

Roy decided to run a search by sex.

"Well waddya know," said Roy. Nine of the ten sick employees were women. The tenth was the guy who had broken his leg.

For some reason male employees were finding it a lot more appealing to come in to work than they had six months ago. But as a matter of fact so were the female employees. Because even nine in a month was significantly down on the number of female employees who had been off sick six months ago.

"Huh," said Roy.

He spread out the rest of the bag of M&M's on his desk, finished off the greens, put the rest in the bowl, and pondered.

He decided to start on the reds.

Half an hour later Roy came out of his office carrying a bowl of blue peanut M&M's.

"Care for a peanut M&M, Stell?" he said to his secretary, or personal assistant as they called them these days.

"No thanks, Roy," said Stella.

Roy wished the manufacturers could hear her. Maybe then they'd rethink this newfangled shade of M&M which they had foisted on a reluctant public.

"Stell," said Roy, wondering how to phrase this. "Have you noticed anything unusual or out of the way in the office recently? Say in the last six months?"

"I can't say that I have," she said. "What kind of thing did you have in mind?"

"Well, I don't exactly know, for sure," said Roy, absent-mindedly eating a blue peanut M&M. He was not entirely surprised by the response. In Roy's opinion the thing to look for in a secretary, or personal assistant, was the ability to take each day as it comes. You don't *want* Einstein. If by some accident you end up with Einstein, you're in trouble. *Big* trouble. Any personnel officer will tell you the same. Stella was no Sherlock Holmes, but then he hadn't hired her to *be* Sherlock Holmes. One of the first rules of recruitment is that if you hire someone to not have certain qualities because you perceive those qualities to be inimical to the satisfactory fulfillment of the job requirements, you should not then turn around and *blame* the person for not having the qualities you chose them not to have in the first place. It may seem obvious, but it's surprising how many people forget this seemingly obvious fact in the heat of the moment.

Roy decided to inconspicuously wander around before going to Reception.

"Hi, Roy," said Lucille, not looking up from her terminal. The tread of the head of human resources, so reminiscent of that of an approaching elephant, had been familiar to her by the end of the first week on the job.

"Peanut M&M?" offered Roy.

"No thanks," Lucille said politely.

Roy only wished the manufacturers could hear.

"Peanut M&M, Stephanie?"

"Don't mind if I do," said Stephanie.

"Take all you want," urged Roy. "I'm just taking them over to Reception."

Stephanie took four. The phone rang.

"Peter Drake's office, how may I help you?"

Lucille didn't know whether the new girl was a lightning rod or not. She liked it that way. It meant for once Joe was doing his job.

Roy hesitated, then moved on to a cluster of desks where no one was on the phone. Lucille took the opportunity to write on the back of a message pad "I wouldn't eat those if I were you."

Stephanie hung up. "Whyever not?" she asked.

Lucille raised an eyebrow. "He goes through the whole bag," she said. "Color by color. So by the time he's gotten down to the blues he's got to have handled them all about four times. One for each color. Then he takes them to Reception. Can you imagine?"

The new girl made a face. "Gross me *out*," she said. She surreptitiously slipped the M&M's into her trash can. "Oh my God, I think he saw me," she said.

Roy realized that the girl had only accepted to be polite. The manufacturers just did not seem to have realized that it wasn't just him. *Nobody* wanted to eat the damn things.

Men were walking between the desks here and there. Was it his imagination, or were they walking with a jauntier step?

Was it his imagination, or was there a different atmosphere about the place?

Roy absentmindedly ate another blue M&M.

The thing was, if morale had improved that was obviously all to the good, but whatever it was it was important for human resources to be kept apprised. Because whatever it was was something human resources could probably improve on. That was why it was important to keep your finger on the pulse. Otherwise you ended up with amateurs, who didn't really understand what was involved in dealing with people, dealing with issues they didn't fully understand. So that later, when things had gotten out of control, it was left to the boys in human resources to pick up the pieces.

On an impulse, Roy stopped off at the desk of Laura Carter, who was secretary, or rather team support coordinator, to two of the younger marketing men. Laura had gone through a bad patch about nine months ago. She had been off sick two and three days a week, and while there was always a valid medical excuse there was a pattern that a blind man could have seen.

What's more, you didn't have to be a genius to see that there was something about the sense of humor of the team that Laura had had trouble adjusting to. Things that members of the team had meant to be taken in the spirit in which they were intended had unintentionally caused offense, and unfortunately one or two members of the team had seen that they had touched a raw spot and had not been able to resist teasing the girl in a way they probably wouldn't have if she had appeared not to mind. Ed Wilson, for example, had an exuberant way about him that most of the girls just took in their stride. Laura, for some reason, had had trouble handling it.

Well, Roy had happened to look at the *names* of the people who had been off sick in the last six months – this kind of thing comes as second nature to an old personnel hand – and one of the things he had noticed instantly was that Laura was not among them. Some people think that with all the hundreds of people in an organization there's no way one man could keep track of them all. They'd be surprised. If you've been in the business long enough there's precious little escapes you.

"Hi, Roy," said Laura, not looking up from her screen.

"Hi, Laura," said Roy. He noticed that Ed Wilson was not in his office. So much the better. "How's every little thing?"

"Just fine, Roy," said Laura. "I won't stop if you don't mind, I'm just finishing this off for Ed."

"You go right ahead," said Roy. "Care for an M&M?"

"I won't just this minute, thanks," said Laura.

You *see*? thought Roy.

"It's good to see you looking so well," said Roy. "It can take some time to adjust to the pressure of a job like this. Sometimes it takes people a while to settle down."

"Well, I had a lot of health problems when I started out," said Laura. "Which didn't help. And I have to admit, looking back, there was a personality clash between Ed and myself, I was brought up in a certain way so there were some things about Ed's behavior that according to the way I was brought up were inappropriate."

Laura sent a document to print.

"I'll have one of those M&M's now," she said. "This is really attractive, having all the blue ones in a bowl. Was that your idea to have a bowl of them in Reception? I always thought that was a nice touch. You know, when I was a little girl I used to wonder why they never had any blue ones, and then one day they brought them out. It was like, Somebody up there likes me!"

Well, thought Roy, there's just no accounting for tastes. But a lifetime in personnel teaches you to take these things in your stride.

"Anyway," said Laura, crunching an M&M, "my mother always told me as long as you respect yourself, sooner or later the message will get through. No matter what kind of upbringing someone has had, as long as *you* know the kind of behavior that is acceptable, sooner or later that fact is going to get across. It may take a little longer to communicate it to someone from a seriously disadvantaged background who doesn't know any better, but eventually you'll make your point."

A good personnel officer knows there are times when you don't know exactly how to respond. When those times come – and they come to the best of us – the best thing is to remain silent.

Roy ate an M&M.

"I have to admit I was getting pretty downhearted at the amount of time that had gone by with no apparent result," said Laura. "And to be fair, it wasn't just Ed, all of the team had an attitude that was not the easiest thing for someone from a different background to accept. But then one day it was the funniest thing. They just seemed to change overnight. I don't know what brought about the change, but I presume it was just that the time had come. They realized *somebody* was going to have to change, and since I had demonstrated in no uncertain terms that it was not going to be I, they accepted that it was just going to have to be they."

"And you can't pinpoint some specific incident that might have triggered the improvement?" said Roy. Through no fault of her own, Laura was not in a position to see the larger picture. Whatever it was that the team had responded to seemed to have had that effect on everyone in the company. You can't work in personnel without becoming something of a cynic, and Roy doubted that the ladylike comportment of their secretary had had such dramatic and far-reaching consequences.

"No, not really," said Laura. "Although I remember they had all had appointments with a gentleman from a temporary agency who was investigating their requirements. It may be that he may have said something in passing which gave them that little additional insight into their behavior."

This was the first that Roy had heard that the representative from the agency had talked to all the men on the team individually. This was highly unusual, and it would have really been more appropriate to clear it with personnel, but Roy couldn't fault the agency. It had delivered some really first-class employees, girls Roy would have been happy to have offered a place on the team with no ifs, ands, or buts.

"Well, I'll leave you in peace," said Roy. "Keep up the good work!" Roy knew the value of an encouraging word even if some people didn't.

He was no closer to the heart of the mystery than he had been when he started out. But that there *was* a mystery was something he didn't doubt for one second. *Something* was afoot. The question was, what might that something be?

Roy was determined to leave no stone unturned until he got to the bottom of it.

Roy took the rest of the blue M&M's to Reception.

At his size, he had to plan ahead. It was no good suddenly making the discovery that he urgently needed to go to the bathroom, since there was no way he could *get* to the bathroom in a hurry. So he decided to stop off on his way back to his office as a precautionary measure.

•

Roy sat on the disabled toilet, a prey to uncertainty. What *was* going on? There were no clues to speak of. What if the trail had gone cold?

He shook his head and sighed. He really should try to cut down. Three jumbo bags of peanut M&M's per day just wasn't healthy. Moderation in all things – that should be our watchword.

The thing was, though, that he *had* cut back at one point. He'd gotten down to one bag a day and he'd stuck to that religiously for a month. But by the end of the month he'd had to concede defeat. Because the problem was, it had impacted negatively on his performance. The human mind is a strange animal, no two alike, and for some reason the activity of going through the different colors of M&M was essential if his mind was to function at its best. And the job was such that a single bag just wasn't adequate to see you through the manifold challenges that you were apt to meet in the course of a day. He had heard smokers make the same observation. Smoking is an unhealthy, anti-social activity that endangers everyone in the workplace, so the No Smoking policy was not up for negotiation, but Roy could understand their point of view, and he was not without sympathy for it.

Roy was about to pull himself to his feet when he heard a funny kind of click. A panel had slid open in the wall beside him. Roy stared. In the hole revealed by the panel were the soles of two bare feet pointing downward. While he watched, some kind of mechanism must have been operating, because gradually the feet moved out into the room. Bare calves came into view. Bare thighs. Bare – Holy *mackerel*.

He was looking at the naked lower portion of a woman. The mechanism had stopped. He couldn't see anything above the waist. As it was he could see plenty. And then some.

I don't believe I'm seeing this, he thought.

This wasn't some casual sexual liaison among the staff. Someone had had to build this contraption and put a hole in the wall. How many people were involved? What would the shareholders think? Was it even *legal*?

Nothing happened.

I gotta get outta here, thought Roy.

He stood up, did up his pants and buckled his belt. He flushed the toilet.

The naked rear end of the woman hadn't moved.

Jesus, thought Roy.

Roy had never had a girlfriend, and though he had been on a couple of dates when he was younger and thinner he had always been shy. This kind of thing was *way* out of his league.

I'm getting too old for this job, he thought. Roy had had to deal with a couple of unsavory incidents in his time. But what the dickens was he supposed to do about this? Who would he even tell? What was he supposed to say? He tried to imagine telling someone, Steve Jackson for example, about the naked lower portion of a woman.

I just can't do it, he thought. A man from the younger generation would probably have taken something like this in his stride. Roy just couldn't deal with it. He couldn't even think of words he could bring himself to speak in the presence of another person. But how could he just walk away from it? It would be irresponsible to bury his head in the sand and pretend it hadn't happened. But what the *hell* was he supposed to *do*?

Besides, there was another problem. How was he going to get out of here? What if he opened the door and there was someone out there? What if somebody *saw*? They'd think he had been involved in this. If you've been in personnel long enough you know how stories get around. There was no way somebody was going to keep something like that to himself. The story would get around, and everyone in the building would think there was something in it.

Somehow he was going to have to persuade the woman to take herself off.

Was there some kind of speaker or something somewhere so he could tell her to go away?

Roy looked around the cubicle, but he couldn't see anything. Unless maybe this thingamajig by the toilet roll was some kind of communication device? He jiggled at it. An unopened condom fell out onto the floor.

Roy picked up the condom and tried to squeeze it back up inside the thing it had fallen out of. Three more fell out on the floor.

He considered trying to shove the four condoms back in, but the way things were going he'd just end up with a whole stream of the darned things piling up on the floor. He stuffed them into the inside pocket of his jacket.

There seemed to be absolutely nothing in the cubicle that would allow above-the-waist communication.

Well, maybe if he just kind of pushed on her legs she would get the message?

But what if she got the wrong idea?

Roy hesitated. This could be really embarrassing.

He had thought that things couldn't possibly get any worse. Suddenly he realized just how lucky he had been when all he had to worry about was how to get rid of the visitor.

The handle of the cubicle turned just a fraction.

Someone was trying to get in.

THE HUMAN STALLION

Sometimes life forces you to learn things about yourself that you would rather not know.

Ed had always known he had drive. He just didn't realize how *much* drive. But after the facility had been in place a month many guys actually found they weren't making that much use of it, whether because of being in a relationship or whatever. So they would send screen messages offering their disability for a bottle of Scotch or whatever, and Ed started picking up extras. Soon he was using it five, six times a day.

Previously he had always thought the female staff unduly sensitive. Now he realized maybe it was not all their fault. They were working with a stallion in their midst, someone who could only work off his energies by using the DF an unrealistic number of times a day. Now that he had the outlet he knew he was a nicer person as a result of it. People had even commented on it.

So he had to give a lot of credit to the people who had devised the program for their insight into the workings of people with drive. It was kind of like going to a gym and working out on a punchbag. Instead of taking whatever it might be out on whoever happened to be standing by, you took it out on someone who was paid to have stuff taken out on them.

Anyway, once he had recognized that he had a problem he made a point of using the facility regularly even on the rare occasions when he didn't feel like it.

Today a message from Mike had flashed up on his screen and he'd been in the middle of something, but he thought Might as well get it out of the way, so he clicked Yes to show he was coming. He had a big fax he wanted to get out, he could give that to one of the girls on his way over. Laura wasn't at her desk, so he stopped off in the next department. Elaine was just standing up from her desk when he came by. He explained that he had an urgent fax that had to go out *now* and he handed it over.

Elaine seemed about to object.

"Look, I don't have time for this," said Ed. "Put it on the machine. Wait for it to go through. Put it in my In tray *with* the confirmation. Any problems, take an aspirin and call me in the morning."

He strode off. He had just reached the door to the Men's when he remembered he'd promised to call someone at two. It was now 2:05.

The lightning rod could wait. It was what she was paid for, after all. He headed back to his office and picked up the phone.

Elaine put the fax on the machine but it kept jamming on autofeed so she finally had to feed it in manually herself. The whole time she was there she was conscious of time passing. Finally the last sheet went through. Then the machine dialed the number but the number was busy. It dialed three times and then it just printed out a sheet saying it couldn't get through so she had to feed all the pages again. This time she got a connection. She left the document on the fax machine and hurried to the Ladies. She was *way* too late.

Ed was back in his office on the phone, she could see. He'd probably want the fax back immediately. Well, too bad.

She hurried into the disabled. Sure enough, the light was on; the guy was already in the other cubicle. No time for the skirt today. He wouldn't be seeing anything he hadn't seen plenty of times already.

She undressed from the waist down, got on the transporter and went backwards through the wall.

Nothing happened.

She glanced at her watch. She wished the guy would just get on with the show so she could get back to work. Ed was going to want that fax back.

Time passed. She pictured the guy on the other side, desperately trying to get it up. If only Joe had installed some kind of way of communicating from one side to the other. She'd tried suggesting it, heck, they'd all tried suggesting it, but Joe just kept saying he'd get on to it as soon as he had the time. They all knew what that meant. Someone had once had an idea for improving the original notification, but getting Joe to do even the simplest little programming was like pulling teeth.

Ed, meanwhile, was getting irritated. He had finished his phone call and hurried over to the Men's, only to find that someone was in the disabled stall. All the other stalls were free, and the company didn't *have* any disabled employees, which could only mean one thing: Someone was helping himself to Ed's disability. Or rather, they were really helping themselves to Mike's dis, which Ed had snapped up for the going rate (a bottle of Johnnie Walker) because he might as well get it over with. So now Ed was a bottle of Scotch down and someone else was helping himself to the proceeds.

Ed rattled the door.

Inside the stall, Roy had suddenly asked himself a question. *Why* was somebody trying to get in? There were five other stalls. You couldn't tell him all five were now occupied. And the company didn't *have* any disabled employees, which could only mean one thing: Someone had turned up *expecting* to find this, this obscenity within the disabled stall and in all probability make use of it.

What this meant was that Roy found himself in a quandary. If he opened the door, he could put a name to a face. He could identify a member of the workforce and challenge him and the whole sordid business would come out. That was obviously the responsible course of action. But there was just one problem.

If Roy opened the door, *he* would be the one who was actually *in* the *stall* with a naked half-woman. All the *evidence* would point to it being *Roy* who had turned up for this little rendezvous. It would be Roy's word against whoever. There would be no actual *proof* that it was, in fact, the other man who had intended to use company time for R&R, and that Roy was just an innocent bystander who got caught in the crossfire.

Someone was pounding on the door with a fist.

Elaine, meanwhile, was wishing she had had time to pick up something to read.

The lightning rods had gradually accumulated a stash of magazines, but Elaine had read all the issues of *People* and *Us Weekly* and *Mademoiselle* and *Elle* and *Marie Claire* and *Better*

Homes and Gardens at least once. *People* has never claimed to be *War and Peace*. It's not really the kind of thing you keep reading and rereading, discovering new layers of meaning each time. It doesn't pretend to be. Nor, for that matter, does *Us Weekly*. People don't go back to the February 1999 issue of *Mademoiselle* and suddenly realize how much they missed the first time around because they were too young to understand. This is not a criticism – that's what people *like* about them. But what this means is that if you're stuck in a waiting room with back issues of *People* which you've already read you're going to have a long wait. A wider range of preread magazines is not going to significantly improve the situation.

What this meant was that Elaine had time on her hands. She had a million things to do, the screen message had come at the worst possible time but then that's men for you, if they have a choice between sex at a time when it's convenient and sex when you have a million things to do they'll go for the bad time every time. In this case, to be fair, the client hadn't specifically picked her and she didn't *have* to accept – she could have let someone else pick up the assignment. But then she'd just have had it hanging over her head for the rest of the day. If she'd waited she'd have ended up having to accept later in the day, probably at an even *less* convenient time. So when it had come up on her screen she'd thought Might as well get it over with. And now here she was, stuck, waiting for Rambo to get off the dime.

She found herself wondering, as she sometimes did, whether it was all worth it. Sure, the money was good, but who needs this kind of aggro?

The fact is, there's no perfect job. You're going to run into aggro whatever you do, so you might as well get paid for it. Most places just pretend the aggro doesn't exist, why would they compensate you for working in an environment that's just one big happy family, you're lucky just to be working with such great people it's not the money that counts it's the people I don't *think* so.

The important thing is just to be clear about your goals. If you go through a lot of extra aggro on a daily basis, and at the end of the year all you've got to show for it is a lot of clothes in your closet, don't go looking for someone to blame if you spend what would have been your retirement selling secondhand clothes. Elaine had opened a separate account for her lightning rod earnings, and she put everything she earned on that side straight into that account. That money was going to put Hayley through college, and Elaine wasn't going to touch a penny of it. She hadn't had a lot of choices in her life, but Hayley was going to go wherever she wanted, no matter how much it cost. Money was just not going to be a consideration. In just six months she'd put $15,000 in the account. For $15,000 you can put up with a lot of back issues of *People*.

Elaine had reached this realistic conclusion, and now she'd been waiting fifteen minutes. *What* was the *problem* with the guy? Many women who provide sexual release for male clients in more orthodox settings have had this reaction to an unanticipated delay, but at least they can see that the client is trying. Elaine had no idea *what* the client was doing. If, in fact, he was doing anything at all. If, in fact, he was even there.

She'd been here sixteen minutes, and in all probability Ed Wilson was wearing a hole in the floor waiting for his fax. Right. You had your chance, Jack, and you blew it.

Roy was still mulling over his quandary when it was solved for him. There was a low whirring noise. The lower portion of the woman began to disappear through the wall. Soon there was nothing to be seen but her feet. Then her feet were gone, and the panel closed, and he was alone in the stall.

Someone was still pounding on the door.

Roy lifted the bolt and opened the door.

I shoulda known, he thought.

He was looking into the irate face of Ed Wilson.

It took two seconds for Ed to realize he'd made a mistake. It was only too obvious why Roy had chosen this particular cubicle when five where free. Ed wouldn't have liked to have to lift 320 pounds of human flesh from a sitting position using nothing but his knees; in all probability Roy didn't like it either.

"Sorry, Roy," said Ed, thinking on his feet. "I thought I left my gym bag in here earlier. I coulda sworn this was the last place I had it, but I don't see it. Guess I musta left it at the gym. Hope I didn't interrupt anything."

Roy had never really cared much for Ed's sense of humor at the best of times. For some reason he could never think of a better come-back than "Ha, ha, ha. Very funny." He was about to say "Ha, ha, ha. Very funny," for want of a better idea, but Ed was already on his way out the door.

And now Roy was in a *real* quandary. Ed Wilson was one of the top performers in the company. Roy knew, none better, just what outrageous demands Ed had made and gotten away with in the past. Ed was always being headhunted, and every time Ed was headhunted he used it as an opportunity to demand some new and more outrageous level of compensation. Every time Ed made some new demand Roy would think This time he's gone too far, this time he's *really* done it – next thing he knew Ed would be driving around in the Lamborghini he'd demanded as a company car.

Well, it was only too obvious that Ed hadn't personally knocked a hole in the wall. Something like this couldn't happen without somebody approving it somewhere. What had obviously happened, incredible though it might seem to an outsider who didn't understand the weird dynamic that operated between Ed and Steve Jackson, was that Ed had made yet another demand and Steve had just given in.

Well, if that was the case, just *who* was Roy supposed to report this *to*? If he took it to Steve, it wasn't going to be Ed Wilson who was sitting at home with the Want Ads.

On the other hand, did Steve really know what he'd gotten himself into? Was something like this even *legal*?

It was a real quandary.

Elaine dressed, returned to the fax machine, picked up fax and transmission sheet, and went over to Ed's office to drop them off. She got there just as Ed came striding up from the Men's Room.

"It took you twenty minutes to send a *fax*?" said Ed, who was in no very good mood. "If I'da known it was gonna take twenty minutes I'da told you to *walk* it over."

"It took five minutes," said Elaine, in no very good mood herself. "The other fifteen I was doing something for Bob that I had to interrupt because you said this was urgent. Bob, just in case you've forgotten, is my boss. I presumed that the urgency of the fax pertained to transmitting the material to the recipient rather than transmitting the transmission sheet to you. I *do* apologize for this unfortunate misunderstanding."

In the old days Ed would probably have said something direct and to the point. But the lightning rods had brought him to a new level of self-awareness which he had not had before; he knew the reason he was ready to strike out at anybody within range had nothing to do with the fax. Besides, he was suddenly conscious of things he would have been less conscious of in the old days. He had always been interested in breasts, obviously, but now he felt an appreciation for a full frontal view, even clothed, which he would once have taken for granted. Besides, he wasn't one to hold a grudge. He liked a girl who could hold her own instead of letting you walk all over her.

"Did anyone ever tell you you're beautiful when you're angry?" he asked grinning.

"Let's put it this way," said Elaine, "it's not exactly an original line."

Ed laughed. He'd had four separate sessions today already, he could live with an isolated disappointment. Besides, Elaine was really attractive. She had dark red hair, and dark brown eyes, and a long, full, sexy mouth. He'd been working hard, no time to play, it had been a long time since he'd connected with someone from this direction.

"OK, I overreacted," he said magnanimously. "I admit it. I overreacted. What can I say? Excess is my middle name. So I'll make it up to you. Can I buy you a drink after work?"

"Much as I'd love to," said Elaine, "I have to pick up Hayley from her homework center after work, and I have other plans for the evening."

"Tell you what," said Ed, who had not gotten where he was by taking polite or not-so-polite negatives for an answer, "I'll take you to pick her up. How does that grab you? We'll surprise her. Turn up in the Lamborghini, make her day. And then I'll just drop you off, unless of course I can persuade you to cancel your plans."

"Why, *thank* you," said Elaine. "What a wonderful idea! Usually I have to use my *own* car to pick her up and drive home in, which means I have to give up my parking space. I then run the risk of not finding one in the morning after I drop her off at school on the way to work, especially if the traffic's bad. *This* way I can just leave the car there overnight and take the bus in, and no matter *what* time I get in I'll know I've got a parking space, because the car will have been there ahead of all the other people who took theirs home and then had to drive in again the next day. If only I'd thought of that before!"

Ed grinned. "No problem," he said. "Gimme your keys, I'll get one of the guys on security to drop it off for you. They owe me a coupla favors, and besides, they got nothing better to do, long as I pick up the cab fare, which I'm happy to do, Elaine, just to show you my heart's in the right place."

Elaine felt herself weakening. Ed was all right when you got to know him, you just had to make it clear you weren't putting up with any bullshit. The person who had recruited Laura Carter to be his secretary had to have been insane, to put it mildly. Or on some weird peanut M&M trip or something.

"Well," she said.

"It's a deal," said Ed. "Five o'clock?"

"Sure," said Elaine, shrugging and giving in. In spite of herself she felt flattered. Ed usually stayed till 9 or 10 at night, at the *earliest*. And here he was basically leaving halfway through the day, and all for her.

At 5:20 the Lamborghini pulled up in front of Hayley's school, which provided an after-school homework center for children of working parents. Hayley came down the sidewalk with her friends, obviously looking for Elaine's Toyota. Then she saw Elaine in the Lamborghini.

Elaine had never seen anything like the look on her face, this kind of 1,000-watt look of amazement, as if somebody had explained that they'd decided to introduce a second Christmas to the year and today was the day.

"Mom?" said Hayley, coming toward the car, and all her friends came with her.

"This is Ed Wilson, from the office," said Elaine. "Ed, I'd like you to meet Hayley."

"Pleaseta meetcha," said Ed, holding out a hand, and they shook hands across Elaine. Then Elaine got out to let Hayley into the back seat, and then she got back in, and then they took off.

"You guys in a hurry to get home?" said Ed, and Hayley said No before Elaine had a chance to say Yes. "Wanna take a drive along the shore?" said Ed, and Hayley said Yes before Elaine had a chance to say No.

They drove out along the shore, which was not too crowded at this time of day, so Ed was able to just test the speed limit once in a while to give them some idea of the general point of a Lamborghini. Then they stopped for hamburgers, and Ed bought eight separate Rodeo Deals just so they could instantly collect all eight Rodeo Gals. They went and sat down, and Hayley just sat there with her chocolate milkshake and the eight Rodeo Gals, each in a different cowgal outfit, and she looked all lit up inside.

Elaine had been on lots of dates over the years, and she couldn't count how many times she'd had to sit there cringing while the guy sat there trying to be nice to Hayley and Hayley sat there being polite and quiet back. She couldn't think of a single one that knew how to talk to kids, or that Hayley had liked. And now here was Ed not even making an effort, it wasn't just the fact of the Rodeo Gals, it was the fact that Ed just naturally entered into things from a kid's point of view. From a kid's point of view, the whole point of being grown up is that you can afford to get the whole set of a special offer all at the same time, so why would you want to wait? Of course, some men might have had just enough of a glimpse of that to buy the whole set, but they would have been so condescending about it to Hayley that it would have been almost as bad as not buying anything at all. Whereas Ed obviously had the attitude, Who knows *when* we'll come back? If we ever do? Who knows if they'll still have the offer? Let's get the whole set now just to be on the safe side. In other words, the attitude of a ten-year-old kid.

Now of course, one way of looking at it was that the reason Ed related so well to a ten-year-old kid was that *Ed* had the mental age of a ten-year-old. And thinking back over some of the stories she'd heard about Ed's sense of humor, Elaine had to admit there was more than a grain of truth in it. But wait just a minute. This wasn't some total idiot who couldn't get his act together, this was the top earner in the company, somebody who had asked for a Lamborghini as a company car and gotten it.

Besides, you can tell something about someone by the way kids respond to them. A kid can usually tell if someone is genuine or full of b.s. If a kid likes someone that tells you something you probably couldn't find out any other way.

So Elaine sat eating one of the eight Broncoburgers, watching Ed eat fries in a way that suggested his manners hadn't undergone much of a transformation since he was ten, and relaxing. It felt weird to *relax* on a date with Hayley around, because usually she was so tense what with sensing all the cross-currents.

•

Roy, meanwhile, was breaking his golden rule. Roy's golden rule was that you should never take work home with you. When you leave the office, leave the office, and make sure you leave the office *at* the office. That was the rule, but Roy was in a quandary, and he had simply not been able to leave that quandary behind when he walked out the door.

Should he tell someone? If so, who?

Not easy questions, and there was no easy answer.

AN UNEASY TRUCE

For the next three weeks Roy went on trying to make up his mind what to do. He hadn't been able to bring himself to use the disabled stall again. He had had to make do with the ordinary stalls, something he hadn't tried for several years and would have preferred not to be attempting now.

He noticed that some kind of romance seemed to be developing between Elaine and Ed Wilson. He was surprised that Elaine would want to get involved with someone with Ed's reputation, and in fact, once or twice he considered the possibility of giving her some kind of subtle hint. If she had any idea what he *really* got up to she'd drop him like a hot potato. But it wasn't exactly the kind of thing you could convey by a subtle hint. Luckily, considering Ed's reputation, there was precious little chance of anything coming of it. So he just kept his distance and hoped the end, when it came, wouldn't be too much of a disappointment to Elaine.

Finally, at the end of the third week, Roy decided enough was enough. He couldn't go on flinching every time he passed the disabled cubicle. The truly brave man is not the man who feels no fear – it's the man who faces his fear and conquers it. So Roy went into the Men's on Friday afternoon, pushed the door to the disabled stall firmly open, and strode in.

The panel in the wall was gone.

Roy walked over to the wall and knocked where the panel had been. It seemed solid, as far as he could tell. Could he have – but he *couldn't* have imagined something like that. Could he?

He paced up and down. Wait! What about –

The wall attachment which had dispensed condoms was also gone.

Roy examined the wall carefully where the attachment had been. There were no screw holes or anything like that, but if he wasn't mistaken there was a new tile in the wall. Besides, now he thought of it, he probably still had those four condoms in the inside pocket of his suit. He slipped a hand into the pocket; yup, still there. So it hadn't been a figment of his imagination.

On the other hand, as proof that something fishy had been going on four condoms were pretty weak – if you were going to try and convince someone else. There was absolutely nothing here now to show that anything had ever happened.

Well, what did it matter? Didn't this solve everything? For whatever reason, whoever had been responsible for it had had it removed. It was gone now. Wasn't that the main thing? He could just put it out of his mind and get back to work.

Unfortunately the human mind doesn't work like that. Now that there was no physical evidence left, now that there was no problem to actually solve, Roy's mind just went on chewing over the mystery. To outward appearances he was the same efficient human resources operator he had always been;

inwardly, he was preoccupied. He went right on wondering how it had actually reached the stage of being put in place, and who had been responsible, and why they had taken it out. Was it because they knew he knew? Had Ed Wilson had a word with someone higher up? Had they realized that if they did not take preemptive action Roy would take it for them?

There's an old saying: An elephant never forgets. If they had been hoping to put him off the scent by removing the evidence, they would have saved themselves a lot of trouble if they had remembered that famous saying.

What had actually happened, of course, was that the probationary period for the lightning rods had come to an end. Over the six-month period the facility had been gradually extended to allow a wider range of employees to participate at strictly performance-related frequencies, as its positive effects on those already participating began to be perceptible. Joe had gone in to talk to Steve, who was absolutely delighted with the results – absenteeism was down, profits were up, everything was for the best in this best of all possible worlds.

"I'm glad to hear that, Steve," said Joe. "So you'd like to make this a permanent arrangement, is that it?"

"For the time being," said Steve.

"There's permanent and permanent, obviously," said Joe. "Two-year contract?"

"Let's do it," said Steve.

"That's what I like to hear," said Joe. "Because I've introduced some enhancements to the product that I'm very excited about. I wouldn't want you to have anything but the best, Steve. That's not the way I do business. These enhancements have worked beyond all expectations on our other sites, and I want you to have the benefit of those developments."

"I'm pretty happy with what we've got in place right now," said Steve, rightly sensing that these enhancements would not be complimentary.

"Sure," said Joe. "But remember, Steve, we're providing this above all as an incentive. It's false economy, if you want my opinion, to cut corners when it comes to making that incentive as attractive as possible."

"What did you have in mind?" Steve asked reluctantly, and Joe explained about the adjustable toilet.

Whatever Steve was expecting, it wasn't this.

"I'm pretty happy with what we've got in place right now," he said again firmly. "I see what you're saying about the ambience, Joe, but I really don't think these guys are that sensitive to atmosphere, if you want my honest opinion."

Joe had been expecting some initial resistance, but he knew he just wouldn't be happy until the original, flawed prototype had been replaced by the model which was now up and running in Kansas City. "Look, Steve," he said patiently. "It's to do with self-perception. I've just installed an absolutely up-to-date facility in Kansas City. What kind of message does that send to your staff if they hear they're trailing Kansas *City* in the level of provision? Do you *want* your staff to feel like a bunch of hicks? Do you *want* them to think they've got to go to Kansas City for state-of-the-art accommodation?"

In other words, did he want to have Ed Wilson singing THEY'VE GONE ABOUT AS FUR AS THEY KIN GO around the office at the top of his voice.

"Well, no," said Steve. "But we've only had this six *months*."

"Sure," said Joe. "But believe me, Steve, once you've upgraded you'll wonder how you ever lived without it."

•

With these words did Joe persuade Steve to approve installation of ten complete height-friendly facilities, thus further improving the cash flow situation. It was something he could feel good about. He had ensured that Steve would not face any unpleasant legal eventualities through making access to lightning rods subject to height restrictions. At the same time, he had spared Steve the aggravation of being aware of this. A good salesman knows that the fact that something is true is not necessarily a reason to share it with the customer. The current provisions for disabled employees caused Steve enough grief. There was absolutely no need to add a gratuitous source of irritation.

It came as second nature to Joe to clean up after himself. The new installations were added to the other end of the Men's and Ladies' Rooms over the course of a single weekend, and on the following weekend, once participants were aware of the change of venue, the old transporter was removed from the disabled cubicle, the panels removed, and the holes plastered up. Joe had no way of knowing that the installation had been seen by someone who shouldn't have known about it. He had no way of knowing just how far-reaching the repercussions of that breach of security would eventually be.

5

TROUBLESHOOTING

A WOMAN IN A THOUSAND

Sometimes your words come back to haunt you. You say something casually, without thinking that much about it. Later it turns out you spoke truer than you knew.

In the early days, when Joe had been trying to persuade women that being a lightning rod was something to be proud of, something aspirational that could fit in with the life goals of a very special person, he had used the phrase "a woman in a thousand."

"Maybe one woman in a thousand could do it," he'd say. "We're looking for that woman in a thousand."

"It's not for everybody," he'd say. "We're looking for the woman in a thousand who is a real team player."

Well, he'd said it, obviously, but really it was just a way of flattering the applicant, the way you flatter someone into buying the *Encyclopaedia Britannica*. Or if the truth be told, what he was probably thinking was that not one woman in a thousand would fall for it. He was looking for the woman in a thousand, all right, the woman in a thousand who was dumb enough to think it was a smart career move to stick her fanny through a hole in a wall and let someone give her the old Roto-Rooter from the rear.

Well, ironically, it turned out he had spoken no more than the truth.

It *was* a job for the woman in a thousand. Or at least, he didn't have a thousand gals on the payroll yet, but of the couple of hundred signed up so far, apart from Lucille, there weren't more than about five with the brains of a headless chicken. The rest, if you wanted his honest opinion, had a damn sight *less* brains than a headless chicken.

It's hard work finding new clients for an innovative scheme like this; it's hard work convincing existing clients that it definitely is for them. All you want from the ladies is for them to demonstrate beyond the shadow of a doubt that the installation is the morale-boosting, productivity-enhancing type of product you made it out to be. All you want is for them to get on with *their* job while you get on with *yours*, which is persuading more companies to go with the flow.

But instead Joe had found himself fielding constant phone calls. He'd be in the middle of a meeting with an important client when the phone would ring. His secretary would tell him it was urgent. He'd pick up, and it would be some gal in floods of tears because some guy slapped her on the fanny.

For the kind of money she was getting you'd have thought she could throw in a slap on the fanny every so often without going into a big song and dance about it, but the gal would go on and on about how she had been given every assurance that she would be treated with respect, this wasn't at *all* the kind of thing she'd been led to believe, she felt that her integrity had been compromised di bla di bla di bla.

"I hear what you're saying," Joe would say. He couldn't help *but* hear what she was saying, she was yelling so loud everyone in the Goddamn building could probably hear every Goddamn word. "Look, I'll give this my serious consideration.

You're right, this raises serious questions. It's too serious to do anything hasty. I'll call you back when I've had a chance to give it some serious thought."

And he'd hang up thinking *Jesus*.

Or sometimes one of the gals would come down to the office and raise Cain. Sometimes they'd come during office hours when there were new applicants being screened, and sometimes they'd come after work and catch him just as he was getting ready to get home for the day – he never knew which was worse.

"If you think I'm going to put up with *this* kind of thing you're very much mistaken!" they would say, just as if he hadn't *warned* them that it was a job for a woman in a thousand.

Joe would generally just let them talk themselves out. When the hullabaloo had subsided he would say, "I couldn't be sorrier, Suzanne (or Julie or Nicole or Yvonne as the case might be). I'm shocked that a thing like this could happen. I need hardly say that I never in my wildest dreams anticipated that one of our clients could step over the mark in this fashion. This is *way* out of line. Totally unacceptable. But the thing is, Suzanne, as I explained when I interviewed you, this is a job for a woman in a thousand. Because as I'm sure you know, this is a very innovative approach. We're *all* feeling our way. Some of the behavioral parameters are still fluid at this stage. I'm sure the client didn't mean to cause offense, he was just feeling his way – "

This was a slightly unfortunate turn of phrase in the circumstances but Joe would speak smoothly on.

" – as are we all. This is all very new. And remember, many of our clients are relatively unsophisticated young men in many ways, the fact that they are high earners doesn't necessarily mean that they have the conceptual framework which would enable them to deal with an unfamiliar situation of this kind with the level of savoir faire you might prefer to encounter. It's that very lack of savoir faire, I need hardly say, which leaves them in such crying need of a service of this nature."

"That's all very well, Joe," the gal would say, "but just how much background in the social graces do you need to know that you don't go around peeing on people?"

"I know, I know – " Joe would begin.

"What kind of shithead has to consult Emily Goddamn Post to ascertain that pee belongs in the receptacle provided? What kind of social *moron* are we talking here? I'm sorry, Joe, but this is just too much. What kind of infantile pervert derives sexual satisfaction from taking out his wiener and squirting pee on people? I mean *Jesus*, Joe, di bla di bla di bla ... "

"I know," Joe would say again. "I know. I couldn't be more horrified. But that's just the point. We're dealing, often, with deeply inadequate individuals. Persons with a very low sense of self-worth. Now unfortunately, as I'm sure you know, in a conventional office that type of person tends to take out his feelings of low self-esteem on his colleagues, in a way that impacts negatively on the effectivity of the team. I'm sorry to say this, but I have to remind you that, as well as the obvious sexual function, providing a safe outlet for that low self-esteem is part of what we here at Lightning Rods are hoping to achieve."

"Sure, Joe, I appreciate that, but *Jesus* – "

"Remember, Suzanne, we don't know the whole story. For all you know the client may have just been taken to task by someone higher up in a way that he perceived as humiliating – he may, unforgivably I know, have taken *out* that humiliation on you. I'm not condoning what happened for one second, let's get clear on that one here and now, I'm just saying we have to see this in a wider context. We have to try to get this in perspective."

And nine times out of ten he would end up having to take the gal out to lunch or even dinner at a fancy restaurant to put the unpleasant experience behind her. Because if he didn't strategically make a suggestion of this kind sooner or later it would occur to the gal that there had to be a way of *identifying* the person responsible and getting back at him. And since the whole *point* of Lightning Rods was to eliminate the spectre of sexual harassment from the modern office this was a deeply worrying thing to have occur to someone you personally introduced into the office for the specific purpose of eliminating that cause of concern.

Over dinner like as not the gal would relax and tease him about the woman in a thousand and tell him she didn't believe for one second that there was a woman on the planet who could just take that kind of thing as all part of the day's work. But that was exactly where she was wrong. Joe knew just such a woman. Only he was beginning to think she wasn't a woman in a thousand after all. A woman in a million was nearer the mark.

It reached the point where if he picked up the phone and heard a woman's voice his heart would sink. Unless, of course, the voice belonged to Lucille.

It was thanks to Lucille that a lot of safeguards were in place that it probably wouldn't have occurred to him to think necessary, but which in the light of later events turned out to be worth their weight in gold. For example, the fake fire alarm was Lucille's idea. Why wait for someone to try not using a condom when you can put the fear of God in them from day one? And it was thanks to Lucille that there was a control on the woman's side of the wall enabling her to lock the door to the disabled cubicle. Because while there was no reason to think the majority of people would not use the facility responsibly, it was just as well they should know that if anybody did get violent he would not be able to get away. Likewise, there was a device that guaranteed that the transporter would not operate if more than one person was in the disabled cubicle. Also, the door of the disabled cubicle could not be opened while the transporter was in operation; it could only be opened after the transporter had gone back to the other side.

This was to foil the type of person who not only fantasizes about a football team and a cheerleader but who takes the sexual outlet provided in his workplace as an opportunity to act out that fantasy in real life. Joe had been in no position to argue – after all, he had had that type of fantasy himself, and after all the lightning rods were living proof that the boundary between fantasy and reality is nowhere near as fixed as we sometimes imagine. And later, when the gals started hassling him over all the perceived slights they had received, he was glad he hadn't argued. He shuddered to think what life would be like if he *hadn't* taken those apparently unnecessary precautions.

What he eventually came to realize was that maybe he had been a tad undiscriminating in the applicants he took on to begin with. He wasn't *blaming* himself, after all what choice did he have? If you're recruiting for bifunctional personnel you not only need the typing skills and what have you, you also need someone who satisfies certain minimum standards of attractiveness, I mean let's face it no one is going to thank you if he goes into the disabled toilet only to be confronted by a quivering mass of lard. And on top of that you need to find someone who is willing to do something that the majority of applicants are going to reject out of hand. Well, basically Joe had started out by accepting anyone who met the grade and wanted the job; now he was paying the price for that.

Because what he was discovering, unfortunately, was that he hadn't ended up with a team of cool, unflappable ladies like Lucille. What had happened was he had ended up with a lot of people who were in it for the money, but who hadn't stopped to think about what the reality of what they would have to do for the money would actually be like. In fact, unfortunately, instead of ending up with the type of person who is trying to achieve some goals, he had mainly ended up with people who didn't have a lot of choices. He'd be looking across the desk at some gal who'd responded to an ad for rusty shorthand and 60 wpm typing, she'd be telling him what her speeds used to be before she stopped working to stay home with the kids, her husband had walked out, suddenly she was trying to meet the mortgage payments which she didn't stand a hope in hell of doing on the level of remuneration you get with rusty shorthand and rusty 45 wpm typing. Well, obviously in one sense Lightning Rods offered her the chance to achieve a goal of keeping the house without working two jobs and never seeing the kids, but someone in that kind of situation is not going to see it in that light. He'd learned that to his cost.

Well, for a while he'd gone on taking calls from dissatisfied personnel, but there's only so much you can take. What he wanted to say was, if you can't stand the heat stay out of the kitchen. But a caring employer doesn't make that kind of remark to an employee on whom a client has thoughtlessly peed. What he was finally forced to do, though it went against the grain, was to hire a staff advisor on a salary of $40,000 a year purely to talk the gals through whatever it was they were feeling. And recruiting the advisor was a job and a half! It took him two months of in-depth interviews, and time he could ill afford to waste, to come up with someone he thought could deal with the type of situation he'd been fielding sin- glehanded for God knew how long. He wished he could have just given the job to Lucille, but Lucille was earning so much as a lightning rod he couldn't afford her.

AN UNUSUAL SUGGESTION

Although he couldn't download responsibility onto Lucille's capable shoulders in the way he would have liked, Joe did continue to benefit from the insights of someone he had identified from the first as one smart cookie. He sometimes suspected that Lucille was not entirely in agreement with the installations as he had originally set them up. The reason he suspected this was that from the first Lucille kept thinking of ways to make the service more to her liking. Unlike the other lightning rods, she never called to cry on his shoulder. Instead she kept calling in with suggestions and advice and comments.

One day he said, "That's a very interesting idea."

And he said, "Um, I was wondering. Would you like to have dinner sometime?"

There was a short pause, and then Lucille said, "Sure."

He said, "Would, um, would Friday suit you?"

And she said, "Fine."

He picked her up after work and drove to the restaurant. She was wearing a pink suit and pink shoes. Her hair and make-up were immaculate.

They had a table in a quiet alcove of the restaurant where they would be undisturbed.

"So how's it going?" he asked.

"It's going just fine," said Lucille, taking a sip of wine.

"And it's not giving you any, that is, obviously I do what I can to screen applicants but I have to say I've had some girls getting pretty upset."

"Really?" said Lucille.

"To the point where I wonder if I was optimistic in hoping applicants could approach it in the spirit intended."

"Well, I don't know," said Lucille, taking another sip of wine. "The way I see it is, the body is nothing to be ashamed of. Nobody gets excited about a company that provides toilets for the staff. Nobody gets excited if they provide a canteen or a gym. Why shouldn't they provide for another physical need?"

Joe was staring wide-eyed. This was a really brilliant way of putting the point that had never occurred to him; he could have spared himself a lot of trouble if he'd thought of it.

"Now the way I see it is," said Lucille, "if you'll forgive my mentioning when we're about to eat, say you go to the bathroom and use the toilet. Well, you don't spend the afternoon dwelling on it, do you? In fact half the time you don't even think about it while it's going on, heck, we all know people who read on the john. The way I see it is this is no different. It takes a little longer than using the john, is all. I usually take a magazine to pass the time. Or I might do my nails."

And now he was staring with his mouth wide open. Lucille was quietly eating her salad. Her nails were immaculate.

Just as well, since he had a delicate subject to bring up.

He said, "Uh, Lucille."

She said, "Mhm?"

"I'm glad you put it in that perspective," he said. "Because I want to discuss something with you."

Lucille took a sip of wine. "OK," she said. "Shoot."

"I've, uh, I've had a request from a client," he said. "He's making kind of an issue of it, but frankly none of the people I've got in place are really what I'd want to trust with something of this nature."

"I'm pretty happy where I am," said Lucille.

"Oh, you'd stay where you are, no question about that. And if you decided you were able to make a contribution to satisfying a valuable client obviously your compensation would be on top of what you're making now."

"Keep talking," said Lucille.

He took a deep breath. There was no way this was not going to be embarrassing.

"I have a request for whipping on the bare butt."

And then, anticipating misunderstanding –

"His butt."

Lucille said, "That's weird."

"You're telling me," said Joe.

"Why would anyone want that?"

"Your guess is as good as mine. The point is, anyway, he's making an issue of it and if I can make him happy heck that's fine with me, but you'll appreciate, well, let's just say this goes a long way beyond what most of the women who work for us would consider appropriate."

"What level of remuneration are we talking," said Lucille.

"I was thinking $5,000 per annum. For a twice-weekly, um, session. As it happens, their conveniences are out by the elevator. You would simply take the elevator to the appropriate floor at the fixed time and go into the Ladies disabled toilet in the usual way, only this time – "

"I get the picture," said Lucille. "*Jesus.*"

"I know," he said. "Ain't that something?"

"So I'd go there and, what, there'd be a whip in the closet?"

"Exactly, all the equipment would be waiting."

"Isn't this going to make a lot of noise?"

"Apparently that's not a cause for concern."

"Huh."

Lucille took another sip of wine, and she said presently, "Look, Joe, I'm not saying I won't do it. But you know as well as I do that this is beginning to be outside the original parameters which were defined in terms of making a contribution to a single employer. I don't have to tell you what this is starting to look like. Well, you know as well as I do that $50 a session is an inappropriate figure in the context. You know as well as I do that he would have to pay a lot more for a similar sort of service in a context where he would be running a high risk to satisfy his needs. To put it another way he is getting added value in the fact that this is risk-free and completely confidential, and in my opinion that value ought to be reflected in the remuneration package."

"What did you have in mind?" he asked.

"$15,000 per annum for two sessions a week. Alternatively, if he would prefer to pay on a per-session basis, $200 a visit."

Lucille had to basically pick a number out of thin air, since she had no idea what the going rate was for this kind of service in circles where it was not seen as an adjunct to secretarial work. Still, it's not a bad rule of thumb to demand three times what somebody offers you. In later years, when she had moved on to the more aggressive mores of the litigation lawyer, she found that the rule of thumb had to be revised upward to a factor of ten or twenty – but what she always said was that, though she might have started out on the conservative side, at least her instincts had always been in the right place.

"Well," said Joe. "Well, I'll see what I can do."

CAREER DEVELOPMENT

Years later, when Lucille was making a million a year as a litigation lawyer, she was sometimes asked to identify the thing that had made the single biggest contribution to her career. A lot of women saw Lucille as a role model, because she had started out the way lots of women start out: She had learned to touch type, she had learned a couple of word processing packages and a spreadsheet, and she had worked in an administrative support capacity for eight years, admittedly at increasingly senior levels, before swanning into Harvard Law School with LSATs in the high 170s and swanning out again into the cutthroat, male-dominated field of litigation. What was her secret?

Lucille didn't say "That's my secret" because if you say something like that it's just an open invitation to all and sundry to pry into your affairs. Besides, there's no point in unnecessarily alienating people.

What she said was that the thing that was the biggest help was the fact that she had taught herself shorthand in tenth grade, even though everybody told her there was no point because most jobs didn't require it any more. She had practiced shorthand all through high school, and she had kept it up at work even when it wasn't needed, and when she went to Harvard Law School she was able to get more out of classes because she wasn't having to scribble at breakneck speed to get everything down. Then every night she made a point of typing up her shorthand notes and making a print-out, as well as saving the notes on disk, with the result that she consolidated the material covered in the lecture. Then when she had to take exams she had already reviewed the material once, and she had typed notes for all her lectures, and she was able to incorporate new material and cross-references into the material she had on disk. So that shorthand everyone told her was a waste of time enabled her to make the best possible use of her time at Harvard Law School, and that was the thing that had made the single biggest contribution to her career.

This is the kind of thing people want to hear from a role model. They want to hear that the role model got where she is today doing something they themselves might well have done, something that maybe isn't a million miles from something they're just naturally doing already. Something everybody undervalues that will one day turn out to surprise them.

They don't want to hear that the thing that made the single biggest contribution was whipping someone on the bare butt twice a week for two years, in a specially equipped disabled stall in the Ladies.

The way Lucille saw it was, most people are not going to get the opportunity to follow up that little tip even if they have the inclination. And nobody is going to come to any actual *harm* learning shorthand. Nobody is going to find themselves out of their depth following a set of study techniques. They may not end up a hot shot litigation lawyer, but they'll improve their grade-point average – that's a heck of a lot more than you can say for most free advice.

The fact is, though, that there's a heck of a lot more to life than a grade-point average.

Lucille had always been able to keep a cool head in a crisis. She had always had an attention to detail. Those two assets helped her to achieve top scores when she came to take the LSAT. The thing is, though, that the LSAT does not test for the killer instinct. Like it or not, we have an adversarial legal system, and there are areas of that system where someone without the killer instinct is going to get pushed to the wall.

What Lucille realized later, when she got on the litigation track, was this. Attention to detail is important, especially in a big case. But it's something that can be delegated. The reason good secretaries and personal assistants have attention to detail is that detail *can* be delegated – it can be delegated to the kind of person who's good at that kind of job. The killer instinct is something else again. You can delegate anything else, but the killer instinct is not something that can be exercised by proxy.

Well, lots of people realize that sooner or later – but for most people the realization comes too late. Or sometimes people get a glimpse of the truth, but they misunderstand it; they think that having the killer instinct makes you a bad person. But the thing is, it's not a *personal* thing. You don't have to personally hate the opposition. In fact, if your emotions are involved in that way, you'll probably be less effective than you otherwise would be. Lucille knew this, because by the time she recognized the importance of the killer instinct she had that instinct on call – and that was *entirely* as a result of her little biweekly extracurricular assignment.

What Lucille realized was that everyone has a little pool of aggression inside them. If you've been given the assignment of whipping someone twice a week, and you want to do a good job, you've got to draw on that pool of aggression. You've got nothing against the guy, heck, you don't even *know* the guy. But if you want to do a good job you've got to be able to bring that whip down like you mean business; you've got to be able to bring a whip down and *draw blood*, and instead of stopping and saying "Oh, I'm sorry, did I hurt you?" or "Oh, excuse me, was that too hard?" you've got to bring it down again just as hard as you did the first time. Or harder.

Well, if you're in court, or you're at the negotiating table, you've got to be able to draw on that same pool of aggression. You've got to be able to mean business. Most women think they mean business if they manage to cause someone a slight stinging sensation – and even then they probably smile and apologize just in case anybody's feelings got hurt. Until you know what it's like to draw blood and hit *harder* the second time you don't know what it *means* to mean business. And the thing is, people can tell.

So in the end it was all for the best. But to begin with it was by no means obvious that the experience would be the valuable, career-enhancing opportunity it turned out to be.

Lucille had always thought she was pretty unflappable; her adjustment to life as a lighting rod had only confirmed this. Even so, she had to admit that the experience of applying a whip to a bare butt was quite an eye-opener. It's not something that secretarial work really prepares you for; you just have to call on your inner resources and hope for the best.

She turned up on the first day not really knowing what to expect. Sure enough, there was a Ladies Room out by the elevators, just as Joe had said there would be. She went in, and it turned out there was just the one stall, adapted for disabled users, and the outer door bolted from the inside. Maybe that was why noise was not expected to be a problem. And sure enough there was a small whip in a cupboard labeled Fire Equipment. There was a button to press to show she was ready to proceed – it had taken her about five months of lobbying Joe to get that one lousy button made standard in all installations. So Lucille pressed the button, and a panel slid open in the wall, and the transporter came through, and sure enough here was the bare butt of the client waiting to be whipped. For reasons best known to himself he had kept his shoes and socks on, so he was wearing well-polished black loafers and black silk socks.

You know, thought Lucille, I don't care *what* you say. This is weird.

Well, she thought, look at it this way. Men are strange at the best of times. Some are just stranger than others. And look, it's his fifteen grand. All I have to do is whip the guy a couple of times a week, for a year, and it'll be *my* fifteen grand.

And she raised her arm and brought it down, and she brought the lash of the whip down with it, and it was *pathetic*.

Lucille gritted her teeth. She was here to do a job.

Come on, she thought. Let's give the guy his money's worth.

She raised her arm and brought it down. There was still no noticeable result, so she thought she must be doing something wrong. She raised her arm and brought it down harder. Then she noticed that there were pale weals on the butt where she had hit it the first couple of times. Then they turned red.

After a while she got the hang of it.

He might not be able to sit down for the rest of the day, but he sure as heck got his money's worth.

THE OTHER 999

Lucille had been coping with the new responsibility for about three months, on top of her regular secretarial and lightning rod duties, when one day she went to the Ladies to freshen her lipstick. She was just blotting her mouth dry when she heard someone sobbing in the height-friendly cubicle.

Lucille hesitated. People used the HFC for all kinds of things – if you ran to work, for instance, it was a good place to change clothes, or if you were going out for the evening you could just change in the HFC. So there was no reason to assume that this was a lightning rod. But what if it was? The problem with any new service is there are a lot of blips and wrinkles that no one could have anticipated, and besides Lucille sometimes wondered if Joe was as rigorous in his selection procedure as he should have been. It was all very well Joe talking about the woman in a thousand, Lucille sometimes thought Joe just hired anyone who walked in off the street who could type, as long as she didn't have any cellulite and said Yes. The reason she thought it was that after just nine months on the job she knew of at least six other lightning rods in the building, and frankly, if Joe had been doing his job, she shouldn't have known one.

Before she could make up her mind the door of the cubicle swung slowly open, and a girl from Supplies walked out. Her face was streaked with tears.

"Diane," said Lucille. "What's the matter?"

"I've done something terrible," said Diane, dissolving into tears once more. "And now I've done it I can't ever undo it. I can't ever be someone who never did it." Tears dripped steadily onto her blouse. "I want to get married, but how can I do a thing like that to Don?"

"A thing like what?" said Lucille.

"Like letting … "

Diane wiped her face with the back of her hand.

"Here, have a tissue," said Lucille.

Diane dried her face with the tissue.

"I was at my wits' end," said Diane. "I didn't know what to do. All I needed was three credits to complete my physiotherapy qualification and then my mother lost her job and if I didn't help her she was going to lose her house and I just, it just seemed like everyone was depending on me, and when this opportunity came along at the time it looked like the answer to a prayer."

"Well, I don't know what it is you've done, or think you've done," said Lucille. "And it's obviously none of my business. But in my opinion you should just let bygones be bygones. Whatever it is, don't let it spoil your life. If you've met someone you want to spend your life with, just think of that as a fresh start and put whatever it is behind you."

"Yes, but you don't *understand*," said Diane. "It's not that *easy*." She spat out a description of the lightning rod facility in a way that was only too obviously not the attitude of the woman in a thousand who saw it as no different from holding hands.

Lucille could see she was expected to be shocked and horrified and surprised. Some people might have acted shocked and horrified and surprised just to throw off suspicion; that wasn't her way. Lucille never bothered to pretend anything she didn't feel; it was too much trouble. If you're going to go around trying to provide people with the reaction you think they want you're going to drive yourself insane. Why bother.

"I see," said Lucille. "Well, obviously if it hasn't worked out for you it might be time to quit. It isn't for everyone. I know quite a few women who've tried it, and some of them found it harder to deal with than they expected."

Maybe that would calm her down. If people went around having hysterics it was going to do the business no good at all.

Diane was staring at her openmouthed. "You know *other* people who do this?" she said.

"Obviously if you're thinking of getting married you may want to give it up," said Lucille.

"But," said Diane. "How can I do this to Don?"

"Does he think you're a virgin?" asked Lucille.

"No but – "

"Well then there's no reason for him to know, is there?"

Diane opened her mouth.

"Look," Lucille said firmly. "You go to the bathroom every day of your life."

"Yes but – "

"There's no *secret* about it. It's common knowledge. But you wouldn't expect to share every little detail with your loved ones."

"No but – "

"You're not planning to tell him every time you change a tampon."

"No but – "

"If you ask me," said Lucille, "this is a lot less unfaithful than sleeping with someone you know, where Don would have reason to be jealous. Here, you've made the physical act about as close as it can *get* to just going to the bathroom."

Diane was still crying quietly.

Lucille handed her another tissue, thinking *Where* does he *get* them?

The fact was, as Joe could have told her, that there simply weren't enough qualified applicants to fill the positions.

MISS PERFECT

As any salesman knows, you think you've covered all the angles and all of a sudden when you least expect it out of left field comes a boomerang.

One day Joe was sitting in the office waiting for his 11 o'clock appointment, and at 10:58 this black gal came in.

"I'm afraid I have an 11 o'clock appointment," he said politely.

"I'm a couple of minutes early. I'm Renée." She held out her hand. He stood up and shook it thinking *Shit*.

He had advertised for a crème-de-la-crème PA. On the surface of it this might look like unnecessary extravagance: If you use somebody like that as a lightning rod, you're talking a 100% increase on a $50,000 salary. Whereas if you used a couple of data inputters, say, you'd get twice the coverage for your dollar.

What he'd decided was that this was a shortsighted way of looking at it.

If you talk to people from an older generation, one of the things they comment on is the fact that it's just not possible to get the same quality of secretary that you could get thirty or forty years ago. Time was you could get a bright gal out of college and she'd get a job as a secretary, sometimes she'd marry and settle down and raise a family, sometimes she'd make a career of it. Well, nobody wants to go back to the days when that was all she *could* do. If a woman is able to do the same job as a man, why shouldn't she do it, and get paid accordingly? But the fact of the matter is, it's had some consequences, and the business world hasn't really faced up to those consequences.

A man who has worked his way to the top of a multi-million dollar operation needs first-class support. Like as not he's dealing with an international concern; he needs to be able to delegate to somebody who isn't looking to take over his job. Time was, he could have *gotten* that support. Today, the kind of person who would be qualified to give that level of support just isn't interested. It's partly the money, and partly the fact that the job isn't going anywhere.

Well, you can't do a heck of a lot about the prospects. Trouble is, you can't do a heck of a lot about the money, either. Because there's no way shareholders are going to stand still for a secretary making $100,000 a year. Plus, all the guys on the career track in the company are going to get pissed off. Any CEO worth his salt knows a top-drawer PA can make more of a contribution to the company than some jack-ass vice president, but just because you know something like that doesn't mean you can *say* it, let alone put your money where your mouth is. One of the first things any manager has to learn is the importance of staff morale.

The result is that sooner or later the PA decides to jump ship. She knows she's never going to make top dollar, so it's Sayonara baby.

What he had speculated, anyway, was that if you offered somebody the chance to fulfill that role and make double the going rate, she would find switching over to middle management a lot less attractive.

The other thing was that there was an important principle at stake. It was important that lightning rods should be drawn from every tier of an organization. Because if you start economizing, if you start saying you're only going to use low-level personnel, sooner or later that's going to stigmatize that whole branch of employment and you're going to have a major problem on your hands.

So he had advertised for a personal assistant to a CEO of a major company, and he had made a few appointments, and the first appointment was for 11 in the morning. He had already had a look at the résumé and been impressed. And now in walked this gal.

She was dressed the way you'd expect someone who planned to work at that level to dress. She was wearing low-heeled Gucci shoes, and a beige cashmere dress, and a silk scarf, and a gold watch. He thought *Jesus*.

"If you'll just fill out this form," he said.

She took out a La Cross pen and filled out the form and handed it back to him.

"Thank you," he said. "And now we'll just get the skills out of the way. There's a word processor in the next room. The program will take you through the tests."

She stood up and walked into the glassed-off cubicle. He could hear a couple of light clicks as she accessed the menu and made her choices. And suddenly it was like a plague of invisible locusts filling the room with their clattering wings. It was like a radio tapdance revival. It was like the dregs of satellite TV, the kind of program that shows 500 simultaneous ping pong matches *live*, and *only* on Channel Who Gives a Fuck. It was like, more worryingly, someone typing 100 wpm. With no mistakes.

She took the typing test, and the word processing test,

and the spreadsheet test, and the slideshow test. She took the numeric keypad test and the shorthand test. She took the spelling test, and the alphabetizing test, and the grammar test. Then she sent the tests to print, and they printed out on a printer behind Joe's desk.

Joe pulled a sheet of paper off the printer and looked at it. Typing. Speed: 120 wpm. Errors: 0. Word processing: Points out of a possible 100: 100. Spreadsheet: Points out of a possible 100: 100.

He cast an eye over the remaining tests, which were similarly demoralizing.

"This is very impressive, Renée," he said.

"Thank you," she said, sitting down again.

"The only thing is, to tell the truth, I'm wondering whether this is really what you're looking for," he said.

"I think I'm the best judge of that, don't you?" said Renée. "Why don't you tell me something about it?"

"Well, the thing is," said Joe.

"You've already made up your mind, haven't you?" she said crisply. "You've wasted my time bringing me in for an interview, and now you've made up your mind."

"You don't understand," said Joe.

"I certainly do understand."

"I know what it looks like."

"What does it look like?"

"But it's exactly the opposite. You're obviously a very bright gal, I just don't think you'd be interested in the type of position we're looking to fill."

"Indeed," said Renée. "Well, all I can say is, what it looks like right now is that you're in flagrant violation of the Equal Employment Opportunities Act."

"I know that's what it looks like," said Joe, "but."

"What exactly is it in my qualifications that you think makes me unfit for this job?"

Sometimes the best thing you can do is just come right out and tell the truth.

"Let me explain about the job," said Joe. He explained about the job.

"So as you can see," said Joe, "with the best will in the world, if we were to hire an African-American the anonymity which is an essential part of the scheme would be destroyed. There's nothing wrong with your qualifications. On the contrary. But we simply have no means of protecting your anonymity in the way that we can protect Caucasian members of the program. I'm sure you can see that it would be very unpleasant for you to have all the men in the office who had made use of the facility coming up to your desk and knowing that you had provided the facility."

The face across the desk from him gave him a look that could have turned a man to stone.

"Do you expect me to believe this?" she asked. "Do you expect me to believe a *word* of this? I've never heard of anything so ridiculous in my life. If this is the best you can do I can only assume that you *have* no legitimate quarrel with my qualifications, that you most certainly *are* in violation of the Equal Employment Opportunities Act, and that the *best* place to pursue the discussion is in *court*."

"Look," said Joe. "Let's not do anything hasty. Let me call one of the girls. I'll have one of the girls come in and explain it to you. Believe me, no one could be sorrier than I am to have taken up your time unnecessarily, and if you like I'll be happy to reimburse you for the morning's work. I realize this is all very new, but I can assure you it's exactly as I've said."

And without giving her a chance to reply he picked up the phone and dialed a number. Lucille answered on the first ring.

"Lucille," he said thankfully. "Look, I'm in the middle of a crisis. Could you take an early lunch hour and come down to the office?"

"What is this regarding?" asked Lucille.

"I, uh, I need you to confirm to a job applicant that the job is as I've described it to her and would not be suitable for an African-American applicant as we would not be able to protect her anonymity."

"I see," said Lucille. "In other words, you're asking me to give up the protection *I'm* entitled to in order to explain it to someone who doesn't like the fact that you've wasted her time."

"Uh," said Joe.

"I assume you're planning to offer me some sort of compensation?" said Lucille.

"Uh," said Joe.

"A thousand dollars," said Lucille.

"What?" said Joe.

"It's entirely up to you," said Lucille.

Joe glanced at the job applicant.

"Yeah, yeah, OK," he said. "Whatever."

Lucille was there in ten minutes.

"I'll just leave you ladies to discuss this in private," said Joe, and he was out of there before you could say Jack Robinson.

Renée sat in the little office and a woman in a pink suit came in and introduced herself. Renée would not have chosen to wear that particular shade of pink, which was too close to bubble gum for *her* taste, but she had to admit the woman was impeccably turned out.

Renée had initially been skeptical. It had occurred to her that there was nothing to stop the interviewer from just calling someone and getting her to confirm his story. But something in Lucille's matter-of-fact manner carried conviction.

Lucille explained that the job wasn't for everyone, and she explained her views on going to the toilet, and she explained that she used tampons and she didn't tend to dwell on them either, and she explained that she was planning to go to Harvard Law School.

"I never really thought of it before," Lucille explained. "Because I certainly don't have that kind of money. But when I first applied to the agency Joe happened to mention that one of the other applicants was saving up money to go to law school. It's a funny thing, but it really stopped me in my tracks. I thought, 'What do I want out of life, anyway?'"

Renée was not usually at a loss for words, but somehow "And what do you want out of life?" did not seem exactly the right thing to say.

"Because if what you want out of life is a lot of *things*, obviously you can get a lot more things if you have more money. I just thought, 'Is that the kind of person I am? Don't I have any goals?' Well, OK, sure, I always thought I'd be PA to the head of a big company one day. I just thought, 'Is that it?'"

I don't believe I'm hearing this, thought Renée.

And Lucille explained that just for the heck of it she had gone out and taken the LSAT and she had turned out to have a real aptitude. "And when I thought about it it actually made sense," said Lucille. "Because attention to detail is one of my strong points."

"I don't like debt," Lucille explained. "I don't care *what* qualifications you have, you can't ever tell what tomorrow will bring. My grandfather lived through the Depression. You can't tell *me* there weren't Harvard lawyers out of a job. Besides, the way I see it is, if you take on a big bank loan other people are calling the shots. I don't know if you're aware of this, but Harvard will make loan repayments for people who are earning less than $35,000 a year if they do pro bono work. Well, that's just fine, but what it comes down to is somebody else gets to decide what they think is worthwhile. Besides which, just because that option happens to be available now doesn't mean it's necessarily going to be available if and when I decide I want to take advantage of it. Well, if I can get around that by going to the toilet a couple of times a day it's a small price to pay."

Gradually Renée stopped feeling insulted that someone had had the impudence to try to sell her a disgusting, pornographic fabrication as a reason for not hiring her. Apparently this was actually true. If it was true, it was still disgusting, but it wasn't an insult that it was the reason she was not eligible for the job.

It simply happened to be in violation of the Equal Employment Opportunities Act.

Now, just because an employer is in violation of the Equal Employment Opportunities Act does not mean you want the job. But Renée had the kind of attention to detail that had been driving her family insane for years, so that she could not help noticing one little detail. The reason the employer was in violation of the Equal Employment Opportunities Act with this particular job was that the whole workplace was one in which an African-American would stand out. In other words, it was the fact that the employer did not have a 50:50

workplace that *made* it impossible to guarantee anonymity. But what this meant was that not having a 50:50 workplace in effect denied whatever African-Americans did happen to be working there access to positions offering double the salary. They weren't given the *choice*. They were just automatically excluded.

In other words, any employer who wanted to implement this program should have simultaneously set the wheels in motion to raise the number of African-Americans in the workplace — *regardless* of whether any actually wanted the job in question. Probably most would *not* choose to be involved in a disgusting scheme of this nature, but they should have the opportunity to make that decision for themselves.

Interesting.

Half an hour later Renée walked out of the office building.

Across the street a narrow park ran along the river. Renée crossed the street and sat down on a bench looking over the water.

"Well, what do you think, Renée?"

Renée (or Miss Perfect, as she was known in her family) watched the eddying brown water for a moment in silence.

At last she said, "I don't know *what* to think."

She crossed one leg over the other and looked down at her polished Gucci shoe. The leather was a dark chestnut, gleaming like oiled wood; her leg, in its filmy Hanes pantyhose, was two shades paler, and her cashmere dress was marron glacé. She had twelve other pairs of brown shoes in her closet because it's important to get the shade exactly right when you are matching earth colors. Some people will wear a pair of tan shoes with an oatmeal dress, or chocolate brown shoes with a red dress; the only thing you can say is, if they're going to go out looking like that, they're probably better off not noticing. It's some kind of consolation to think that most of the people around them won't notice either.

If you actually care about how you look, on the other hand, you'll take the trouble to get it right. Sometimes a dress needs matching accessories: sometimes a red dress *needs* red shoes and a red bag. At other times neutral accessories are called for. But just because something is neutral doesn't mean it goes with everything, it's important to get it right. Renée had dyed Italian leather sandals in magenta, coquelicot, chartreuse, peacock blue, lime green, lemon yellow, and frosted orange. She had suede loafers in lavender, lilac, ivory, cream, tangerine, royal blue, charcoal grey, and black. She had ankle boots in three shades of navy blue, four shades of brown, black suede, black leather, and black leather with black suede trim. In addition to the sixty other indispensable pairs of shoes she had a list of things that most people get wrong:

> Never wear gold jewelry with blue. If you're going to wear blue, you need a silver watch. If you can't afford the watch, don't wear blue.
> Never wear gold buttons.
> Never wear coins or medals as buttons.
> Never wear fake coins or medals as buttons.
> Never wear cloth buttons with a metal rim.
> Never wear self-covered buttons in man-made fibers.
> Never wear self-covered *velvet* buttons. Cotton, silk, linen, and wool are acceptable; anything else is in bad taste.

Never wear a belt that ties. If it doesn't buckle, it
shouldn't be there in the first place.
Never wear anything with a button-down flap.
Never wear anything with a pocket that zips.
Never wear anything with a drawstring.
Never wear *anything* with epaulettes.
Never wear anything two tone.
Never wear a raincoat that doesn't match your shoes.
You probably need a minimum of ten.

There were about 200 other principles on the list, and even in
the fashion magazines people sometimes got some of them
wrong. Some people think this kind of thing is trivial; they
think as long as they get the important things right the rest
doesn't matter.

The fact is that being perfect is a matter of habit. If you
want to get things right, practice by getting everything right.
If you always get *everything* right, down to the last detail, when
the important things come along you'll be ready for them.
Otherwise, you waste more time than you save wondering
whether something is *worth* taking the time to get right. And
even if you decide it is, you won't know how to get it right
if you try.

Miss Perfect had been perfect ever since she could remember. Her clothes were always folded, sorted by color,
and put away. Her toys always looked as good as new. Her
schoolbooks had paper jackets to protect them. Her notebooks
were always pristine, filled with notes that fell automatically
into perfect outlines in perfect handwriting. Her homework
was always on time, and it always got an A. College was the
same, and so was every job she had ever had. That was why
she was ready to be PA to a CEO at the age of 28.

"I don't know what to think," she said again, clasping her hands around her knee and looking at her beautifully manicured thumbnails, and thinking of the fact that Lightning Rods was in flagrant violation of the Equal Employment Opportunities Act.

Renée sat on the bench, swinging her shoe.

This detail was going to go on niggling at her. She could tell. *All* details niggled at her. Sometimes she thought she would rather not have to find closet space for 100 pairs of shoes; she didn't *want* to own shoes in twenty-two separate shades of navy blue. But if her shoes were wrong for her dress the color just niggled at her and niggled at her and niggled at her until she gave in and bought another pair. If a button was loose on a blouse it niggled at her. If her watch didn't agree with the talking clock, it niggled at her. This was going to just go right on niggling at her.

"You need a lawyer," she said, but something was niggling at her.

The thing that was niggling at her was the calm, confident way Lucille had shared her ambition to go to Harvard Law School.

The thing that was niggling at Renée was the fact that all these things were niggling at her. Because if you have the type of mind that is simply not *able* not to notice details maybe you *don't* need a lawyer.

Maybe you could be a lawyer yourself.

Renée had noticed for years that the people running the country did not bring the level of perfectionism to the task which she brought to organizing name tags for a conference. The problem was that to do the job the way she would want to do it would drive even her insane. She had enough trouble just organizing a conference to her own satisfaction.

She swung her foot back and forth.

The fact is that not being able to not pay attention to detail can actually be a liability. Just because Renée was not able to not pay attention to every single little detail did not mean she thought it was actually *worth* it. Au contraire. Sometimes it got really irritating. That was why she had decided to apply for a new job. It wasn't just the money, though the money was part of it. She had thought maybe a job that was more of a challenge, that carried more responsibility with it, would justify the level of perfectionism she would not be able to help bringing to it.

Well, wasn't it just possible that the reason she kept looking for new jobs was that she was not doing the kind of job that would *ever* justify the level of perfectionism she brought to a job? Wasn't it possible that the kind of job that would justify that level of perfectionism was always going to be one where you couldn't avoid making *some* mistakes? Maybe the time had come to learn to live with that. Instead of looking around at the way other people were running the world, and letting it niggle at her, she could do something about it. Go to Harvard Law School. Become a Justice of the Supreme Court. All you had to do was look at the job the current appointees were doing to see where there was real scope for improvement.

"I think you're getting a little carried away here, Renée," she said.

A dog trotted by. It squatted in the grass and squeezed out a long, narrow, soft brown turd, then trotted gaily away.

Renée looked at the turd in the grass.

Suppose someone offered you the chance to go to Harvard Law School, and all you had to do was pick up a turd a couple of times a day, *wearing plastic gloves*, on top of your regular job. It would be kind of disgusting, but no worse than cleaning toilets. She had taken a part-time job as a chambermaid when she was fifteen to save up and buy a computer; did she have any regrets? No way.

The difference would be that you would be getting a chance to have a completely different life. Wouldn't you do something kind of disgusting for a couple of years to have a chance you wouldn't otherwise have? You know you would.

"I think we're talking about something rather different here, Renée," she said.

Suppose someone offered you the chance to go to Harvard Law School, but you had to do something *really* disgusting for two years. Suppose you had to agree to shovel out a stable all day long for two years. Two years of shoveling horse shit and at the end of it you could go to Harvard Law School. Or what if it was something even more disgusting? Suppose you had to work for two years at a sewage disposal plant. Two years of shoveling human shit and at the end of it you could go to Harvard Law School, no strings attached.

At the end of the day, you're just talking about pieces of the planet. Your body is a piece of matter on the surface of the planet. The shit is also matter. You use one object on the surface of the planet to move around other stuff on the surface of the planet. And what you buy with moving all that stuff around is the use of your mind.

If you're a personal assistant, chances are you won't have to deal with anything that's physically disgusting. You can leave that to the cleaners. Or at least, you can leave most things to the cleaners. If you're the type of person that things niggle at, you will probably find yourself cleaning your keyboard with a toothbrush, or noticing that there is some kind of disgusting gunk on the phone that will *have* to come *off*. But by and large the job is not offensive to the senses.

On the other hand, you have to clutter up your mind with a lot of stuff that you might well prefer not to give house room. That's always going to be part of the job; you are never going to reach a stage where you can clear the decks and focus on major issues. And the fact is, plenty of people who go to law school are no better off. They come out with these loans to pay off, and before you know it they are counting themselves *lucky* to be cluttering up their minds with tax loopholes.

You could argue that a deal that asks you to do something physically disgusting for a limited period, and gives you free use of your own mind in exchange, is actually not such a bad bargain.

You could argue that the type of person who could come up with this kind of argument is wasted outside the law.

Renée stood up suddenly. She had noticed a small pharmacy on the ground floor of the building. She crossed the road again, and in the pharmacy she bought a pair of plastic gloves.

She returned to the park. The turd lay undisturbed in the sweet young grass. She drew on both gloves, and she picked up the turd in her right hand and went back to sit on the bench. She crossed one leg over the other, resting her arm on her knee. Her hand in its plastic glove rested on the cashmere of her skirt; the turd reposed in the plastic-gloved palm of her hand.

She sat looking at it coolly.

If you are fastidious you actually spend a lot more time than other people dealing with things that disgust you. Most people don't notice their surroundings; they don't notice a thin film of soap around the bathtub, they don't notice the streaks of dirt on their windows after it rains, they don't notice the flecks of grease on their stove or the grime in the cracks at the bottom of their trash can. They don't have to deal with things that disgust them because hardly anything does. As long as they have a toilet that flushes and a shower that works they think they're living in a clean environment. But if you're fastidious you *notice* all this stuff that nobody else sees, and you have to deal with it on a daily basis. Because you know *one* thing for sure. If *you* don't deal with it, nobody *else* is going to.

At last she stood up. It was as if her body knew what she wanted to do better than she did. It walked to a disposal unit that said "Pet Waste Only" and it lifted the lid and dropped the turd inside. Then it walked to a unit that said "Litter" and it peeled off the plastic gloves and dropped them in. Then it turned and crossed the street and went back into the building.

AFFIRMATIVE ACTION

"I've decided I want the job," said Renée, sinking gracefully into the chair in front of Joe's desk.

Joe laced his fingers together on the desk.

"Renée," he said, in a low, unhurried, thousand-dollar-suit voice. "As I'm sure Lucille explained to you, much as we'd *like* to take on someone with your qualifications we just don't have the openings. Didn't Lucille explain that to you?"

"Yes, she did," said Renée. "She said it wasn't for most people, and it was for the woman in a thousand who could make a real contribution to the organization and expected to be compensated accordingly. Now, as I'm sure you're aware, any organization which, by the underemployment of African-American personnel, excludes all African-Americans from this sort of opportunity *regardless of their qualifications*, is in violation of the Equal Employment Opportunities Act."

Joe sighed. For this he had paid Lucille $1,000? He might as well just have gone out and bought another suit for all the good it had done.

"Look, Renée," he said. "With the best will in the world, what you're asking is impossible. In the first place, just increasing the number of African-Americans in the workplace is not going to solve the problem. Even if you had an office

196

that was staffed 100% with African-American personnel you *still* wouldn't be able to guarantee anonymity, for the simple reason that then you're talking about personnel with a range of pigmentation among themselves, with the result that there would be no way to keep people who made use of the facility from identifying the members of staff who had provided it. I'm sorry, but we've got to face facts. And besides, if you think about it, where will it all end? You could just as well say that an office should be 50% Hispanic-American, or 50% Chinese-American, or what have you. I'm sorry to disappoint you, because you're a pretty exceptional applicant and I hate to see talent go to waste, but you've got to be realistic. No single office is going to be able to be that big of a melting pot."

Renée crossed one leg over the other, and clasped her hands around her knee.

"Joe," she said. "You seem to be laboring under a misapprehension."

"Oh really?" said Joe.

"Yes," said Renée. "You seem to think this is my problem."

Joe hesitated.

"You seem to think it's up to *me* to come up with a solution," said Renée. "But *you're* the one who's got I don't know how many companies into a mess. Thanks to you every single one of your clients is now in flagrant violation of the Equal Employment Opportunities Act. That's not *my* problem. It's *your* problem."

Wow, she thought. This is *great*.

Renée had never realized just how satisfying it could be to be confrontational. As a PA you hardly ever get to do this kind of thing. Once in a while you can tell an airline, or a caterer, or a courier, that their level of service is unsatisfactory. You can tell people that your boss is on another line.

But how often do you actually get to tell someone that he's racist and it's up to him to do something about it? Never, that's how often.

Joe was thinking *Shit*. He was also thinking that the female of the species is more deadly than the male. Whoever said that was absolutely right.

"Look," said Joe. "I hear what you're saying. I'll tell you what. I'll have a word with Lucille. I'll see if she has any ideas."

Lucille agreed to throw in another visit to the office as part of the original thousand-dollar package.

"Look, Lucille," said Joe, when Lucille strolled into the office at 5:37. "I don't know what you said to this gal, but it seems to have had exactly the opposite of the desired effect. She's got some bee in her bonnet about Harvard Law School."

"Oh really?" said Lucille.

"Now I'm absolutely the last guy in the world to want to stand in the way of people's aspirations, but there's a time and a place for everything. With the best will in the world you know as well as I do that there's no way we can guarantee that ladies in different colors of skin can be inconspicuous."

"I see what you're saying," said Lucille.

"You can talk about the Equal Employment Opportunities Act until the cows come home, you're not going to change the basic facts of the situation. For the love of Mike, does she *want* people going around making insinuations and innuendos?"

Lucille sat in the chair in front of the desk and crossed one leg over the other. "Calm down, Joe," she advised. "This isn't getting us anywhere. What you're saying is what? She wants the job, and she says it's up to you make any necessary arrangements to guarantee anonymity?"

"You got it," said Joe. "Jesus."

"Well, she's got a point," said Lucille.

"What?" said Joe.

"She's got a point, said Lucille. "You are in violation of the Equal Employment Opportunities Act."

"Whose side are you on, anyway?" asked Joe.

"I'm just stating a fact," said Lucille. "The way I see it is, you're lucky this came up now. Gives you a chance to do something about it before things get out of hand."

"But," said Joe.

"Let me think about this for a minute," said Lucille. She swung her foot thoughtfully. She was wearing a pair of filmy Hanes pantyhose which made her legs a very pale tan.

Hm.

"Well, I've got an idea," she said when the minute was up. Lucille was a stickler for detail. When she said a minute she meant a minute. Not 59 seconds. Not 61 seconds. A minute.

"OK, shoot," said Joe.

"Well, the way I see it is, the problem is basically with people seeing bare legs in their natural skin color. I don't see why you couldn't just issue some kind of solid colored tights, or maybe something in rubber or PVC, with just a slit at the crotch. Apparently a lot of men find the idea of entering through a hole in a piece of clothing quite stimulating, so my guess is you wouldn't have any complaints from the customers. And it would solve the whole problem of people with different colors of skin, which when you come down to it is probably relevant to a lot of the people you've already got working for you. What happens if someone spends a couple of weeks in the Bahamas? You never really thought it through that far."

Joe opened his mouth to protest. Then he shut it again. PVC would spoil *everything*, but there was no way he could explain that. He didn't really like to think about what Lucille might think about how he had happened to have the idea in the first place, so he tried not to think about it. But one thing was for sure, if he said it would spoil it, it would be only too obvious that he thought there was something *to* spoil. Namely, a scenario that derived from the type of fantasy that involved an element of the unexpected. If somebody just happens to be clad in black PVC from the waist down, it is really stretching probability too far to imagine that she isn't expecting something to happen. It defeats the whole point of the fantasy. The whole thing would be *ruined*, and there wasn't a damn thing he could do about it. The Equal Employment Opportunities Act had him over a barrel.

The thing that was really unfair was that in his fantasies he had given *plenty* of opportunities to black gals, and for that matter to gals from all *kinds* of ethnic backgrounds. It's just that there is a difference between reality and fantasy. In a fantasy, nothing ever has any repercussions. In real life, you have to weigh pros and cons, in case someone gets hurt.

Unfortunately there was also no way he could explain this to Lucille, while as for Renée! Something told him that for all her ranting about the Equal Employment Opportunities Act Renée would not appreciate being told that her employer had had black gals, or rather African-American gals, in his game show fantasy. If you're a salesman you tend to have a sense for these things. He could be wrong. But he sure as hell wasn't about to go trying to find out.

PVC

For the next couple of days Joe tried to put a brave face on things. He tried not to think about the PVC with a slit in the crotch which the Equal Employment Opportunities Act was going to force him to implement. If he thought about it he was just going to get depressed, and in sales you can't afford to get depressed. You can't afford to go around thinking What's the point? That negative take on the product will communicate itself to the customer, and before you know it all the hard work you put into getting your foot in the door will be down the drain.

Sooner or later, though, we all have to face the facts. So he went home at the end of a long day and forced himself to confront the whole issue of PVC.

Now, whenever you don't like something you have two alternatives. One alternative is to change the world. The other is to change yourself. In this case, changing the world was not an option. The Equal Employment Opportunities Act was here to stay. Like it or not, PVC, or a reasonable facsimile thereof, was going to be a feature of the lightning rod installation for the foreseeable future. But if you can't change the world, one thing you *can* try to change is your attitude.

Joe poured himself a stiff Bourbon and turned his mind to the question of PVC.

Essentially, the problem boiled down to the fact that PVC lacked spontaneity. But supposing the gal was wearing a pair of tight PVC pants, and she was doing some exercises, trying to do a split or something, and the pants split. All of a sudden she hears someone outside – no, wait. The *mailman* rings the *doorbell*. And she can't go to the door because her pants just split and she isn't wearing any underwear! So she goes to the window, and it's really stiff so she can only get it up a few inches, and she sticks her head through, and she has to lean way out so she can see the mailman, because she has to tell him to leave a parcel by the door. Then she gets into a long argument with the mailman because the mailman says she has to sign for it, and while she's arguing the *lodger* comes up from behind and sees the hole in the crotch and takes advantage of the situation. Or *wait*, maybe the gal is staying with her sister and her sister's husband. She borrowed her sister's PVC pants to do exercises in, but they're too tight, not that she's fat or anything she just has more curves than her sister so she has to lie on her back and *squeeze* into those PVC pants, and she couldn't wear any *underwear* because the *pants* are so tight, and then she stands up and bends over and the pants split right up the crotch. So then she hears the doorbell and she thinks Oh shit, it's the mailman, and she goes to the window and leans right out and then the *husband* comes in and he sees the PVC pants with the split up the crotch only he thinks it's his *wife* –

Already Joe could see that PVC had a lot more potential than he had originally given it credit for.

He went back to the bedroom and loosened his clothes and experimented with various fantasies involving PVC and his final conclusion was that they were at least as effective as the game show. There was a real buzz about it. Why had he ever thought PVC lacked spontaneity? Treated properly, PVC could be just as unpremeditated and spontaneous as any other type of clothing. This was actually something you could feel good about incorporating into the product, something that would add value.

He sat up and swung his feet to the floor. He shook his head, thinking of Lucille with rueful admiration. He wouldn't be fooling anybody if he pretended he had actually *liked* shelling out a grand to get out of a jam, but if this PVC was the stroke of genius he was beginning to think it was, the idea was the bargain of the century at a measly 1K.

Plus, it would mean his worries about the Equal Employment Opportunities Act were a thing of the past.

EQUAL OPPORTUNITIES

Joe introduced the PVC enhancement to all his operations. He gave Renée a placement as a bifunctional crème-de-la-crème PA. He put RODS IS AN EQUAL OPPORTUNITIES EMPLOYER on all his ads. And in his innocence he thought all his problems were over.

In fact, his problems were just beginning.

6

A FINE ROMANCE

TIME MANAGEMENT

Renée prepared for the new job the way she prepared for everything – thoroughly.

The way Renée looked at it was this. You were selling use of your body for short periods of time in exchange for the chance to make the best possible use of your mind. Well, why not take it one step further? Why not set aside the actual time allocated for non-secretarial functions and put it to use? Learn a language? Study accounting? *Do* something with the time, so that at the end of a year, say, you'd look back and what you'd see was that you'd worked on a language a couple of times a day. On top of being paid for the time, you'd have a new asset that no one could take away from you.

She spent quite a lot of time thinking about which particular project would give her a real sense of achievement. What she finally decided was that this was the ideal opportunity to read Proust's masterpiece, *A la recherche du temps perdu*, in French. The amount of time lightning rods were typically expected to be on duty would be just right for working through a French text. On the one hand she wouldn't be reading a lot at any one time, so she wouldn't get discouraged. On the other hand, it was quite a long book, so by the time she finished she'd probably have enough money for Harvard

Law School. She could look at the volumes on her shelf and see how far she had to go.

So she went to the university bookstore and bought the complete set, and she started at page one, paragraph one on her first day on the job.

Sure enough, the idea worked perfectly. The fact that she had to struggle with the French meant she didn't have a lot of attention to spare for anything else that might be going on. She'd go through as much text as she could, underlining words she didn't know with a pencil. At night she'd look up the words and read through the passage again. The next day she'd read on. Within a month she was having to look up fewer words. Within six months she was reading the French almost as well as she read English – and that was *entirely* the result of doing it on a daily basis.

So unlike most lightning rods she was able to look at something she'd actually accomplished with the time. It was no different from reading a book while you have a massage, or a jacuzzi, except that she'd done it on a daily basis for six months. Instead of cluttering up her mind with bad feelings, she had actually *improved* her mind. And by the time she reached the end of *A la recherche du temps perdu* she'd have earned $100,000 just out of time spent reading Proust.

Pas mal.

Years later, when Renée was making constitutional history as a Supreme Court Justice, she was sometimes asked to identify the thing that had made the single biggest contribution to her career.

A lot of women saw Renée as a role model, and a lot of African-Americans saw Renée as a role model, here was someone who had worked in subordinate positions for years, admittedly at increasingly senior levels, before swanning into

Harvard Law School with LSATs in the high 170s and swanning out again to glide with apparently effortless ease right on up to the Supreme Court. What was her secret?

Renée didn't say "That's my secret" because in her opinion coyness was in bad taste.

What she said was that there was no one single thing, but she made a point of doing things right first time. Effective time management was also important.

She did not say that there's nothing like being on the receiving end of a proactive sexual harassment management program for letting you in on a big secret.

No matter how mundane and routine the job in hand, most people don't know what they're doing half the time. If they're setting up something new that's never been tried before, you can make that 98.2 % of the time. It's only when you're in on something from the beginning, when staying in the air for 12 seconds counts as heavier-than-air powered flight, that you understand just how much is left to do. Something leaves the drawing board and the spectators cheer when it crashes into the sand, because at least 12 seconds elapsed before the crash. Naturally enough, the inventors think they've really achieved something if they can move on to just keeping it in the air without crashing. Naturally enough, if they break that 12-second barrier, all *kinds* of faults get overlooked in the excitement.

What Renée realized was that exactly the same thing applied to the country as a whole. It was set up from scratch by people who managed to overlook minor details like slavery and a whole sex. Naturally enough, with that level of glaring oversight to fix, it was easy for people to overlook the faults that remained. Because the thing is, we grow up with the laws we've got, and we assume they're right because they're what we're used to. What we don't realize is that some of those laws were written by people like Joe, and the rest were written by people trying to clean up after people like Joe. That's why they leave a *lot* to be desired.

What Renée realized was that the more important something is, the less likely people are to fix mistakes. They're going to assume that if it's that important, somebody must have known what they were doing. Or they're going to assume that anything seriously wrong would have been fixed after all this time. They're not going to realize that the people who set it up didn't know what they were doing 98.2% of the time. They're not going to realize that the people who fixed it were just trying to bring it into line with an acceptable, 50% level of cluelessness. So if something leaves a lot to be desired, it's up to you to do something about it. Because if you don't, you know one thing for sure: nobody *else* is going to.

That simple piece of knowledge gave Renée the determination that carried her all the way to the Supreme Court. *Pas mal.*

And in addition to letting her in on the big secret, Lightning Rods also gave her the opportunity to put that newfound knowledge into practice.

Joe would have been the first to admit that Renée was a real asset to the firm. In fact, he had to mentally retract all the harsh things he had thought about the Equal Employment Opportunities Act. Because the fact was, his first impulse had been to take the easy way out and tell the applicant to go elsewhere. It was only because he had been legally obligated to come up with a solution that he had gone to the trouble and expense of introducing PVC.

As it turned out, the PVC *alone* was a real improvement on the product. It solved the perennial problem of inappropriate urination. It enhanced the enjoyment of most participants in the program. Also, he had hired a truly exceptional applicant. And if it hadn't been for the Equal Employment Opportunities Act all that talent would have been squandered.

The only thing was, Renée seemed to be even more demanding than Lucille. Not a day passed without Renée calling up to make comments and recommendations. Usually when a lightning rod made a suggestion Joe would promise to make a note of it and give the matter careful consideration. He tried this once with Renée.

"And when can I expect to see some action taken?"

"Uh, I can't really say before I've had a chance to think about it in greater depth," said Joe.

"When do you expect to have a chance to think about it? Tonight? Tomorrow?"

"Uh ... "

"I'll give you a call tomorrow afternoon. I don't see any reason why this shouldn't be resolved by next week."

Joe had never realized that a crème-de-la-crème PA had so much in common with a bulldozer.

He had then tried his other tried-and-true response, which was to explain that the suggestion could not be implemented on the software in its present form, but that he would do everything in his power to integrate it into the software the next time he updated the program.

"And when will that be?"

"Uh ... I'm not sure. I've got a lot of commitments, so I'm not exactly sure *when* I'll be able to get around to this. But I'll certainly do it just as soon as I've got a moment to spare, I can assure you of – "

"Do you mean to say that you do the programming *yourself?*"

The fact was that Joe was too embarrassed to hand it over to a computer expert, who would be bound to look at what had been done so far and sneer.

"I prefer it that way," said Joe. "I developed the product, and it works best if enhancements are introduced by someone who knows it inside out."

"Well, there's something to be said for that, of course, but this is pretty urgent. Can't you just do it this weekend?"

"I don't think this is something that can be done in a weekend," Joe said firmly. "It's pretty complicated stuff."

"Really? It looks pretty straightforward to me. What language are you using?"

"Just English for the time being," said Joe. "We don't really have enough Hispanic clients at this stage to justify bringing it out in Spanish. Though obviously, should the need arise, Lightning Rods will be ready and willing to meet that challenge."

There was a short silence.

"I mean what programming language are you using," said Renée.

"*Oh.* Oh, *right,*" said Joe. He mentioned the name of the program.

"Then it shouldn't be a problem. I'm familiar with the basics, anyway. I'll come in this weekend and deal with it. I'll expect to be paid overtime, obviously."

"Uh … "

"Fifty dollars an hour. Anything else I need to know? Good, then that's that taken care of."

After that Joe just gave up and allowed himself to be bulldozed over on a daily basis until the system met Renée's exacting requirements. It cost him about $5,000 in overtime for all the programming. But when the dust settled he realized it had actually been worth it. It was like getting the Princess and the Pea to design a mattress. Once Renée had smoothed out all the little wrinkles in the system that bothered her, the final result was something that made the whole spectrum of lightning rods happier. Phone calls to the office dropped right down. Joe even began wondering whether he really needed that counsellor.

Unfortunately one of Renée's innovations, while invaluable in itself, was to have far-reaching and dangerous repercussions.

Renée was irritated from the first day by the unprofessional approach of her fellow lightning rods. For one thing, there was a stash of magazines in the HFC. For another, *twice* in one *week* she came in and found someone's PVC just lying on the floor where somebody had just *left* it instead of disposing of it properly. For another, nobody seemed to worry all that much about the anonymity which was supposed to be an integral part of the program. She was only 20 pages into *Du côté de chez Swann* when she spotted her first other lightning rod. By page 40, she could identify no fewer than 10.

One of the main reasons seemed to be that many of the lightning rods should never have been hired in the first place. Instead of managing their time so that their minds were otherwise occupied they seemed to dwell on the physical aspects of the job in a way that was bound to lead to trouble. Sooner or later they'd get depressed, feel a need to confide in someone. They'd bottle it up inside, see someone coming out of the HFC, jump to conclusions, assume it was another lightning rod, feel the urge to come out. Well, if they *had* to talk about it the *last* people they should be talking to were people in their own company.

Renée tried to get Joe to do something about it, and Joe just tried to avoid the issue.

At last she'd had enough. "Look, Joe," she said firmly after Joe had avoided the issue for about five minutes. "This is completely unacceptable. You can't tell *me* your clients wanted this kind of working environment. You promised them complete anonymity at every level; well, right now anonymity is as full of holes as a Swiss cheese. Clearly members of the program need more support from the company than they're currently getting."

Joe tried to interrupt but Renée proceeded implacably on. "Now, in my last job, as PA to the Senior Vice President, I also oversaw an in-house online network for support staff. Staff could raise any problems they were experiencing in a forum where other members of staff could respond; at the same time, if I saw any issues related to performance that needed addressing, I could raise those issues at an early stage. There's absolutely no reason why something similar should not be put in place for the entire lightning rod network. Since I've had experience of setting up and running something like this in the past, I'm prepared to take this on – design the software, organize installation and supervise the network. My guess is that most difficulties can be resolved internally; anything we can't deal with can be referred to the parent organization."

"Uh … "

"I'll want another $15,000 a year on top of what I'm getting now. At the end of the first year I'll let you know if that needs to be revised upward."

"Uh ... "

"Good, then that's settled."

Renée set up the network. She introduced a magazine compartment within the transporter. She laid down the law on such matters as correct disposal of skirts and PVC cladding. She gave the lightning rods a forum in which to air their views. And every so often she would offer tips of her own.

If Renée had stuck to advising people to learn a language in their spare time, Joe could have gone on sleeping the sleep of the just. But one day, when Renée was nearly halfway through *Du côté de chez Swann*, the question came up of the effect of the job on people's relationships. Many lightning rods said that the job made them less interested in sex outside work, and that it sometimes had a negative effect on their relationships. One said her boyfriend was always complaining, because he worked in the same company and he knew she wasn't working that hard so he couldn't see why she was always tired.

Renée pointed out that if her boyfriend worked in the same company, the company was providing an outlet for his needs. There was absolutely no reason for his girlfriend to feel guilty. Renée had meant to be supportive, but it generated a lot of controversy, because the lightning rod said if she thought her boyfriend was using the facility she would never be able to think of him the same way again.

As it happened, Elaine sometimes checked out the network, and she thought the network facilitator had made a good point.

In fact, it made Elaine see her work as a lightning rod in a whole new light.

What Elaine thought was that a lot of men in relationships were probably using the facility, and if you thought about it just having that facility could make a relationship stronger than it otherwise would be. One of the things that can put a strain on a relationship, after all, is the fact that men tend to equate a relationship with sex on demand. Well, if they can actually *have* that sex on demand in the workplace, it stands to reason they should be able to keep that demand under control in other contexts. It stands to reason that the relationship is less likely to be damaged by demands for sex at inappropriate times and in inappropriate contexts. It stands to reason that the relationship will stand a better chance of success.

The point made a big impression on Elaine. And having made an impression on Elaine, it also had an impact on Ed Wilson.

DEPRIVATION

As a frequent flier, Ed was well placed to notice new developments in the lightning rod installations. When PVC was introduced he was not unappreciative. But the fact was, his impromptu date with Elaine had reminded him of just how much of a woman there is above the waist. The more he used the lightning rods, the more he kept remembering how much he was missing.

After that first excursion to Rodeo Bill's Ed had started inviting Elaine out on a fairly regular basis. For some reason, though, he never seemed to get any closer to making contact. Elaine refused to go out without Hayley on school nights. She refused to stay out late on school nights because Hayley had to do her homework. She refused to let him unbutton one single button in case Hayley came in with a question about her homework.

The fact was that Elaine had given a lot of thought to the discussion on the lightning rod network. And the way Elaine saw it was, providing sexual release for people was part of her job. When she left the office she was off duty, and she could do what she damn well liked. Usually, of course, if she went out with someone for a few weeks, she might start to feel like she should do something, because she would be aware that he was probably getting frustrated. But why should she feel guilty about someone who was *already* getting an outlet at the office? If someone can get hot meals at the canteen, why the hell should his girlfriend have to cook? Especially if she happens to actually work in the canteen? Besides. Men come and go, but if things go wrong with your kid you can't just trade in and trade up. No kid wants to worry about coming downstairs in case some guy is getting hands-on experience of her mother's Wonderbra.

The result was that Ed was getting more frustrated than he would have believed was possible for someone who was using the lightning rods five or six times a day.

Sometimes Ed, Elaine, and Hayley would drive out in the Lamborghini while Ed discovered just how much can be taken in by peripheral vision if a D-cup is lurking in the periphery. Sometimes they would go back to the house and play Scrabble, and Ed would just leave the board to peripheral vision the better to savor the full agony of strictly hands-off experience of a Wonderbra.

Hayley, meanwhile, was gradually accumulating a whole roomful of complete sets of special offers. Every time they went to a fast food outlet Ed would compulsively buy however many meals it took to collect the whole set of whatever it was that happened to be the special offer. It wasn't too bad if you could *pick* the remaining, missing parts of the set each time you bought a meal; where it got embarrassing was with the kind of deal where the prize just came in a sealed wrapper that you opened later. Ed would just keep buying meals until the prize turned up. No matter how long it took. They once sat in a Lucky Leprechaun for five hours because they only had four out of a possible five lucky toadstools, free with every purchase of a Magic Meal (just $2.95 with medium-sized drink and medium fries).

One hour to eat the first three Magic Meals, open their wrappers and find they had two out of five toadstools.

Half an hour buying and throwing away another twenty Magic Meals to get a third toadstool.

Half an hour buying and throwing away another thirty Magic Meals to get up to four.

Then Elaine put her foot down. People were starving. It was *obscene* to be throwing away food like that just to collect a Goddamn lucky toadstool. If Ed wanted to go through with this he could prepurchase however many Magic Meals it took and then eat the meals later.

Three hours of prepurchasing five hundred Magic Meals and going through five hundred wrappers to come up with the fifth and final lucky toadstool.

They never did eat all those prepurchased meals, because Hayley said just the thought of a Magic Meal made her want to puke, and Ed said he felt the same way so he'd just give them to the homeless. So at the time it looked like nearly $1,500 had been thrown away on a stupid plastic toadstool. Which just shows how shortsighted we can be. It turned out that only twenty of that fifth toadstool had ever been made, so that a complete set of lucky toadstools was incredibly rare. Within ten years it was worth $50,000 – and that was just *one* of the complete sets Ed picked up for her when she was ten.

Years later, when Hayley was a millionaire, people used to think the way she got started was through her connections. It was having a stepfather who was a multi-billionaire that made the difference. What Hayley would say was that Ed did two things for her. The first was, he gave her a lot of stuff that got caught up in the collectability craze, so that all those complete sets represented a large capital amount when she was in her early twenties. The second was, he taught her that if you want something, you should just give it everything you've got. Don't worry about looking dumb; don't worry about what other people will think; just *go* for it.

What Ed would say was: "She's a sweet kid."

What he would think was that he would never have been crazy enough to buy 553 Magic Meals if he hadn't have been in a state of advanced tit deprivation.

In later years, of course, features were standard which in the early days would have seemed inconceivable luxuries. Today a heater is standard in all cars. Time was when people would heat up a brick in the oven and wrap it in a towel. Today we take car radios for granted; well, the time is still within living memory when, if you wanted a radio in the car, you had to take it out of your living room and put it on the front seat. In the same way, users of the early lightning rods could not have imagined that one day a video panel at eye level would be standard; the idea that you would one day be able to choose between seeing the back and head of a virtual partner, or just getting an eyeful of breasts ranging from mango to melon, would have seemed unthinkable. In the early days users were expected to look after themselves. Soon the Men's HFC had its own stash of magazines. Then Joe had the bright idea of providing the magazines, because he could get a good deal on bulk orders, and keeping them in a concealed compartment. He tried it out in Kansas City and when it proved popular he made it standard in all his installations, and *that*, if you can believe it, was what passed for high concept in 2000.

Whether a more sophisticated product would have made life easier for Ed Wilson will never be known. As it was, precisely *because* Ed Wilson was using the product so much more regularly than most clients, he was one of the first to become dissatisfied with its shortcomings. There comes a time when screwing someone from behind with nothing to look at but the wall gets stale; there comes a time when even screwing someone from behind while reading a magazine does more harm than good. All the magazine does is make you aware of all the features that are inaccessible because there's a wall in the way.

Studies on the baboon in captivity have shown that primates in captivity take out their frustration on each other. Ed Wilson chose to take out his frustration on Roy.

From the point of view of Lightning Rods, he could not have chosen worse.

7

A HIGHER POWER

THE BIG BREAK

Ironically, the thing that kicked Joe's problems into the major league was the very thing that made him think there was now no stopping him, i.e. the fact that he got his first big break.

His first break, obviously, had been when he had found the one company in a thousand prepared to take an innovative approach to the problem of sexual harassment. But that was a break he had had to work for. He had had to write to 1,000 companies, and he had had to handle all the various forms that rejection can take from 999 of them.

But his first *big* break came through something he had done absolutely no work for at all.

What happened was that Borelco started attracting interest from a big player. Steve had built Borelco up over the years and did not want to see it swallowed whole. In a move to parry the acquisition, he entered into a merger of Borelco with a company about its own size, Namier & Swanson, Inc. Naturally all kinds of finagling had to go on as to how the employment conditions of the two companies were to be made commensurate.

One thing that Steve knew Borelco would have to bring along as part of its culture was the lightning rods, because the men who had grown accustomed to the facility would have bitterly resented being made to give it up after the merger. It would have caused everything to get off to a bad start. But it was not all that easy a subject to raise with the other side.

"Look, Steve," said Joe, when the difficulty was explained. "If you want my honest opinion, there's absolutely no point in going out of the way to make trouble for yourself. If you think about it, everybody just takes it for granted that all parties concerned provide toilets for the staff; what's more, nobody is going to go to the trouble to specify what people are supposed to be doing in the facilities provided. What I suggest is that you simply explain that Borelco has been a pioneer in introducing height-friendly toilets to all its sites; this is a record you're proud of, and you don't want it lost in the confusion of the merger. Once the necessary construction has taken place on all former NSI sites you simply explain that you've found it most effective to outsource implementation of your sexual harassment policy, and you can leave the rest to me."

The net result was that they extended the facility to NSI, thus doubling Joe's business at a stroke.

A by-product of the merger, whose significance Joe was only to understand much later, was that Steve began to appreciate the possible benefits of restructuring, not to say downsizing, human resources. Steve had been finding Roy a pain in the butt for years; now, for some reason, some kind of friction seemed to be developing between Roy and one of the top earners in the company. Might the merger not offer a tactful way of easing Roy out the door? Unfortunately the CEO of NSI had been finding *his* head of human resources a pain in the butt for years, and he got in first with the ax – unlike Steve he was *way* ahead of the game, and as soon as the merger was mooted a strategic downsize was the first thing he thought of. So Steve had to not only keep Roy but give him a bigger team to foist blue M&M's on. He'd lost out this time. But the seed had been planted.

About six months or so after the merger it occurred to someone that BNSI, as it was now called, was now up to the fighting weight of the company which had originally threatened a takeover. So they merged with Vesey Syndicates, forming BNSV, and once again they took the height-friendly toilets and outsourcing of sexual harassment management with them. Then BNSV merged with Sinclair Products, and BNSVS kept the lightning rods, and by now the concept had extended right across the country without Joe having to do a thing.

He didn't have to do any work at all apart from keeping up the supply. That certainly kept him on his toes, but nothing compared to what would have been involved in drumming up that kind of business from scratch.

Because the thing was, every time there was a merger there would be a complete structural reorganization. People were getting made redundant to here and gone, they had other things on their minds than the realignment of the sexual harassment policy. Plus, if there were some new faces around, people didn't make much of it because they had other things on their mind. *Plus*, things were changing all over the place, so no one was going to question something like some construction on the disabled toilets. That was the *least* of their worries. So unlike the word of mouth referrals, where there was a lot of persuading to do after you got your foot in the door, here a succession of companies were just his for the asking.

By this stage, obviously, Joe was not able to carry the whole show on his own shoulders. He had had to recruit for that person in a thousand who is able to put across an innovative product to people who can be expected to be initially unreceptive or even hostile. He wasn't looking for hot shots — experience had taught him that this was not a job for prima donnas. He was looking for people with a genuine understanding of the dilemma facing the modern employer. He was looking for people with a genuine understanding of the dilemma facing women trying to put themselves through school, or bring up a family singlehanded. People with a genuine desire to help people resolve those dilemmas.

He was not wholly satisfied with the crew he had signed up so far, but a good businessman makes the best of the material he has to hand. We have to deal with people the way they are, not how we'd like them to be. A good businessman knows that and acts accordingly.

Anyway he had three guys on the sales team, and he had also taken on staff for the recruitment side, so that he was well positioned to take advantage of his big break when it came. The first merger took place just a year after Steve had approved the trial run, and within another two years Joe had installations in all 50 states of the Union.

On the positive side, Joe was never going to have to worry about cash flow again. Besides which, Lightning Rods was now the temporary personnel provider of first resort for one of America's largest corporations: This gave it a credibility which it had not had when it had only had a few small, relatively obscure clients on its books. People would come to Lightning Rods just looking for a temp. This was all to the good, since it offered further protection against the possibility of ghettoizing bifunctional staff. Not to mention a chance to spread the word if the opportunity presented itself.

On the negative side, Steve had finally succeeded in downsizing Roy out the door. He'd been foiled again after the second merger, when yet again someone *else* was quicker on the draw and someone *else's* albatross was given the old heave-ho. Third time around he knew better. No sooner had forces been joined than Steve made it clear, in subtle ways, that he would not be heartbroken if Roy walked the plank. Joe watched from the sidelines, little guessing that the outcome of the battle had relevance to himself; as far as he was concerned, he didn't care who ran human resources as long as they didn't interfere with the temp outsourcing. In this he was making a serious mistake.

Roy put up a good fight, but he knew it was time to quit. He was up to six bags a day; things couldn't go on like this. So he gave notice, accepted a big pay-off, and went home to brood. For some reason, the incident of a couple of years earlier kept coming back to haunt him. He had nothing to lose now by mentioning it, and one night, when he had had one too many to drink, he happened to mention it to his brother-in-law.

This, too, in itself, might have had no adverse consequences for Joe, but for one thing.

When Walter had left the Army after 'Nam, he had thought at first that he'd had enough of killing people.

Then he'd changed his mind.

THE NET CLOSES

One day Joe was sitting in his usual booth at the back of Stan's Grill, eating a char-grilled burger and drinking an ice-cold Bud. It was the end of a long day, and when he'd had a long day he liked to come to Stan's to unwind. Stan's was almost empty — it almost always was, which was one of the things Joe liked about it, though presumably it wasn't such a source of satisfaction for Stan.

Joe was just about to order another beer when a stranger walked in. He looked around, then walked down the length of the room with firm, even steps, and he stopped at Joe's table.

"Mind if I sit down?" asked the stranger.

Joe looked at the room of empty tables. He looked up at the stranger.

"What's going on?" he asked.

The stranger took out an ID from his inside pocket. "Walter Pike. FBI."

Holy shit, thought Joe. "Please sit down," he said.

The stranger seemed to know everything there was to know about Lightning Rods. Names, places, dates — the works. Also, he seemed to have a terrifying grasp of the law. He kept pointing out various legal irregularities relating to the services provided.

Joe couldn't really think of anything to say so he just kept saying, "Is that so? I didn't realize the law said that." It was no more than the truth, since Joe's attitude to the law was that it was something best kept at a safe distance – but for some reason the stranger seemed annoyed.

"Look, Joe," said Walter at last. "You don't seem to understand the gravity of the situation. You're in big trouble. You've been operating this service of yours in all 50 states, which means that you're not only in breach of Federal regulations on about 25 counts, you're also in violation of something like 892 separate laws at the state and local level."

"Huh," said Joe.

"You're in deep kimchi, pal," said Walter, and he began to list the various statutes which had been flagrantly breached. Walter had watched a lot of *Dragnet* as a boy; he knew just how to make a criminal feel like dirt.

Joe thrust his hands in his pockets and waited for it to end. If you start up an innovative business something like this is always in the cards. You go into it with that knowledge. The important thing is to decide ahead of time what's important to you.

There's an old saying that goes something like this:

Lord, help me to have the patience to accept the things I cannot change, the courage to change the things I can, and the wisdom to know the difference.

Now, the United States of America, with its 50 states, has one of the most complicated legal systems in the world. You're never going to change that; learn to live with it. *Because* the legal system is so complicated, it takes a lot of training to get on top of it, so that American lawyers are among the most expensive in the world. You're never going to change that either. What that means is that in the early stages, when you're just starting out, you can't afford to pay a lawyer to find out what the law requires. If you're starting up a new business, there's always a possibility that some aspects of the business may not be within the strict letter of the law. But if you are doing something that happens to fall foul of the law, you don't have a hope in hell of doing something about it.

What you need is the wisdom to recognize that fact, and the patience to accept it. If you can't deal with it, fine, don't start up a business. But if you're going to take that attitude, you might want to think about where the country would be if everyone had waited to get the green light from the law in its current form.

The thing you have to remember is that the law is made by human beings, with all the flaws and imperfections that that implies. Like all of us, they're just doing the best they can. They're not telepathic. They're not scientific geniuses. They can't tell what the world is going to be like tomorrow, let alone ten years down the line, let alone however many years have elapsed before you happened to come along with your idea. In other words, there may well be laws in place which are inappropriate to the world in which your idea can give people a chance to lead happier lives. But the only way to determine whether that is the case is to give your idea your best shot and see whether it takes off.

If it does reasonably well, you'll be able to afford a lawyer to tie up any legal loose ends that may have been left hanging. If it does spectacularly well, so that some of America's largest corporations have made it a part of their business enterprise, you may well be able to bring about any little adjustments to legislation that may be necessary to square the law with what people turn out to need. If it doesn't do so well, or if it does really well but prejudice stands in the way of legal reform, you can always just retire to the Cayman Islands with whatever profits you have managed to accumulate in the interim. The Cayman Islands have beautiful white sandy beaches washed by brilliant turquoise seas, and if you can't be content to spend your declining years in that kind of environment you're obviously the kind of person who's going to be miserable *wherever* they are, you might as well be in jail for all the difference it will make.

This was the way Joe had looked at the question of the law when he started out. Now of course, most of his clients had probably assumed that he had actually cleared the legalities before hanging up his shingle; they would probably be pretty upset to find they had been embroiled in something that was not strictly legal. But some of these clients packed a big punch. If they decided a facility was essential to the effective running of their operations, they could deal with the law a whole lot more effectively than Joe could. Even if they were upset, they would not let their emotions rule them; they would determine the level of value of the service, and take measures accordingly. And it was Joe's bet that not one of his clients would want to go back to the bad old days of unread guidelines and embarrassing workshops and sexual harassment tribunals, the days of not knowing when or where the ax would fall, the days when the most minor and dispensable of employees could suddenly turn up with a suit for a million bucks in damages.

Still, there's no point in gratuitously alienating an FBI agent. However philosophical you may be about being in breach of Federal regulations, if an FBI agent starts going into detail it's only polite to show concern.

"Gee," said Joe. "That's terrible."

Something in Walter's expression suggested he had not shown enough concern.

Sometimes the best thing you can do is just tell the truth.

"Well, the way I see it," said Joe, "is what would our Founding Fathers have done?"

"What do you mean?" asked Walter.

"Well, the reason we had the Revolution in the first place was no taxation without representation, am I right?"

"Sure," said Walter.

"But if you think about it, that was really just part of a larger issue, which was that people were being governed by laws which were none of their making. The fact of the matter is, Walter, that the overwhelming majority of laws in this country were made before you and I were even born, by people who couldn't *represent* us because we didn't exist. Now I don't know if you know this, but Thomas Jefferson said each generation should make its own laws and not be bound by the laws of its parents."

"I didn't know Jefferson said that," said Walter.

"Many people don't," said Joe. Joe had learned the fact in eleventh grade, in his American history class, at a time when the class was still called Americanism versus Communism, and he had never forgotten it. "And as a matter of fact," Joe went on, "we can actually *see* why that should be so. If your parents were anything like mine they were probably quite conservative on sexual matters. What Jefferson saw was that you have to make your laws fit where you're at now."

"Well, that's very interesting," said Walter, "but – "

"Also, the South had every right to secede," said Joe, drawn on by process of association to the other thing he remembered from eleventh grade. "If you think about it, they

234

had just as much right to break away as the colonies did to break away from England in the first place. The only actual difference was that they were on the same continent. Well, you're not going to tell me we should write to the Queen of England and apologize and explain that it was all an unfortunate misunderstanding. You're not going to *tell* me it's all right for *Hawaii* to secede because it's off in the Pacific. Nossir. Which isn't to say that slavery is not a terrible wrong. I'm not saying for one second that Lincoln was not a great man, I'm just saying sometimes we have to keep our heads and not get carried away by the Gettysburg Address."

"Well, I see what you're saying," said Walter. "And I have to say I never thought of it that way before. But for all practical purposes the law is the law."

"I accept that," said Joe. "I'm just pointing out that when Thomas Jefferson takes a different view, we have to ask whether we haven't gotten side-tracked somewhere along the line. Maybe we've thrown the baby out with the bathwater. Maybe we've failed to separate the wheat from the chaff."

"Well, Joe," said Walter. "You may be right, and you may not be right. That's not for me to decide. I don't make the laws; that's not my job. It's my job to enforce the law in its present state."

"I appreciate that, Walter," said Joe. "I know you're just doing your job."

"At the same time, it's sometimes necessary, in the interests of national security, to take a larger view."

As soon as Joe heard that he knew his *immediate* problems were over. He might end *up* in jail, but at least Walter wasn't going to haul his ass off to jail in the near future.

"Stan," he called over, "another coupla beers over here."

•

The beers came, and Walter said, "But you're right about one thing. Times *have* changed. That's why I think this has such a big contribution to make to the nation as a whole."

"In what way?" asked Joe.

"Well, for better or worse, the sexual drive of men in office is one of the biggest nightmares national security has to deal with. It opens the person in question to pressures you really don't want a person in that position to be under. Blackmail. Coercion. Extortion. In the old days, when the press knew their place, it wasn't so bad. JFK could do what he damn well wanted and the press would just look the other way. Today it's a whole different ball game."

"You can say that again," said Joe.

"Now the way I see it," said Walter, "is that by incorporating anonymity into your program you have actually stumbled on a feature that could make it very very helpful to men in authority. The whole worry about who someone has been involved with and what she might say would wither away. Because the thing is, the problem isn't *somebody* knowing what the guy has been up to – in the interests of national security, the Bureau has got to be kept apprised at all times. The *problem* is there's been no way to keep the *girl* from knowing."

Walter gave a world-weary smile. "Now don't get me wrong, Joe, but I think we can both agree that the product is not up there with Marilyn Monroe. But times, as I say, have changed. I think our leaders today recognize that they can't expect the same liberties people in their position could avail themselves of twenty or thirty years ago. I think the advantages of the program will make it very very attractive. And if we can work together to put something in place that deals with this issue effectively, I can guarantee you we'll find a way to get around the various statutes you are currently in violation of."

The fact is that every FBI agent looks back wistfully to the rapport between J. Edgar Hoover and the Oval Office. Ideally, the FBI should maintain that record of achievement. In fact ideally the FBI would establish that level of rapport with the incumbents of every public office at the state as well as national level. And it would be even more ideal if the FBI could have that kind of rapport with everyone in the country.

Now as soon as Walter started investigating Lightning Rods it had occurred to him that that ideal was nowhere near as unattainable as it had seemed heretofore. If the FBI had input into an innovative employment agency of this nature it would be *bound* to raise its levels of rapport to heights hitherto undreamed of. And of course there were all kinds of ways the Bureau could help to broaden the client base in directions where rapport had top priority.

Joe hesitated. In a way he was being offered an easy way out. With the FBI on his side he could stop worrying about the law. Or rather, to be accurate, he could go *on* not worrying about the law, safe in the knowledge that the FBI had everything under control. And I don't care *what* kind of hot shot you've got as a lawyer, no matter *what* you're paying he's never going to match that kind of guarantee.

On the other hand, he was used to running his own show. If he let the FBI in, they might well end up making a lot of demands that he would be in no position to refuse. *Already* Walter was talking offhandedly about doing away with something that was absolutely essential to the integrity of the firm: the anonymity that Joe had guaranteed both clients and staff. Now of course, it hadn't been possible to get things up and running without explaining the nature of the service to potential users – but knowing who the service has been *offered* to and knowing who actually *uses* it are two very different things. The computer generated opportunities and made them available to participants, who could accept or decline as they saw fit. Neither Joe nor anyone else knew what participants chose to do – no one knew except the actual participant himself.

On the other hand again, how much choice did he actually have?

"Something you got a problem with?" said Walter. An FBI agent has to know when a show of force will be effective, and when to give someone a little space. If you're trying to get someone to cooperate with the Bureau on a long-term basis, it's usually better if they feel they've made the choice of their own free will.

"It's just," said Joe.

"Just what?" said Walter. "Remember, I'm here to help you. The Bureau thinks you're doing some very important work, Joe. The thing is, though, that you've cut a lot of corners. A free society is only possible if everyone in it plays by the rules. People can't be allowed to treat the law with contempt, Joe. That's where the FBI comes in."

"It's just that anonymity really is essential to the product," said Joe. "People who make use of the product are placing their trust in Lightning Rods. They're relying on Lightning Rods to *protect* their anonymity. After all, if they wanted they could always get *satisfaction* elsewhere. Anonymity is our key selling point. If we take *away* that anonymity in my view we'd be cheating the client. And that's not how I do business."

"I'm glad you brought that up, Joe" said Walter. "It's important to get these things out in the open. We can't afford to have any misunderstandings if we're going to be working together."

Joe didn't like the sound of this. He signaled to Stan for another couple of Buds.

"I'll tell you how I see it, Joe," said Walter. "I can see a place for anonymity in the private sector, unless, obviously, an individual in the private sector was giving cause for concern. In which case obviously we'd want to keep track of his movements. But in the public sector a different set of rules apply. The thing is, though, let's not get obsessed with a single issue. Let me explain where I think you can make a real contribution, and see how it grabs you."

"OK, shoot," said Joe. He remembered suddenly that he was speaking to someone who carried firearms. "Let me rephrase that," said Joe.

Walter laughed. "That's all right, Joe. We're trained to only resort to violence as a last resort. You have absolutely nothing to worry about. You're in safe hands."

Joe gave a half-hearted smile.

"Let me explain where I'm coming from," said Walter. "The thing is, Joe, you don't understand what it's like for people in public office. I'm not just talking about the ones who make the headlines – the ones with strong sexual urges beyond their control. In some ways those are the least of our worries. The fact is, anyone in that kind of position is under constant pressure. They go into office thinking they'll be in a position of power, and what they discover is that they're constantly having to appease people. The ones we at the FBI *really* worry about are the ones who just repress it. You don't know when, or how, they're going to blow. Now as I see it, a service such as yours could provide a safety valve for people who could otherwise do a lot of damage – *without* making them vulnerable to unscrupulous people who would take advantage of their *need* for a safety valve."

"I'm sure it would do all that and more," said Joe. "My point was just that I'm not comfortable with introducing the element of surveillance – "

"What I'm saying," said Walter, "is that in the circumstances of the public sector anonymity is not viable. Appropriate monitoring is indispensable. What I want you to ask yourself, though, is whether the greater good achieved, by making the service available to these vulnerable individuals, wouldn't outweigh the sacrifice of this particular feature of the product."

Joe sighed.

"I see what you're saying, Walter," he said. "But this really is a radical departure from the Lightning Rods philosophy as I understand it."

"I understand that, Joe," said Walter. "But the thing you have to remember is, as things stand, legally you could be closed down tomorrow. Maintaining the service in its present form is not really an option at this present time."

Joe finished off his Bud and put down the can.

"The thing to remember," said Walter, "is that the Bureau would identify suitable venues for installations. We would provide a range of locations that you, as a private businessman, would have difficulty accessing."

A good FBI agent knows when his words have struck home. Walter could tell that the subject was beginning to lean in his direction.

"That's why I'm saying, you should try to avoid getting obsessed with a single issue," he said persuasively. "Essentially, we're offering you the chance to stop worrying about the legalities and develop the product to its full potential."

There comes a time when you have to recognize that you can't always do things exactly according to plan. Like it or not, Joe was beginning to accept that this was one of those times. And compared with serving several concurrent life sentences the offer was not unattractive.

"This is a rare opportunity for you to serve your country and make a profit at the same time," said Walter.

"You're on," said Joe. "And you know, Walter, it's really not as bad as it looks."

"Oh really?" said Walter. "How do you figure that?"

"Well, at least I'm not in violation of the Equal Employment Opportunities Act."

DOING GOOD BY DOING GOOD

Joe was not entirely comfortable with allowing the FBI access to what had previously been strictly confidential information. For about a month, in fact, he found himself going home early and spending time on fantasies that a successful businessman usually doesn't feel the need for. A successful businessman does not usually need to revisit *The Adventures of Superdick*, however much they may have thrilled him in seventh grade. He does not need to solace himself with a story about a sexually demented superhero, drugged by an evil genius, and the superhuman sexual powers of a 13-inch Kryptonite-powered dick. But for some reason none of the more sophisticated fantasies which Joe had developed over the years seemed to help.

After a while, however, Joe began to see that there had been more than a grain of truth in what Walter had said. He began to see that Lightning Rods and the FBI were able to achieve a synergy that produced results.

Joe worked closely with Walter on introducing lightning rods to the public sector, and he could see for himself that in many cases it made all the difference to someone who, albeit sexually indiscreet, was in other respects the better candidate. One timely installation had worked wonders for a candidate whose two previous campaigns had been marred by mud-slinging of the worst kind. The candidate had pledged to clean up three dead rivers, a project Joe felt strongly about, and for once he was able to keep his campaign focused on the issues rather than on unsavory personal details. When it came to the issues it was no contest, and he won hands down. So that was something to feel good about.

Also, Joe was able to go major league on height-friendly facilities in a way he wouldn't have been able to, on his own, for *years*. If ever. He had installations in forty-nine state capitals, not to mention DC and NYC. The important thing was not just the actual number of buildings involved; it was what it symbolized. Something like this sent a message to people. An elected government should represent *all* its citizens. If it forgets about the little guy, something has gone badly wrong.

So Joe tried not to think about what the FBI might be up to, and just focus on the positive. The way he saw it was, what you do when you grow up isn't always what you imagined as a kid. When you're a kid you always think you're going to be an astronaut, or a quarterback, or something like that; you can't understand why so many grown-ups spend their lives doing boring things like selling vacuum cleaners. When you grow up there are some financial facts you have to face. Sure. But you also recognize that there are different ways of making a contribution. Nobody ever dreams of growing up and going into sewage disposal – and yet we would all be dying of horrible diseases if someone didn't make a career of doing just that. Well, Joe had found a way of cleaning up the world in an area that was *just* as important. And in the process he had *also* found a way of making the world a more welcoming place for people who had happened to be born short through no fault of their own.

Sometimes, when he was feeling uneasy, he would think of Ian, still back in KC (as the natives call it) reading about John Foster Dulles. Unless some new hero had supplanted JFD. The thing Joe would think was that he had come across Ian for the briefest of encounters and then gone on his way. But Ian just went on being short, day in, day out; it was something the guy had to live with on a daily basis. And the main thing the guy had to live with was people going around stereotyping him as short. Which, if you think about it, is pretty stupid. Joe was 5 feet 10 inches tall. When he was feeling lonely, did he go around looking for other people the same height because they'd be sure to have a lot in common? No, he did not. And it wasn't just some little idiosyncratic eccentricity of Joe's, either. *Nobody* goes around looking for someone their height to make friends with. Because having the same height in common with somebody else is about the *least* interesting thing you can have in common. Well, if how tall you are kicks in as a significant fact below a certain height, and if it gives you something in common with other people that height, it doesn't take a genius to see that *height* is not the operative factor. It's other people's perception of that height.

The way Joe saw it was, you can't do much about people's perceptions. But at least other disadvantaged groups get some perks to go with it. Well, when was the last time you heard of someone being hired as the token dwarf? Never, that's when.

Joe could only stand by while Walter did his best to promote rapport between the Bureau and candidates for political office. But when it came to installing appropriate facilities it was another matter. In fact, as soon as Walter had outlined the new opportunities that would arise, Joe had thought through the nature of the facilities from scratch. This was a chance to make an impact that would not come again.

If you're an ideas man you don't just stop having ideas because cash flow is not a problem. You go right on having new ideas, and when you have an idea you want to see that idea in action. One of Joe's ideas was an idea for height-friendly ATMs. You could have a screen and keypad that could slide up and down the wall according to preference, and not one but *two* potential slots for the card and the cash. You could have some kind of gadget that would automatically adjust the screen depending on which slot you put the card in, though it would probably take some pretty fancy programming. Or you could just have some kind of manual device, a button or a handle of something, and the user could select the appropriate cash slot from a menu. Unfortunately he hadn't been able to think of a way to justify it to the client.

What Joe now decided was that he was going to just put his foot down. He wasn't even going to *argue* with people. He was going to just go right ahead and let the chips fall where they may. If you have height-friendly ATMs and toilets in government buildings that sends a message to the business community. They may choose to ignore that message. But at least they can't say you didn't send up the smoke signals.

That was how Joe made the best of things. He was getting involved in politics, after all, and people who get mixed up in politics soon discover they can't have everything exactly the way they want it. All they can do is try to achieve some good in the areas where their hands aren't tied – because they sure can't do a heck of a lot where their hands *are* tied. And they're bound to be tied some of the time. That was what Joe discovered working with Walter. An uncomfortable discovery in many ways, but he had to make the best of it.

•

Walter, on the other hand, felt pretty damn good about the way things were going. In the first place, he was serving his country to the best of his ability. In the second place, the new development was doing his career no harm at all. And in the third place he had the satisfaction of seeing the FBI strike a definitive blow against one of its oldest and deadliest enemies.

When Walter had joined the FBI its energies had been divided. Communism was still a threat to national security, and taken seriously as such. Also, the war on drugs took its toll. Not to mention organized crime. There simply wasn't the *manpower* to take on the CIA, and the FBI was to pay the price for that understaffing. While the FBI's attention was otherwise engaged the Agency's sphere of influence grew by leaps and bounds. Of course, in some ways the CIA was its own worst enemy – even just reading the papers you could tell it was just one balls-up after another, and the papers didn't report *half* of what those clowns got up to. You might well think it was only a matter of time before operations were handed over to an organization that knew what it was doing. Unfortunately it didn't work that way.

Well, what comes around goes around. If the lightning rod level of surveillance, with the level of control it implied, became a reality, the FBI would at last be able to control one of the greatest existing threats to national security.

8

THE FUTURE IS OURS

COMPETITION

Joe's synergy with the FBI was a major factor in extending the operations of Lightning Rods. Ironically, however, the thing that kicked Lightning Rods into a whole different ball park was that Joe suddenly started facing competition.

In the early days Joe had gone out of his way to underline the difference between a lightning rod installation and prostitution. Because the concept was so new prostitution was the first thing people thought of, and a lot of groundwork had to be done to enable people to understand the distinction between the two categories.

In fact, of course, as it turned out, some of the most effective lightning rods had had careers in the more traditional branches of commercial sex. For some reason it was easier for someone with that kind of background to pick up a few office skills and move over to lightning rod work, than for someone with an office background to expand her repertoire the other way.

In retrospect, maybe that wasn't so surprising. Women who made the move across from, say, secretarial work were making a lot more money than they were used to, but they also had to get used to working conditions that presented a whole new range of challenges. Women who came the other way tended to see things differently. In some cases, they might actually see their take-home pay go *down*. Others might find they'd only achieved parity. And they might well find they were working longer hours to *achieve* that parity. What they were looking for, in other words, was not primarily a big financial pay-off. What they were looking for tended to be closer to all the things Joe had initially outlined as the main attractions of the job.

As one woman later explained, she had originally started out with an escort agency because the money was good; then she had built up her own clientele and the money was even better. But there's something about that whole lifestyle that gets you into the habit of spending everything as soon as it comes in, or even before – at one point she had owed something like $30,000 on her credit cards. You keep meaning to save, but you never do, and every once in a while you wake up and look in the mirror and you look like shit and you realize the money is going to keep going out but sooner or later it's going to stop coming in. Trouble is, it can be quite hard to find some other line of work that pays enough to make it even conceivable.

So from her point of view, lightning rods was ideal as a second career. At 17 she had hated the idea of a nine-to-five job, but at 27 she was able to see the attraction of a job that came with a healthcare plan and a pension plan and a reasonable guarantee of employment when she was 37 or even 47 or 57. There would obviously come a point when the lightning rod element of the job would be removed on grounds of seniority, but by that stage she would be qualified for a responsible mainstream position. Besides, the high earnings of the lightning rod segment of her working life would be reflected in her pension.

And besides. Quite apart from the long-term financial implications, in many ways lightning rod work was a lot less stressful than what she was used to. One of the things that gets on your nerves after a while is having to interact socially with people you wouldn't choose to mix with if you had a choice. Not to mention having to watch physically unattractive people get undressed – that gets old *real* soon. Lightning Rods removed that whole factor of the equation. It was really only after it was gone that you realized how much of your life you'd spent with a big fake smile plastered across your face.

In the early stages, when nobody had heard of Lightning Rods, women who might have been interested in this kind of career move didn't know it existed. Recruitment, as a result, was *hugely* labor-intensive, and even after the recruits had signed on they required a level of through-care which was not really in the spirit in which they had been invited to join in. Later, as word started to get around, things improved considerably. Lighting Rods started to attract a type of applicant who had already resolved whatever conflicts she might experience relating to providing a service with a sexual component. The numbers on the register continued to grow steadily but counseling costs leveled off. The ratio of recruitment time to successful applications fell dramatically. In many ways, the new development was a welcome one.

As is the way of these things, however, every silver lining has a cloud. As word spread through the mainstream sex industry of the opportunities available for women who were concerned about the future, it reached others with a different agenda.

People were not slow to see that there had to be openings for more than one operator in the new field. Naturally enough, however, they brought their own preconceptions with them, preconceptions formed in an industry with its own scale of values. Coming from that background, they were not always able to appreciate just what it was that Joe had been trying to achieve. They tended, as a rule, to focus on the economics of it, and, in many cases, to misunderstand what they saw, overlooking the value built into the system which was made possible by the economics.

Joe's first challenger was a man who had started out in the escort agency business. Ray had escort agencies in ten major cities, and it was in that light that he automatically interpreted the lightning rod concept.

His first thought, before he had time to go into the concept in any detail, was just that this could offer a solution to a problem that sooner or later anyone who runs an escort agency is going to have to confront. The problem, essentially, is that you are dealing with a highly time-sensitive commodity. Every girl has a sell-by date, and unfortunately individuals may not necessarily have the degree of self-awareness which would enable them to recognize the arrival of that date and take appropriate action without input from a third party. Nobody wants to hurt anybody's feelings, but if you have an agency with a reputation to uphold sooner or later you're going to have to spend some time getting people to face facts.

That can be a difficult process, especially if someone is going to have to go through a period of financial readjustment as a result. You don't like to see someone walk out the door knowing she is going to have to make some compromises. You don't like to see someone walk *in* the door when it's all ahead of her, knowing the kind of choices she is potentially going to have to make a few years down the line. There are, obviously, individuals who take the kind of financial precautions that mean they don't have to make those choices when the time comes, but those individuals do tend to be in a minority, and unfortunately there is little you can do.

What Ray initially thought, anyway, was that a lightning rod agency could be a way of easing the girls over into a less time-sensitive environment. It *had* to be an environment that was less intolerant of physical deterioration than an escort agency; what that meant, obviously, was that there would be a window of opportunity which would give a girl the chance to capitalize on her experience while picking up some new skills. It was a more humane way of dealing with a problem that was not going to go away, and it also made good business sense. If a girl looks after herself she can have the body of a 25-year-old well into her thirties – problem is, the face is the first thing to age. Well, by the looks of things, anyone who *did* look after herself could go on profiting from it, and enabling her agency to profit, *well* after the age when she would otherwise have had to start being realistic about her expectations.

So he set up an agency with branches in the major cities where he already operated. He had a lot of contacts in the business community, and he was able to pitch the service at cost-conscious companies because he did not have the over-heads in terms of counseling, recruitment, and so on. The only thing was that he did not achieve the level of integration of lightning rods into the workforce that Joe had aimed for, because it would be pretty obvious who in an office was going to the Ladies seven or eight times a day. Also, he never really grasped the intricacies of managing bifunctional personnel. He made the mistake early on of hiring one girl out as a bifunctional receptionist. Being an over-deployed lightning rod she had to be away from the switchboard on a more or less hourly basis, and the company went through the roof.

After a while he decided it was more trouble than it was worth.

Word of the new agency came to Joe's ears, of course. Some of the girls who came to Lightning Rods had started out with Lightning Escorts, so Joe was able to get a pretty clear picture of what his rival had to offer. Frankly, it didn't worry him. It wasn't worth worrying about. It was only too obvious that the guy was totally out of his depth.

When Mel started out, on the other hand, he had a couple of escort agencies, but he also had a wider range of interests. What it meant was that he was able to see a basic difference between escort agency work and lightning rod work which had somehow been missed. An escort has to have personality to be successful; a lightning rod, on the other hand, keeps personality on the other side of the wall.

Then Mel looked into the economics of it, and he frankly couldn't believe his eyes. Here you had apparently otherwise sane businessmen shelling out hundreds of thousands of dollars, sometimes *millions* of dollars, to provide staff with randomly accessed pussy. He kept adding up the figures and saying I don't believe it. Finally he believed it. And as soon as he believed it he knew there had to be money in it.

The wastage in the system was so humongous that anyone who understood the first thing about business could undercut it by 50% and still make an obscene profit.

Because the first thing that struck Mel was that the guy who had dreamed all this up had confused two totally separate issues.

One issue was the question of protecting the anonymity of the men availing themselves of the facility. This was a valuable feature, no two ways about it. Instead of men going out and jeopardizing health and reputation you got everything safely boxed off so that release was available in a protected environment. The thing to remember is that you never want to entrust your health or reputation to the type of person who would provide paid sex in the first place. That's a good rule of thumb. This was the first facility Mel had ever seen that even began to address that concern.

But the issue of protecting the anonymity of the personnel providing the service was a completely separate issue. Considered from a purely business point of view, there was no advantage to it whatsoever. In other words, there was no need to go to all the trouble and expense of incorporating highly qualified female staff into the scheme at grotesquely inflated salaries. If you eliminated that constraint, you could have a specialized pool of talent already in position and constantly available throughout the day.

If you do that, you are instantly able to cast your net that much wider. Because you can then provide the facility within an office building serving a multitude of clients – many of them small companies that would not find it practical to have a lightning rod as a member of staff.

The thing that the guy who had come up with the idea had not seemed to realize was just how much pussy is out there, or how economically it can be provided. Because the guy had obviously come from a pretty sheltered background, so he did not understand the obstacles confronting many potential applicants. Say you take a woman who has made it into the country somehow, back home she wouldn't even have an indoor toilet but here she has all kinds of conveniences you and I take for granted. Someone like that would count herself lucky to get the minimum wage for a forty-hour week, especially if for a lot of the time she just waited for people to come in. Well, if someone is willing to put in the work we should give them the chance to stand on their own two feet, because that's what this country is all about.

Now if you have the potential to have the facility on demand, one thing you have to think about is the economics of it. The way he saw it was the economics of it were completely cock-eyed. Lots of companies provide a canteen for their staff, and they may even subsidize the meals, but they sure as hell don't provide them free of charge.

What that meant was that there was a lot of scope for turning this into a credit on the balance sheet. For instance, you could offer a subscription which included so many uses of the facility per month. Guys who for whatever reason felt the need to make extensive use of the facility could pay accordingly, guys who weren't interested could just leave it be.

The more he thought about it the more insanely underexploited potential leaped out and grabbed him by the balls. Any working girl knows a john likes to try things he can't necessarily get from his girlfriend. Guys these days go online, they realize there's *more* to life than pussy, there's anal, there's double, their girlfriend doesn't see eye to eye, this is something they would expect a facility to accommodate. Why would a businessman try to *penalize* this expectation, when he could be getting bigger bucks for his bang? Get *real*, people.

So he drew up a proposal for a streamlined operation, and a lot of people who had been interested, but who had felt they could not go the whole nine yards, decided that it actually made a lot of sense.

THERE'S MORE TO LIFE
THAN MONEY

There are people who would feel threatened by something like this. You go away on a business trip with a monopoly on an innovative product for helping firms negotiate the minefield of sexual harassment. You come back to find that not only do you not have a monopoly, but somebody else is offering a no-frills service for less than half the price. Many people would find that very, very threatening.

It's not until something like this comes up that you find out what kind of a person you are. Joe came back from a business trip and one of his sidekicks broke the bad news, and it was obvious that Mitch was worried.

"I don't have to tell you what this means, Joe," said Mitch. "There's a lot of people will find this very attractive. Especially the whole concept of having the guys pay for their use of the service, something like that is going to practically sell itself."

"Well, let me have a look at my mail," Joe said, just as if Mitch had announced nothing more serious than the death of an office plant. "See if anything interesting has come in."

He went into his office and started opening letters, and the interesting thing was that he didn't feel threatened in the *slightest*. What he actually felt was *relief*. Years later he would tell the story and people would never quite believe that you could feel that way when a hitherto unsuspected competitor has suddenly turned up to undercut you by 50%. That's because most people don't see the larger picture. They focus on what's in front of their nose.

Most people never think about the fact that you only ever get one life to live, and a business is just a part of that life. If you don't think about how your business fits into your life as a whole, one day you're going to wake up and find you sold away the only life you were ever going to get for the sake of the bottom line. Well, there's only so much money you can spend in this life, and the thing you've got to remember is, the one thing you can't buy back, no matter *how* much money you have, is time. A billion dollars won't buy back one single minute.

From a purely financial point of view, you can't beat a monopoly. If people want the product, they have to come to you, and you can pretty much name your price.

But from the point of view of getting what you want out of life, it depends what the monopoly is.

If you have a monopoly on something that carries a lot of prestige, something that makes people look at you with respect, that's fine and dandy. You also have the monopoly on all that prestige, and good luck to you.

But if you have a monopoly on something that people look at askance, it's not so cut and dried. If your product is something that attracts a certain amount of odium, all that odium has only one place to go. It goes straight to you.

It doesn't matter what precautions you may have taken to make sure the product has no undesirable side effects. People will just go on associating the product with all the undesirable side effects it would have had if you hadn't taken those precautions. It's no good reasoning with them, in fact you won't ever get the *chance* to reason with them. They'll just make up their minds out of prejudice, without even giving you a *hearing*, and the only thing you can do is learn to live with it.

But suppose someone comes along with a similar sort of product, only stripped of all the features that were built in to protect people from undesirable side effects. The product is cheaper, so a lot of people are going to be tempted. A lot of people are going to find, to their cost, what it means to have full-fledged prostitution going on right in the heart of their office. A lot of people are going to discover, too late, just what kind of effect that has on staff morale. They'll find out just what it means for people to be working on a daily basis in that kind of degrading environment.

Gradually, word will get around.

Before you know it, you'll be able to point to the unholy mess that ensues when you cut corners. The fact that you charge *twice as much* shows that you are offering a quality product, a BMW instead of a Datsun.

What Joe saw, in fact, was that the appearance of this sleazeball on the scene was the one thing wanting to give Lightning Rods, Inc. respectability. It wasn't just that it would be the lesser of two evils. It would be seen as the champion of family values, of corporate ethics, of responsible business practice. Companies that might have hesitated to even let Joe in the door because of what people might think would now be calling *him* up. Because the fact was, he had a product no company could afford to be without. Now they'd be able to admit that.

What he saw was that this was his chance to be part of the mainstream. Because let's face it, nobody likes to be a pariah. Nobody likes to be someone people can't afford to be

seen in public with. Nobody likes having to arrange a convenient time to meet when there's no one around but the cleaners.
Nobody likes having to lie about what they do.

What this cheapskate was doing was letting Joe off the
hook. Joe had been carrying the can for close on four years
now. He was almost thirty-seven. If he played his cards right,
there was no reason why he shouldn't spend the rest of his
life as a respected member of the business community.

You can't put a price on something like that. Once you've
got enough money so you can have whatever you want without counting the cost, you don't *need* to keep piling up more.
You don't *need* the business of 100% of all the companies in
America; if you had it, you wouldn't know what to do with it.
Once you've got the money you need, you can start to think
about all the other things that matter. For instance, suppose
you could appear on the cover of *Newsweek* or *Time* magazine
as Businessman of the Year? Suppose you could get an honorary degree from Harvard? You can't buy something like that.
You have to earn it by being perceived to be an outstanding
individual. It's not enough for you to *be* outstanding – other
people have to recognize you for what you are. And here this
piece of slime had upped and handed Joe a life of distinction
on a platter.

Well, thanks for the favor, buddy. Sayonara, and see you
in St. Louis.

Joe came out of his office when he had finished looking
through his mail, and did his best to reassure Mitch. He didn't
say anything about the honorary degree from Harvard, which
might not carry that much weight with Mitch – Mitch was a
nice enough guy, but limited in his outlook. But he gave an
inspiring pitch about BMWs and Datsuns, pointing out that

people had never really fully appreciated the BMW until the Datsun came on the scene. He pointed out that *Playboy* had never really been seen as all that tasteful and intellectual until *Hustler* came along.

"I guess," said Mitch.

"Mitch," said Joe. "I want you to do something for me."

"Sure, Joe," said Mitch.

"I want you to go out and buy a copy of *Playboy* and a *Hustler* and read through the magazines, comparing the two. Look at the type of advertisers they're attracting. Look at the type of article they're running. And what I want you to do is ask yourself what type of reader each magazine is catering to. Then I want you to ask yourself what kind of implications you think that has for us. If you're still worried, come back and talk to me and we'll talk this through."

"Yeah, OK," said Mitch. "Do you want me to do this now?"

"That's exactly what I want," said Joe. "Why don't you take the rest of the afternoon off, and we'll talk tomorrow."

The main reason Joe had suggested it was he thought it would do Mitch good to spend the afternoon reading a couple of recreational magazines and getting paid for it. Mitch tended to take things too seriously. The entertainment business is just that – a business – and it's easy for people at the business end to forget that it's meant to be fun. If you lose sight of that, before you know it you'll have lost touch with the very people who are your bread and butter.

The way Joe saw it was a little recreational reading would help Mitch to loosen up and stop stressing about something that was really not that big of a deal.

SOMEONE TO TALK TO

While Joe was obviously not stressed by the new development, he found as the day wore on that he would have liked to have someone to talk to who also saw that it was no cause for concern.

Now, having sent Mitch home, he suddenly got the idea of inviting Lucille out to dinner. He called her up and Lucille said Sure in the cool way that still unnerved him after all these years. All these years he'd known her, and he'd never invited her back to his pad.

As soon as money was not so much of a problem Joe had bought a loft apartment. He had furnished it in black leather and chrome, which looked pretty snazzy, and he had bought an expensive sound system in case he brought anyone back and wanted to play some music. He had not had much chance to spend a lot of time there, but it was a good investment. Besides, every once in a while he would come back into town and go to this prestigious address and take the elevator to the penthouse. And he'd walk through the door and think This is mine, and remember the days when he'd lived in a disgusting trailer. The apartment never got the chance to be disgusting, because he had a cleaning lady twice a week.

He took Lucille to dinner at a restaurant, and at the end of the meal he suddenly thought Well, here goes nothing, and he asked if she would like to come back to his place and listen to some music.

"That sounds very nice," said Lucille.

So they went back to the penthouse together. So far, Joe had only bought two CDs: a Miles Davis CD that the sleeve said was a classic, and a CD featuring the Brazilian jazz artist Carlos Jobim. Jobim was the guy who had written "The Girl from Ipanema," as well as some other songs Joe hadn't come across before. Most of them were in Portuguese which was probably why he didn't recognize them. If you're using music to create an atmosphere the thing you have to avoid is buying the type of music that is labeled easy listening, what you have to do is seek out music that sounds like easy listening while being real music. That was what made the Miles Davis CD ideal, especially if you turned the sound right down.

Lucille seated herself on the black leather sofa.

"Now what can I get you to drink?" asked Joe.

"I'll have a Diet Coke," said Lucille.

Joe's heart sank. He thought he had thought of everything. The first thing he'd done on moving in had been to stock the bar with every drink known to man, expense no object. And he thought he'd covered the mixers. He had six kinds of mineral water of both the still and sparkling varieties; he had tonic water and soda water and bitter lemon; he had fruit juices up the gazoo. He had Coke, Pepsi, Canada Dry Ginger Ale, and 7 Up. He even had Mountain Dew. Most people's idea of a swinger is probably not someone who drinks Mountain Dew, but hey. If you're a self-made millionaire you're entitled to do as you please in your own home. Anyway, whatever, for some reason it just hadn't occurred to him to buy diet drinks.

"Lucille," he said. "I'm really sorry about this, but it just so happens that I'm all out of Diet Coke. I've got Perrier? Plain, lemon, and lime? Maybe a lime Perrier on crushed ice? How does that grab you?"

"I'll have a Scotch on the rocks," said Lucille, crossing her legs. Lucille was wearing a sleeveless white dress. While not built like Dolly Parton, Lucille definitely had assets that were wasted in her present line of work. Joe found his eyes drifting down. He hastily forced them to keep going as if he had just accidentally happened to take in her breasts on the way to looking at her hemline on the way to, um, her face.

"Coming right up," said Joe, heading for the bar.

He returned with two glasses of Scotch and a plate of cheese and Triscuits and a bowl of peanuts.

Joe was beginning to see that he now faced a social dilemma which had never been faced in the whole history of the human race. What do you say to someone if there is a one in five chance that you have had a close encounter of a ventro-dorsal nature through the wall of a disabled toilet? It's one thing if you're just having a casual conversation, the way they did when they met for lunch or dinner. But what if you're sitting on a sofa back at your place, with mood music playing in the background? Almost anything you do will look like you're taking things for granted because there is a one in five chance that you have already effected an entry through the rear of the premises and because whether you actually did or not the person gave her consent to such entry.

If it had been anyone other than Lucille it might have been that it would have been fair enough to take certain things for granted, especially taking into consideration the fact that she had agreed to come back with him. But Lucille was a real dark horse. You never knew where you stood with her.

Joe took a sip of Scotch and ate a peanut.

Prostitution is degrading to all parties concerned, but one thing you can say about it, a man who has spent a certain amount of time dealing with hookers probably develops his social skills. Whereas the whole point of lightning rods was that it was a purely physical transaction, with no *social* interaction of any kind; that was what enabled it to keep the atmosphere of the office from being poisoned. That meant that however often you found physical release for your needs, you were never going to be any further along in terms of talking to members of the opposite sex.

Joe was still mulling this over, while making polite chit-chat with Lucille, when Lucille said, "What's that noise?"

There was a kind of high-pitched whining noise coming from the back of the apartment.

"Oh, that's Elroy," said Joe. "It can get kind of lonely, living all on your own, so I thought I'd get me a dog. There's a dogwalking service to walk him when I'm out of town. Means I don't have to come home to an empty apartment. I thought I'd better keep him back in the study in case you didn't like dogs."

"I don't mind dogs," said Lucille. "Maybe you'd better let him out. He sounds kind of upset."

Joe went back to the study and opened the door and Elroy did five or six leaps up to shoulder height to say hi before tearing out to the living room to bark frantically at Lucille.

"Will you cut that out?" said Joe.

Arf! Arf! Arf!

Lightning Rods*

"Now Elroy, I'm warning you," said Joe. "You keep this up and you're going straight back to the study, so don't say I didn't warn you."

Arf! Arf! Arf!

Elroy suddenly spotted the corner of the rug. He hurled himself at it and started gnawing on it, growling.

"Hey!" said Joe. "That's a three-thousand-dollar rug, Elroy."

Grrrrrr.

"I'll get his ball," said Joe. He rummaged in the telephone table and got out a greying tennis ball. "Elroy! Elroy! Looka here!"

Grrrrrr. Grrrrr. Grrrrrr.

Joe bounced the ball in the direction of Elroy. Elroy leaped up and grabbed the ball and started tearing around the room.

"Elroy! Hey! Over here, boy!"

Elroy rushed up with the ball. Joe grabbed it and started to wrestle him for it.

Grrrrr. Grrrrr.

Elroy's tail was spinning like a propeller. If a dog had the aerodynamic properties of a helicopter he'd have taken off.

"You doggone son of a gun," said Joe. "What kind of a no-good hound do you think you are, anyway?"

He managed to regain possession.

Arf! Arf! Arf! Arf!

"What kind of dog is he?" asked Lucille.

Joe flicked the ball into a corner with a quick snap of the wrist. Elroy went after it.

"I couldn't tell you," he said. "Some kind of mutt. I think there's some beagle in him somewhere. The way I see it is, what use is a pedigree that you've got to pay hundreds of dollars for? It's personality that counts."

Elroy was back with the ball, jumping up and down. A dog is not able to use language; it's not able to say "Nyaa, nyaa, nya nya nya, bet you wish *you* had a disgusting spit-covered old tennis ball" – at least not in so many words. It has to jump up and down and wag its tail to get the message across.

Grrr. Grrr. Grrr.

"What I did was, I got him out of a pound," said Joe, retrieving the ball and throwing it. "The way I looked at it was, even if I'm not around that much and somebody else has to look after him, at least he isn't *dead*. And he has a pretty good life."

Elroy got the ball and disappeared behind the sofa with it.

Grrrrrrrrrrrrr.

Joe rolled his eyes. "Elroy, just how do you expect us to carry on a conversation with you making that kind of a racket?"

Grrrrrrrr.

"Did you pick 'Elroy,' or was that the pound?" asked Lucille.

"It was my idea," said Joe. "It's kind of a tribute to Elvis, in the first place because it starts with 'El,' and also Elvis was The King and 'Elroy' means 'the king' in Spanish. I thought it was kind of appropriate because the minute I laid eyes on him I thought of that song 'You ain't nothin' but a hound dawg.' I don't think he actually has any hound blood in him, it was just something about his character made me think of it."

"I see," said Lucille. "Well, it does seem to suit him."

Grrrrrarf! Grrrrrrarf!

"No, the pound had a totally different system," said Joe. He was feeling more at ease for some reason, there's nothing like a cute animal for breaking the ice. Now that he was more relaxed his eyes were just sort of *aware* of the Partonesque aspects of Lucille instead of zeroing in on them like targets painted with invisible bull's eyes. He put his hands in his pockets and walked over to the table and picked up his drink. "The pound had these ten names that it used in rotation, they used the names of the seven dwarfs plus Snoopy plus those two Dalmatians in *101 Dalmatians*, and when they'd gone through the list they'd start over again, so you'd get Sneezy II unless Sneezy I had been adopted or put to sleep, in which case the name would be available again."

"Huh," said Lucille. "Sounds kind of depressing."

"You're telling me," said Joe.

"Isn't it kind of inconvenient? I mean, if you start with seven dwarf names plus Snoopy plus Pongo, that's nine boy's names and only one girl's name."

"I wondered that," said Joe. "I got into a conversation with the receptionist while they were drawing up the paperwork. She said it just depended on who was admitting them, sometimes you get someone who thinks Snoopy is unisex so they just hand out all the names on a first-come first-serve basis, and sometimes you get somebody who gets really fixated on it and names all the female dogs after the female Dalmatian."

"Perdita," said Lucille.

"That's right. Perdita I, Perdita II, Perdita III, sometimes they'd have twenty-five Perditas all at the same time."

"I never heard of such a thing," said Lucille. "You know, it really makes you wonder sometimes."

Joe picked up his drink and took a sip of Scotch. The conversation didn't really seem to be going anywhere. He thought suddenly If it hadn't been for me, guys all over the country would still have to be having this kind of conversation every time they needed a release for their physical urges, we'd be right back where we were four years ago!

Because it wasn't exactly that he wasn't enjoying himself, but imagine what it would have been like if there was no alternative. He didn't have to imagine it, because he'd been there. He knew what it was like. Everyone knew what it was like.

If I die tomorrow, I've made my contribution, he thought.

He started telling Lucille about the guy who was offering the cut-price service. He made his comment about BMWs and Datsuns, and he made a joke about getting an honorary degree from Harvard.

"I don't think you have anything to worry about," Lucille said calmly.

Joe thought that anyway, but it was good to hear someone else say it, especially after watching the three stooges quietly panicking.

"In fact, I don't think this guy has thought things through. If you ask me, there are a lot of ramifications that he hasn't even considered. As long as you have the full-service lightning rod installation, you have a way of removing any possibility of inappropriate contact. If a particular lightning rod happens to be related to a member of staff, you can ensure that the computer never generates that pairing. How's *he* going to achieve that? As I understand it he's offering supply on demand, it isn't going to *be* computer-generated because a guy can just walk in any time day or night provided he's prepared to pay. It's just asking for trouble. Sooner or later you're going to end up with someone accidentally paying for contact with his own flesh and blood. Well I'm sorry Joe, but that's just plain wrong. No reputable company is going to want to be associated with something like that. I'm not saying he won't find a market – there probably *are* people who'll rush into something like that to cut costs, without thinking about the consequences. But there are plenty of companies that wouldn't touch it with a bargepole."

Wow, thought Joe. He remembered all over again what it was that had attracted him to Lucille in the first place. She was one smart cookie. This was an absolutely brilliant point. It was bound to come in handy when his customers started asking how this other guy could offer the prices he was offering. The way he looked at it, it was practically unanswerable.

The really great thing about it was that it just helped to position Lightning Rods, Inc. as the defender of family values. I'll take the high road and you take the low road, buddy, and I'll be in Scotland afore ye.

Lucille looked imperiously around the room as if to say How dare someone do something that disgusting on the same *planet*. Joe had to hand it to her. The gal had style.

Partly because Joe was not spending much time there, there were not that many books in the room. There were some glass and chrome shelves on the same wall as the built-in sound system, and on them there were just the two CDs and a few paperback books. If you want to succeed in business it's up to you to make the best possible use of your time; the thing you have to remember is, you'll have *plenty* of time to catch up when you've made your pile. Think of all those hours you'll have to kill in the nursing home – one day you'll be glad you saved up something to do. But there are times when business is so stressful you have to get a grip on yourself, if you don't *make* yourself unwind you'll find yourself making bad decisions. Better to spend a couple of hours quietly reading – at least it doesn't do any actual *harm* – than to rush around trying to plug holes in dikes that don't exist.

This was the way Joe looked at it, and since he had been spending a lot of time on planes in the past year or so he had ended up doing quite a lot of reading. If he finished a book on the outward journey he usually just left it at the hotel, but if he brought it back with him he would put it on one of the shelves to give the living room a lived-in look.

Lucille was looking at the shelves without comment. Now her eyes swept away.

"Oh, you have the *Encyclopaedia Britannica*!" exclaimed Lucille.

As a former rep Joe had been able to get himself a good deal. It was a lot of money, but then you never know when you're going to need to look something up – if you have a crazy schedule, you could do worse than just have a *Britannica* in the home. The Internet is a wonderful thing, but it multiplies a millionfold the dual hazards of creative reportage and fantasy enhancement; if you *need* the straight poop on some area of research which you have over-hastily sketched in for a client, the *Britannica*, with its team of accredited experts, will give you a wealth of bibliographical citations not easily refuted by casual recourse to the wackos at Wikipedia. In this type of eventuality focus is all-important; the apparent saving represented by an online subscription or CD, with the attendant opportunities for XXXX-rated distraction, may too easily prove a false economy.

Lucille stood up and walked over to the two-shelf unit provided for the work. She took out a volume of the *Micropaedia* and flipped it open to a page.

"I just love this old thing," said Lucille. "When I was a kid I used to think it would be just wonderful to have one of my own. It just *smells* so good. It's got that nice clean leather smell on the outside, and then on the inside that smell of clean new pages, it always smells as though you're the first person to ever open to that particular page."

Considering how rarely Joe had call to consult it, Lucille almost certainly *was* the first person to open to that particular page. "I know what you mean," said Joe. "Sometimes I just open it to any old page just to see what's on it."

Lucille was reading her page with a smile. "You learn something new every day," she said. "If you don't mind my asking, how much does it actually cost?"

Old habits die hard. *Britannica* salesmen treat the price of the encyclopedia as classified information, to be released only to customers who have shown they can be trusted. "Oh, I got a special deal," said Joe. "I don't know *what* they're asking these days."

Lucille sat down on the unit. She crossed one leg over the other in the kind of movement that attracts a mental whistle. She opened the volume to another page. "All these people you never heard of," she said. "All these facts. It makes you want to just curl up and read it for hours."

Every salesman knows that it's a numbers game. Joe suddenly realized that he was looking at exactly the kind of customer he had spent all those fruitless months in search of. If one person in twenty in Eureka, Mo. had had this kind of attitude, he would never have stopped selling encyclopedias in the first place. His whole life would have been different.

A salesman has to face facts; that's one of the saddest things about the job. Because what you realize is just how many things are the way they are because people could not make a living out of appealing to people's better nature. He himself had taken pride in selling the *Britannica* when he had first started out; the vacuum cleaners had been his second choice, and the lightning rods had been his third choice. We live in the kind of world where people end up with their third or fourth or fifth choice because there just isn't the money in their first choice. Every once in a while you get this glimpse of what the world would be like, not if everyone was perfect, but if just a *few* more people were just a *little* bit better than they are. You get this glimpse of a world where people could get by, maybe not with their first choice, but with a close second.

Elroy came out from behind the sofa, whining softly. He came over to stand by Joe, and dropped the tennis ball temptingly on the floor.

Joe nudged it with his foot. Elroy snatched it up, growling and wagging his tail.

Joe thrust his hands in his pockets again. Snap out of it, Joe, he told himself. We don't choose to be the way we are. There's something in a dog that has evolved to get excited about a ball. For whatever reason, whatever it is that makes people get excited about the *Encyclopaedia Britannica* has evolved in relatively few people. The average man has evolved to be interested in sex more than the average woman. You're making a living out of a world you didn't make, out of people who evolved the way they happened to evolve. All you can ever do is try to increase the net sum of human happiness to the best of your ability.

I know, he said, but —

But nothing, he said. Sure it would be nice if there were more people like Lucille, but she's a very special lady.

He remembered the spiel he had come up with in the early days about looking for the woman in a thousand. That was Lucille all right.

He was feeling kind of down, if the truth be told.

Lucille looked up. "Is anything the matter?" she asked.

"No, not really," he said. He sat down on the unit, facing her across the open *Micropaedia*. "It's a funny old world," he said.

Elroy dropped his ball hopefully on the floor. Joe didn't have the heart to get into the game. Lucille picked it up with a gingerly thumb and forefinger and tossed it away from her; Elroy scampered after it in hot pursuit.

Everyone gets discouraged from time to time. It's what you do with it that counts. Joe sat looking rather glumly at the upside-down page, thinking about family values.

Sometimes your own mind can actually be more of a mystery to you than the most enigmatic of strangers.

He was just sitting there, thinking You have to deal with people the way they are. Not how they ought to be. That's what being a successful businessman is all about.

All of a sudden he thought: But the reason they're not how they ought to be is there are so many obstacles in the way. Most people want to do what's right. It's just hard. The more people sincerely want to do what's right, the more important it is to help them. They have to accept the way they *are*, and learn to deal with it, if they're ever going to stand a chance of improving.

And suddenly he had an incredibly brilliant idea.

GENIUS STRIKES AGAIN

Joe had thought of an idea so audacious only a genius or a lunatic could have come with it.

The idea was, what if it had been a mistake to concentrate initially on a secular environment?

Events were to prove that he was no lunatic.

He'd made a mistake. A *big* mistake.

But it took genius to *recognize* that mistake.

To be fair, sales is all about targeting.

It's a numbers game.

Target, target, target, target.

Some people are always going to say no.

Now a good salesman can turn that no into a yes. Granted. The question is how long you have to spend turning a no around. A good salesman picks people who are likely to say yes without wasting his time.

Well, in his innocence, he had imagined that a highly Christian environment would not be amenable to the type of product he had to offer.

He said later that he could look back and weep.

One thing you learn in sales is never take anything for granted.

He was a long way from reaching saturation in the type

of organization he started out on, but one thing you learn in sales is to look ahead.

Time doesn't stand still.

Four years ago he had had the field all to himself; now suddenly out of a clear blue sky he had El Cheaparooney to contend with. It was time to move on to pastures new.

Well, if there was one segment of the market where El Cheapo didn't have a hope in hell of finding takers, it was in that part of the country where people care about family values.

So he approached a couple of companies that he had left off his initial list.

What he did was he made most of the points he usually made, but he left out the material about the baboon.

Instead he made the point that a girl who has been brought up in a Christian home should not be subjected to inappropriate behavior and led into temptation at the office. A business has an obligation to protect the purity of its female staff. At the same time we are dealing with fallible human beings. A man may try to do right but fail. A business has an obligation to protect the men on its staff who while trying to follow Christ's path suffer the weakness of the flesh. Which is better: to leave a man to consort with prostitutes, endangering his health and that of his family, endangering his reputation – knowing that if he is discovered the disgrace will ensure that the downward path is swift and sudden! Or to provide an outlet, a hygienic outlet for those carnal frailties?

Joe had been arguing of late, to clients in the secular community, that untold man-hours were being lost to the scourge of cyberporn, thereby making the physical release offered by Lightning Rods an indispensable safeguard to productivity. The argument proved surprisingly adaptable to the Christian setting.

"Remember," he would say, "he that commits adultery in his heart has committed adultery as much as if he had done the deed. But a man who is afflicted by impure thoughts is drawn back again and again to the source of the poison. Is it not better that a man should commit a single impure act, in a couple of minutes, than that he should stain his thoughts with impurity for hours at a time? Is it not better, if he cannot resist temptation, to fornicate once in the flesh than a hundred times in the heart?"

With these words did he persuade both of the companies he approached. He was then able to tell new prospects that he knew of at least two companies with a strong commitment to Christian values which had implemented the scheme.

"Look at Mary Magdalene," he would say. "Let him who is without sin among you cast the first stone."

AND AGAIN

Now it was in the course of his dealings with the Christian community that an idea came to him that was breathtaking in its simplicity.

It goes without saying that the vast majority of firms with Christian values were always going to be hostile to a scheme which accepted man's fallen nature and tried to do something about it. You've got to expect that when you're dealing with a fundamentally conservative group of people. He obviously had to feel his way very carefully, going by hints that people threw out, the odd name dropped in seemingly casual conversation. By and large he managed to steer clear of firms where there was nothing doing, and to zero in on the ones where he stood some chance of success. But as every salesman knows, you can't win 'em all.

He had an appointment one day with a man who according to the scuttlebutt was a likely prospect.

For some reason the man did not respond as expected. He just kept staring at Joe.

"Is this true?" he said at last.

"Scout's honor," said Joe.

"I never heard of such a thing," said the man.

278

"Well, obviously it's quite a new concept," said Joe. "It runs the risk of being misunderstood. Confidentiality is one of the things we guarantee our clients. That's why, to all outward appearances, my agency is just like any other employment agency."

"And people use you? You've been in business a long time?"

"Four years," said Joe. "Long enough for copycats to spring up all over town. If I could just make this one point, it's especially important for a Christian firm to not settle for cheap imitations. Sure you can get cheaper, but money isn't everything. I don't need to tell you that the ideal of Christian forgiveness and charity can sometimes seem to be more honored in the breach than the observance, as it says in the Lord's Prayer, forgive us our trespasses as we forgive them that trespass against us, but if somebody gets known to have sinned the attitudes of his fellow sinners can sometimes be the biggest obstacle to getting back on the upward path."

Jim avoided his eyes. Up to this moment Jim had probably been hoping that Joe hadn't heard about him; now he was probably guessing that he probably had.

"Now the copycats, to offer the prices that they offer, can only make a profit by using the very cheapest materials. Mexicans, Nicaraguans, not that there's anything wrong with that, but you see what I'm saying. And believe you me, that's what we're talking. Whereas Lightning Rods has always made it a policy to use only the highest quality of staff. Which means you're not going to have a lot of people wandering around the place who are going to attract attention. They'll look just like the people you've already got on your staff."

"But in that case," said Jim. "You mean . . . you mean there's no way to tell?"

"That's exactly what I do mean," said Joe.

"This is dreadful," said Jim. "I knew things were bad, but I didn't know they were *that* bad. What is the country coming to?"

Joe was already listening philosophically, waiting for the interview to end. If you're a salesman you can tell when a lead isn't going anywhere.

"I have a twenty-year-old daughter, just moved up to New York," said Jim. "I didn't like the idea a whole lot to begin with. Now for all I know she's working in this sort of environment – "

"Well, if she is, she'll probably be finding she's treated with a lot more respect than she would be in offices that haven't made an installation," said Joe. "Which is just the point I was trying to make just now."

"As far as *I'm* concerned, I'd be willing be pay over the odds just to have a guarantee that a scheme of this kind *wasn't* in place," said Jim.

And that was when Joe had his brilliant idea. "Well, Jim," he said, "if I should happen to hear of such a company I'll be sure and let you know."

Joe went back to his motel. The slight disappointment about losing the sale was more than compensated for by his excitement over his new idea, which had the simplicity of genius.

The new idea was this. Suppose you offered a firm the chance to outsource its whole human resources department to an independent contractor – a contractor which guaranteed its staff provision to be 100% lightning rod free. America is a country which accommodates a wide range of perspectives – there were *bound* to be people out there who would prefer to work in a guaranteed lightning rod free environment, whether because they had been brought up by religious fundamentalists or whatever. Well, where there are people with a fanatical preference you *know* there's got to be money in it.

Five years ago there would have been no market in catering to that preference, because the actual concept of the lightning rod protected workplace did not exist. He had *created* an opening for a product, he had turned into a marketable *product* something people had previously just taken for granted, just by bringing into existence the opposite of that product! Well, if an opening for a product has arisen, *entirely* thanks to you, it's only fair that you should be the first to profit from it.

Of course, some people would probably argue that there were plenty of reputable employment agencies already in existence that never had gotten involved in the provision of lightning rods and never would. Anyone who wanted to steer clear of proactive sexual harassment prevention could just go to Manpower or Kelly or whatever and know they had absolutely nothing to worry about.

That just showed how little they knew. Sure, you can go to Manpower and get the type of product they've been providing all along. But what you're not going to get is the type of safeguard that someone who's been in the lightning rod business from the ground up is automatically going to build into a product.

Because look. If you're going to offer a cast-iron guarantee that no physical outlet will be provided for drive-orientated individuals, and believe you me there are just as many of those among the Christian community as anywhere else, a responsible employer has to ensure that those employees are protected in some other way.

Well, say a young woman for whatever reason doesn't like the idea of working in a firm where there are lightning rods on the premises. She doesn't object to provision being made for one kind of physical function, she doesn't get up in arms about the fact that there are toilets in the building, but for whatever reason she doesn't care for other types of physical function being provided for. *Fine.*

In that case there's absolutely no reason why she wouldn't be willing to make some concessions to a firm that was prepared to offer the kind of environment she wants to work in. As a safeguard to the firm that has made an offer of that kind, at no small risk to itself, she should be prepared to sign a waiver certifying that no sexual harassment charges will be filed against individuals or the firm if some form of behavior takes place which would not have taken place if a physical outlet had been provided.

To put it another way, a firm that has an anti-lightning rod policy owes it to itself to hire the type of employee who is prepared to offer it that kind of safeguard in exchange for the more conservative type of working environment provided.

Which is where an employment agency with an affiliate in the lightning rod side of the business has such an edge. If you've spent as much time as Joe had talking to people recoiling in horror and revulsion at the very *idea* of a lightning rod, you couldn't help but know there was a definite market for a product that guaranteed staff would never even have the *possibility* of rubbing shoulders with one. No two ways about it, it had been stressful at the time – it's discouraging to lose a sale at the best of times, let alone get the kind of looks people give you if you have transgressed one of their socio-sexual taboos.

But it meant he now knew just how strong the feelings were that the original product aroused; he knew just how many people out there would think no sacrifice too great to avoid using it.

Well, if people feel that strongly about something, you *know* there's got to be money in it. Manpower and Kelly and the more conventional agencies didn't even know there was something to feel strongly *about*.

What it meant was that he had an edge. There was going to be a window of opportunity, just when lightning rods started to be publicly known and public feeling would run high, when a firm that had thought through the implications of the LRF office would be well positioned to pick up the ball and run with it.

Joe walked up and down his motel room. "Joe," he said, "I really think you're on to something."

He walked up and down grinning and thinking Boy oh boy oh boy.

The beauty of it was, of course, that it would consolidate his position as a defender of family values. People would see that all he was trying to do was make the world a better place. Because whatever people may tell you, money *isn't* the only thing in life. And the beauty of it was, no matter how you looked at it, he was going to make one heck of a lot of money.

He decided to call Domino's to order in a pizza.

If you want to be a rich man, you need to be able to do two apparently contradictory things. On the one hand, you need to be able to operate at the level of people with a lot of money without losing your cool. Good restaurants, fine wines, fast cars – you need to be able to look like you take that for granted. But on the other hand, you can't afford to get cut off from your roots. Because at the end of the day it's ordinary people, with all their strengths and limitations, that wealth is based on. If you lose sight of that, you won't have your money for long.

"You know what," he said pacing up and down, waiting for the pizza to arrive. "I actually think this unexpected competition is a good thing. Because if this guy hadn't come along I would probably have just gone along getting stuck in a rut, instead of opening up new markets. The way I look at it is, the guy has actually made me a present of two totally new markets that a guy like that is in no position to exploit."

He walked over to the window and opened the curtain.

The motel had been built fairly recently by an exit off I-95. From where he stood, he could have been looking out on anywhere in the country. He could see a McDonalds, and a 7-Eleven, and a Waffle House, and a TCBY.

Every single one of those represented an idea that someone had had to have, an idea whose value had probably been far from obvious at the time. When did they actually start *having* 7-Elevens, anyway? At one time having a store that was open from 7 in the morning to 11 o'clock at night had been a real innovation, something no one had thought of before. People had probably said "Why would anyone pay those kind of prices at 11 p.m. when all they have to *do* is wait and go to the grocery store the next day? Or fine, maybe people might go if they're desperate, but how's a store supposed to survive on its takings between 7 and 9 a.m. and 6 and 11 at night?" Well, the answer is before you, buster.

Or take a Waffle House. Probably when someone came up with the idea everybody had scoffed and said *nobody* is going to want to eat *waffles* after 11 a.m. at the absolute *latest*, who ever heard of eating waffles throughout the day?

There's nothing like the feeling that you've had an idea that everyone expected to fail, and gone and made a success of it. And yet it's funny to think how big a part luck plays in these things.

If I hadn't walked to the 7-Eleven that day and seen that heron, I might be selling vacuum cleaners to this very day, he thought.

"You've been lucky so far, Joe. You've already succeeded at what you set out to do. But don't ever take that for granted. There's bad luck as well as good in this world. You can't afford to rest on your laurels."

The sky was darkening, but it was not yet dark. In the west the molten gold of the setting sun slipped through the hills, and in the darkening hollow the yellow arches and the 7-Eleven and the Waffle House and the TCBY were glowing in the golden light. High above a flock of geese sped southward in a V formation, and on the highway the cars and trucks sped north and south.

He remembered standing on a beach in early morning watching the pelicans. A pelican does what it's designed to do. A sandpiper does what it's designed to do. A goose instinctively heads south in a V-formation in a V formed of other geese instinctively heading south. It doesn't check out the beach and experiment with a sandpiper lifestyle. It does what it's designed to do.

The thing about animals, though, is that they live in this incredibly beautiful world without noticing. It can be the most beautiful morning since the world began and a bird will be out there going after worms, oblivious to the beauty that surrounds us. Whereas a human can just stop the car and get out and look around and think What am I doing with my life?

We all have a choice, thought Joe. Every single one of us has a choice. Look at all those hundreds of people driving up and down I-95. Every single one of them could pull over to the side of the road. There's nothing to stop someone pulling over to the side and looking around at this beautiful sunset and choosing to follow a different path.

What he thought was, An animal can't decide to be a better animal. It doesn't know the difference between right and wrong, so maybe there's no such thing as *being* a better animal. It just has to do what comes instinctively. Whereas sometimes what comes instinctively for a human can be actually wrong. That's why it's important to remember that there's more to life than being a success. Sure, if you do something it's important to give it your best shot. But it's also important to be a good person. You can't ever take that for granted either.

"Look at Ian," Joe told himself. "Here's a guy who never did anybody any harm, one day he's just sitting on the bus minding his own business, looking forward to reading page three of *The John Foster Dulles Book of Humor*, and out of the blue some guy from Keene, New Hampshire asks him a question and gratuitously makes an allusion to his size. Instead of making an offensive reply right back, which would have been only too easy to do, the guy just quietly answers the question. If that's not turning the other cheek, I don't know what is. The fact is, he's a better person than I am. By a *long* shot. I may have done something to raise public awareness of the need for height-friendly facilities, but I've got a lot of work to do on myself. A *lot* of work."

He stood looking out. TCBY, 7-Eleven, and the Waffle House were now in shadow.

Suddenly — whether by accident or through the

mysterious workings of some higher power – he felt the need to take a leak.

He walked into the bathroom, and a big grin broke out on his face. A sign on the wall said: FOR YOUR COMFORT AND CONVENIENCE WE HAVE INSTALLED AN ADJUSTA™ HEIGHT-FRIENDLY TOILET. FOR MAXIMUM SAFETY IN USING THE ADJUSTA™, PLEASE FOLLOW THESE SIMPLE INSTRUCTIONS. Underneath the instructions was a sign in red letters. PLEASE DO NOT ALLOW CHILDREN TO PLAY WITH THE ADJUSTA™. THE ADJUSTA™ IS NOT A TOY. PENALTY FOR MISUSE $200.

Joe pressed the height button and the Adjusta went whirring right on down and stopped a few inches above floor level. It obviously wasn't hooked up for the lightning rod application, so there was no need for the facility to take it below the floor; no, they'd just installed it as their standard john. Joe pressed the seat button and the seat went right on in to the point where a two-year-old could have sat on it without falling through. Far out.

He stood there pressing the buttons while the Adjusta went up and down and in and out because hell, he *invented* the damn thing. It gave him a warm, happy feeling just finding it there unexpectedly. Because this was a major chain motel. All over the United States people would be checking in and whether they had little kids with them or just happened to be personally on the small side they would find conveniences that did not discriminate. Plus, you just *knew* those kids would get a real kick out of trying it out. Whatever the motel management might decree.

Then he remembered that he had come in here for a reason. He answered the call of nature, and he was just zipping up his pants when something occurred to him. If you're an ideas man you never know when or where your next idea is going to hit you. It can happen at the craziest times, times when the *last* thing you'd think you'd be thinking of would be ways to improve the lot of your fellow man.

What he suddenly thought was that he had designed a toilet that went down, and later he had enhanced the product with a seat that went in. It had never even crossed his *mind* that you could have a seat that went *out*.

"You know, Joe," he said. "There *is* something you can do. Something you can get to work on right now, before you start introducing a product into new markets in a form that may not be appropriate to those markets."

Because the thing that occurred to him, thinking back to that incident all those years ago on the bus, was that he had been *way* too judgmental about the guy with the paunch. So he was fat. Is that a crime? What right did *he* have to go around condemning people? Sixty per cent of Americans are obese. Or it might be more. Was he going to go around condemning sixty per cent of the population?

"Because the thing is, Joe, it's no good saying lots of *other* people feel the same way. You're in a position where that kind of attitude has consequences. You saw for yourself the trouble the guy had finding a seat he could fit into. This could have been an opportunity for you to think seriously about the product. But no, you went and introduced enhancements that would benefit one person in 14,000, without even *thinking* of enhancements that could be of value to the male half of sixty percent of the population. Well, I'm telling you here and now, Joe, that's not just bad moral sense – it's bad business sense. And here you are, thinking of moving into the *Bible* Belt – a region of the country that has *way* more than its fair share of persons in the jumbo category – and instead of taking reasonable precautions you're about to do just what you did when you were starting out and didn't know what you were doing. Rushing in without stopping to think."

Sometimes you have to be hard on yourself. It's easy to make excuses; sometimes you have to just refuse to accept those excuses. He walked back into the bedroom and started pacing up and down.

On the toilet side, of course, it wasn't strictly true that the Adjusta benefited only a small minority of the population. But all you had to do was look *around* you to see that there were a lot of people whose needs were not being catered for. If somebody happens to have thighs that are four feet in circumference, you don't have to be a genius to see that a toilet seat with a maximum span of fifteen inches, and a rim three inches wide, is *not* what the doctor ordered. In fact, if you think about it, the whole rim concept starts to look like a blind alley. What you want, at least in *public* conveniences, is a bench with a hole in it. An *adjustable* hole to accommodate persons of small stature. It's obvious when you think about it, but then sometimes that's all genius amounts to – seeing something that's obvious when you think about it that nobody ever thought about before.

Joe was still pacing up and down when something else occurred to him. For whatever reason, he had suddenly remembered a program he had once seen on the Discovery Channel about sumo wrestlers. One gross detail of the sumo lifestyle had stayed with him all these years, and this was the fact that the guys were so fat they couldn't wipe themselves – that little job got delegated to some other lucky son of a bitch.

Well, it may be gross, but you can say this for the Japanese, unlike us they're not ashamed of the body so they actually dealt with the problem. In our society, on the other hand, people are so totally grossed out by this kind of fact of life that even *toilet* manufacturers don't want to know. Because if you think about it, it would be the easiest thing in the world to fit every john with a kind of upside-down shower head, so people could clean down there at the press of a button without having to actually get within arm's reach. But as far as *our* society is concerned the hygienic problems of people of above-average size are just that: *their* problem. You'd think people would be *ashamed* to condemn their fellow-citizens to substandard hygiene in public conveniences. It doesn't work like that. What people *do* is, first they provide inadequate facilities; then they blame the *fat* person for not achieving a standard of cleanliness that can only *be* achieved with adequate facilities.

The more Joe thought about it, the more he couldn't believe he'd never thought about it before. Instead of addressing the problems of the obese individual responsibly, insofar as those problems impacted on his own line of the country, he'd just sat back and jeered. Well, in all probability that jeering had cost him an obscene amount of lost business. All he could say was, if he was going to take that kind of attitude, he had it coming to him. Because the more he thought about it, the more he could see the oversize market had significant implications for the lightning rod trade.

"For better or worse, Joe, we live in a society where fat is not perceived to be physically attractive. If sixty per cent of the population are perceived to be physically unattractive, you *know* there's a lot of sexual frustration going on there, which in an office environment can be deadly."

It was dark outside. Where the highway snaked through the hills the bright white headlights, the small red taillights of the north and southbound cars were all that could be seen.

"Besides which, it's not just a question of purely commercial considerations. A better business environment is important in achieving a better balance sheet. Sure. But there's more at stake here than money. Because the thing of it is, if a class of people is perceived to not be physically attractive, a disproportionate proportion of those people are going to be turning for satisfaction to commercial sex *anyway*. With all the risks that entails. Well, if people are *already* disadvantaged by their appearance, it's just not right that they should be *further* disadvantaged by being put at the mercy of prostitutes and pimps. Surely we, as a society, should not be forcing oversized individuals to choose between sexual deprivation and disgrace. Surely we should not be *adding* to their burden but, on the contrary, doing what we can to lighten the load."

The McDonalds, the TCBY, the Waffle House, and the 7-Eleven were brightly lit, and the parking lots they stood in were lit by tall streetlights whose dull yellow light fell here and there on the scattered cars.

"*Besides* which, there are other people we should be taking into account. What if someone gets married and *then* puts on the pounds? You just *know* something like that is going to put a strain on a relationship. The couple may have all *kinds* of things in common, there's just this one little source of friction. If you were able to *remove* that source of friction you'd be doing everyone a favor."

The geese were fifty miles further on their journey, winging their way swiftly southward in the soft night sky.

"It's up to you to start taking your responsibilities seriously and do something about that. There comes a time when it's not enough to just go on taking. There comes a time when you have to give something back."

Joe stopped by the window. High above, in the black sky, was one bright star.

"I'll try to be more considerate in future," he vowed. "I'll try to be a better person. I'll try to let my success be a force for good. After all, all any of us can ever do is try. All you can *ever* do is do the best you can."

THAT'S ALL, FOLKS

Opinion will probably always be divided as to the ultimate value of Joe's contribution. It would be hard to find anyone with a bad word to say for the Adjusta; many people, however, would have thought better of Joe if the height-friendly conveniences had been his sole claim to fame. The lightning rods seem destined to remain controversial.

The narrow purview of the program, focusing as it does on the presumed needs of heterosexual men, has attracted widespread concern among heterosexual women and the GLBT community alike. Its unquestioned dismissal of hard-won gains in the realm of sexual expression, many fear, has grave implications for the prospect of genuine equality in the twenty-first century.

Others have challenged the very foundations of the enterprise.

When a top litigation lawyer and a justice of the Supreme Court have come up the lightning rod route, it's clear that the program offers genuine opportunities to the right individuals. What's more, the successful marriage of a former lightning rod and one of the country's richest men, a self-confessed heavy lightning rod user, shows that the facility is not necessarily damaging to the private lives of participants.

And even the bitterest enemies of the program admit that the sex scandals of the late twentieth century seem to be a thing of the past. The lightning rods achieved exactly what Walter hoped they would achieve: They took the lid off the pressure cooker. Insiders at the Department of Homeland Security, moreover, have voiced unqualified admiration for this safeguard to our imperilled democracy.

On the other hand, the successful lightning rods were all pretty exceptional individuals. Joe's original quest for the woman in a thousand was an apt one. He might have added to that a quest for the man in a thousand who could see the work in the same light: In spite of several media campaigns to re-educate the public, most men continue to be uncomfortable with women in their family making this kind of contribution to the corporate environment. Critics argued that the vast numbers of women involved in the program inevitably placed pressure on people who are *not* exceptional and couldn't be expected to be. In fact, some people took this to the extreme of arguing that it should never have been decriminalized in the first place.

There is a streak of Puritanism in the American psyche that goes right straight back to the Pilgrims, and that streak has been an unmitigated blessing to the American criminal since time immemorial. What these critics fail to recognize is that if a demand exists for a service, and you criminalize that service, the only people who benefit are organized crime. As it happened, however, Joe was working hand in glove with Walter Pike, and as everyone knows, organized crime doesn't stand a chance when the FBI is on the job.

•

Joe had stopped worrying about the legalities, or rather he had stopped thinking he might one day have to *start* worrying about the legalities, as soon as he and Walter shook hands on the deal. And in fact Joe had nothing to worry about.

Walter had nothing but praise for Joe's outreach work among the Christian community. He was equally supportive of Joe's plans to develop a service for people who were uncomfortable with the concept of a lightning rod. He reiterated that Joe had nothing to worry about, and as it turned out Walter was as good as his word.

To insist on a strict observance of the written law over the laws of necessity, of self-preservation, of saving our country when in danger would be absurdly sacrificing the end to the means – nobody puts these things better than Thomas Jefferson, and Walter was second to none in admiration for our third President. Still, there's no point going around *looking* for trouble. Nobody at the FBI likes breaking the law unnecessarily. In the long term, if inappropriate legislation happens to be in place, the simplest thing is to just get rid of it and replace it with something feasible. It's just a matter of knowing who to call.

There are pieces of legislation which would leave everyone better off which would be political suicide for a politician to be seen to vote for, let alone propose.

Every politician knows that. Luckily, over the years ways have been found to get around one of the drawbacks of a democratic system. For example, a good way to get around the problem of the vote is to tack the piece of legislation on as a clause in some other piece of legislation, something everyone would *want* to be seen to vote for, like Hurricane Disaster Relief. Hurricane Disaster Relief is a good example, as a matter of fact, because everyone is going to realize you have to get something like that passed into law with a minimum of delay, you wouldn't expect someone to hold up a bill like that nitpicking at this or that amendment.

That just leaves the politician who has to put his John Hancock on the actual proposal that is going to get tacked on. A tried-and-true method of getting around this problem is to frame the language of the bill in such a way that it does not specifically mention the thing that would be political suicide. A skilled politician knows how to express himself so that the language will permit a desirable set of events to fall within the law, without allowing it to appear that he anticipated anything of the kind.

If something is in the interests of national security a man with the good of his country at heart will do things he might not do for purely personal gain. A member of Senator Johnson's staff drew up an amendment relating to Vending Machines and Workplace Stress Reduction, so that it was ready to spring into action at the first suitable opportunity. He included a school milk provision just to be on the safe side.

It sometimes happens that nature is not as dramatic as we might like her to be. For some reason there just weren't any floods or other natural disasters of a scale to hit the national press. He was beginning to think he was going to have to tack it onto a Fisheries and Forestry act, which was always a possible – sometimes you can get away with slipping the legislation into something so boring you wouldn't expect anyone to read it. But luckily a small hurricane swept in out of the Gulf of Mexico in the nick of time. The Vending Machines and School Milk Amendment got quickly added to the Hurricane Ethel Disaster Relief

Bill, which was rushed right through out of concern for the victims of Hurricane Ethel.

There's an old Chinese saying: Politics is the art of the possible.

That's true as far as it goes. But there's something else that's important to remember. The father of our country said it best, so we'll let George Washington have the last word.

In America anything is possible.

ACKNOWLEDGMENTS

David Levene introduced me to *The Producers*. Mel Brooks wrote "Springtime for Hitler." I'm especially grateful to Jeffrey Yang and the staff at New Directions for their enthusiastic support, and to Edward Orloff for excellent business advice: I wish more agents were like him.

Dear readers,

With the right book we can all travel far. And yet British publishing is, with illustrious exceptions, often unwilling to risk telling these other stories.

Subscriptions from readers make our books possible. They also help us approach booksellers, because we can demonstrate that our books already have readers and fans. And they give us the security to publish in line with our values, which are collaborative, imaginative and 'shamelessly literary' (Stuart Evers, the *Guardian*).

All subscribers to our upcoming titles

- are thanked by name in the books
- receive a numbered, first edition copy of each book (limited to 300 copies for our 2012 titles)
- are warmly invited to contribute to our plans and choice of future books

Subscriptions are:
£20 – 2 books – two books per year
£35 – 4 books – four books per year

To find out more about subscribing, and rates for outside Europe, please visit: http://www.andotherstories.org/subscribe/

Thank you!

CONTACT

To find out about upcoming events and reading groups (our foreign language reading groups help us choose books to publish, for example) you can:

- join the mailing list at: www.andotherstories.org
- follow us on twitter: @andothertweets
- join us on Facebook: And Other Stories

This book was made possible by our advance subscribers' support – thank you so much!

Our Subscribers

Adam Mars-Jones
Adrian Goodwin
Adrian May
Agnes Jaulent
Ajay Sharma
Alannah Hopkin
Alasdair Thomson
Alastair Dickson
Aldo Peternell
Alec Begley
Ali Smith
Alice Nightingale
Alison Hughes
Alison Layland
Alison Macdonald
Alison Winston
Amelia Ashton
Ana Amália Alves
Ana María Correa
Andrea Reinacher
Andrew Blackman
Andrew Marston
Andrew Tobler
Angela Thirlwell
Ann McAllister
Anna Athique
Anna Holmwood
Anna Milsom
Annalise Pippard
Anne Longmuir

Anne Meadows
Anne Withers
Anne Marie Jackson
Annette Nugent
Apollo Libri Kft

Bárbara Freitas
Barbara Glen
Barbara Latham
Barry Wouldham
Ben Thornton
Benjamin Morris
Brendan Franich
Briallen Hopper
Bruce Ackers
Bruce Holmes
Bruce Millar

Caroline Barron
Caroline Perry
Caroline Rigby
Catherine Mansfield
Cecilia Rossi
Charles Boyle
Charles Day
Charles Lambert
Charlotte Holtam
Charlotte Ryland
Charlotte Whittle
Charlotte Williams

Chloe Diski
Chris Stevenson
Chris Watson
Christina
    MacSweeney
Christopher Marlow
Ciara Breen
Ciara Ní Riain
Clare Bowerman
Clifford Posner
Colin Holmes
Constance and Jonty

Daniel Carpenter
Daniel Gallimore
Daniel Hahn
Daniel James Fraser
Dave Lander
David Attwooll
David Johnson-Davies
David Roberts
David Wardrop
Davida Murdoch
Debbie Pinfold
Deborah Bygrave
Deborah Smith
Deirdre Gage
Denis Stillewagt
Dominic Charles

Echo Collins
Eddie Dick
Eileen Buttle
Elaine Rassaby
Eleanor Maier
Emily Evans
Emma Kenneally
Emma McLean-Riggs
Eric Dickens
Erin Barnes

Fawzia Kane
Fiona Quinn

Gabrielle Morris
Gavin Madeley
Gay O'Mahoney
George McCaig
George Sandison
Georgia Panteli
Geraldine Brodie
Gill Saunders
Gilla Evans
Gillian Jondorf
Gillian Spencer
GillStern
Glynis Ellis
Graham Foster
Gregory August
    Raml

Hannes Heise
Helen Collins
Helen Weir
Helene Walters
Henriette Heise

Henrike Lähnemann
Howdy Reisdorf

Ian McAlister
Ian Mulder
Imogen Forster
Isabelle Kaufeler

Jane Whiteley
Janet Mullarney
Jeffery Collins
Jen Hamilton-Emery
Jennifer Cruickshank
Jennifer Higgins
Jennifer Hurstfield
Jenny Diski
Jerry Lynch
Jillian Jones
Joanne Hart
Joe Gill
Joel Love
Jon Lindsay Miles
Jonathan Evans
Jonathan Ruppin
Joseph Cooney
Joy Tobler
JP Sanders
Judith Unwin
Julia Sanches
Julian Duplain
Julian I Phillippi
Julie Van Pelt
Juraj Janik

K L Ee
Kaitlin Olson

Karan Deep Singh
Kasia Boddy
Kate Griffin
Kate Pullinger
Kate Wild
Katherine
    Wootton Joyce
Kathryn Lewis
Keith Dunnett
Kevin Acott
Kevin Brockmeier
Kevin Murphy
Kristin Djuve
Krystalli Glyniadakis

Larry Colbeck
Laura Bennett
Laura Jenkins
Laura Watkinson
Lauren Kassell
Lesley Lawn
Liam O'Connor
Linda Harte
Liz Clifford
Liz Tunnicliffe
Loretta Brown
Lorna Bleach
Lorna Scott Fox
Lucy Greaves
Lynda Graham

M Manfre
M C Hussey
Madeleine Kleinwort
Maggie Holmes
Maggie Peel

Margaret Jull Costa
Maria Pelletta
Marijke Du Toit
Marion Cole
Martin Brampton
Martin Conneely
Mary Nash
Matt Riggott
Matthew Bates
Matthew Francis
Michael Bagnall
Michael Harrison
Moira Fagan
Monika Olsen
Morgan Lyons
Murali Menon

N Jabinh
Nan Haberman
Natalie Rope
Natalie Smith
Natalie Wardle
Nichola Smalley
Nick Nelson
Nick Stevens
Nick Williams
Nuala Watt

Odhran Kelly
Oli Marlow
Owen Booth
Owen Fagan

P D Evans
Pamela Ritchie
Patrick Coyne

Paul Dowling
Paul Hannon
Paul Myatt
Peny Melmoth
Pete Ayrton
Peter Murray
Peter Vos
Philip Warren
Phyllis Reeve
Polly McLean
Poppy Toland

Quentin Webb

Rachel Eley
Rachel McNicholl
Rebecca K Morrison
Réjane Collard
Richard Jackson
Richard Soundy
Rob Fletcher
Rob Palk
Robert Gillett
Robert Leadbetter
Robin Woodburn
Ros Schwartz
Rosie Hedger
Ruth Martin

Samantha Schnee
Sean McGivern
Selin Kocagoz
Shazea Quraishi
Sheridan Marshall
Simon Pare
SLP

Sonia McLintock
Sophie Moreau
  Langlais
Steph Morris
Stephen Abbott
Stephen Bass
Stewart MacDonald
Sue Bradley
Sue Halpern
Sue Mckibben
Susana Medina

Tamsin Ballard
Tania Hershman
Tess Lee
Tess Lewis
Thomas Long
Thomas Fritz
Thomas Reedy
Tien Do
Tim Warren
Tom Russell
Tom Long
Tony Crofts
Tracey Martin
Tracy Northup

Vanessa Wells
Verena Weigert
Victoria Adams

Will Buck
William Buckingham

Zoe Brasier

Current & Upcoming Books by And Other Stories

Title: *Lightning Rods*
Author: Helen DeWitt
Editor: Sophie Lewis
Proofreader: Wendy Toole
Typesetter: Alex Billington for Tetragon
Set in: 9.8/14 pt Swift Neue Pro, Verlag
Series and Cover Design: Joseph Harries
Format: 210 x 138 mm
Paper: Munken Premium Cream 80gsm FSC
Printer: T J International Ltd, Padstow, Cornwall

The first 300 copies are individually numbered.

FSC
www.fsc.org
MIX
Paper from
responsible sources
FSC® C013056